The SEVEN TORMENTS of Amy and CRAIG

(A LOVE STORY)

The
SEVEN TORMENTS
of Amy and CRAIG

(A LOVE STORY)

DON ZOLIDIS

△ HYPERION / Los Angeles New York

First Hardcover Edition, October 2018
First Paperback Edition, September 2019
10 9 8 7 6 5 4 3 2 1
FAC-025438-19214
Printed in the United States of America

This book is set in Minion Pro, Eveleth/Fontspring; Feltpen Pro/Monotype
Designed by Tyler Nevins
Title lettering and design by Liz Casal

Library of Congress Cataloging-in-Publication Control Number for
Hardcover Edition: 2017056666
ISBN 978-1-368-01006-1

Visit www.hyperionteens.com

SUSTAINABLE
FORESTRY
INITIATIVE
Certified Chain of Custody
Promoting Sustainable Forestry
www.sfiprogram.org
SFI-01054
The SFI label applies to the text stock

For Anne

PROLOGUE

I know it says *A Love Story* on the cover of this book. And it is a love story. But I want to mentally prepare you for it. The couple doesn't get together at the end. There is no happy ending. Spoiler alert.

I guess I probably should've said "spoiler alert" first instead of including it after I just revealed the spoiler, but what are you going to do? Not read the next sentence?

So, yeah. Prepare yourselves.

ONE

Breakup Number Three

January 22, 1994.
Janesville, Wisconsin.
Palmer Park.
11:54 p.m.

I didn't see this one coming either.

We were sitting in her car. She drove a 1980-something Subaru hatchback. Light silver. Spots of rust. The best thing about it was the four-wheel drive, which allowed Amy to navigate the icy roads of southern Wisconsin. It also had heat, which was a particular bonus. There was virtually no way to turn off the heat, however, so now it was emitting a blast of hot air reminiscent of the open mouth of hell.

I didn't really care about that, although it did make things more awkward and smelly than usual as we made out.

We were still wearing our winter coats. She had on a puffy

green fuzzy thing that I always thought looked like a field of moss, and I was wearing my black I'm-troubled-and-artistic woolen trench coat, which stretched down over my knees and got tangled in our legs.

There was also the matter of the gearshift—the Subaru was manual, so as we groped over six or seven layers of clothing, we'd occasionally get stabbed in the ribs.

Basically, it was awesome. Even though I wasn't exactly sure whether I had just felt her boob or a strange bunch in her sweater.

The windows had fogged up, and we separated, gasping for breath, a hot sticky, sweaty mess of raging hormones. If anyone was outside the car, it would be pretty obvious what was going on. Of course, seeing as how it was near midnight in late January in the most heavily forested part of Palmer Park, the only likely pedestrian would be the abominable snowman.

R.E.M. was on the radio. It was that song "Everybody Hurts," which was being played every hour by every radio station like some kind of horrible curse. It was about as romantic as a song about preventing suicide could possibly be.

"This song just pretends it's deep," I grumbled.

Amy pulled some of her blond hair out of her mouth, while I kept going.

"Everybody hurts sometimes? Wow. I never would have guessed. Thank you, Michael Stipe."

Amy didn't say anything, which was probably good because I was about to get on a roll. I have to say, though, that my thoughts about R.E.M. weren't entirely spontaneous—I had practiced this speech before in the shower. I was sure it was hilarious and would improve her mood if the kissing hadn't done the trick.

"Like, are there people out there who think this is a revelation? Like they're going through life, *Huh, I bet those people never hurt*, and then this song comes on and they're like, enlightened? *Oh, I guess everybody does hurt.* Please. The whole theme of the song is like, *Sometimes things are bad.* R.E.M. should be working as guest artists in a kindergarten." That was my favorite part of this bit. Imagining the quintessential college band of the '80s showing up and teaching five-year-olds about colors.

Amy wasn't laughing.

She was looking down at her hands. Her hair fell in a yellow curtain around the sides of her face.

My stomach started twisting up into knots. I broke into a cold sweat. These moments had been happening more frequently lately—Amy would stop, her eyes would glaze over, and you could tell that she was contemplating my utter destruction. At least that was my assumption.

"I've been thinking," she said finally.

"Shit."

"I think—"

"Wait. Hold on. I won't talk about R.E.M. anymore. I'm sure they're cool."

"That's not what—"

"Is it the coat? Is that the problem?"

"Craig." She said it like my sister said it. Like *Shut up, Craig.* I shut up. "I don't know that I can do this."

"Do what?"

But I knew what. Amy turned just a bit to look at me and I could see the tears forming in her eyes. Down came the knife into my heart. Stab. Stab. Stab.

"I don't think I can be your girlfriend." Her words hung in the air for a moment. R.E.M. continued to whine forlornly on the radio. I no longer noticed the heat pouring out of the vent.

I had tried two different approaches to the Amy-dumping-me problem previously. Those two approaches were

1. Cry and
2. Cry more, then hug her mom. (Don't ask.)

So it was time to try something new: arguing.

"Wait a minute. You said you weren't going to break up with me anymore!"

"I know. . . ." She fumbled for a Kleenex.

"But now you're breaking up with me?! This is not cool! You didn't want me to be clingy, so I'm not clingy, I did that—"

"Craig—"

"I'm wearing the hat! Look at this!" I yanked the hat she had given me off my head. "I'm not even a hat person, and I'm still wearing this! For you! I'm wearing this hat for you!"

(Okay, I admit, my arguing technique was not technically the best.)

"Can I say something?" she sputtered. "I don't care about the hat."

"Clearly," I fumed.

She looked up at the ceiling of the car, exasperated. "There are things going on that I can't tell you about. . . ."

"Oh, like before?"

The air froze between us. That was mean. I knew it was mean.

Amy disintegrated. She chewed on her bottom lip and I could see the tears running down her face now.

"Was this your plan?" I said. "Bring me out here into the middle of the woods like a mafia killing or something?"

"No . . ."

"No witnesses. No one will ever find my body."

"Craig—"

"Why were you making me out with me first if you were gonna dump me?"

"I'm not dumping you."

"We were going out earlier tonight, and now, apparently, we're not! That's a dumping."

"Okay, maybe a little," she conceded.

"I'm sorry I made the comments about R.E.M."

"I'm not dumping you because you don't like this song!"

"Well, I don't see why you're dumping me at all."

Amy pulled her hair behind her ears. "I just can't do this."

It felt like a dozen boa constrictors had slithered into the car and were crushing my chest. I reached for anything that could save me. "Like, think about how great we are. We don't ever fight, we don't—"

"We fight all the time."

"No we don't!"

"We're fighting right now!"

"This isn't a fight. This is a discussion. It's a thoughtful discussion. You're discussing doing something stupid, and I'm explaining to you why it's a bad idea."

"Craig," she said gently, "I don't want to hurt you." This is what she always said while she was hurting me. It was as if someone was taking an ice pick and stabbing it through my eye. *I don't want to hurt you. Stab. Stab. Stab. You're only making it worse by screaming and crying. Stab. Stab. Stab. This will feel much better when I do the other eye.*

"If you don't want to hurt me, *why are you hurting me*?!"

"I don't want to hurt you more. In the future." She stopped for a second. Her blue eyes looked silver in the dim light. "I'm sorry."

There was no arguing my way out of this. The snakes were breaking my ribs.

The reality of the situation sucked the air out of my lungs. We were breaking up. Again. For the third time. No more Amy. My senior year in high school had been utterly consumed by her and now it was evaporating. My plan for prom was gone; no more seeing her Monday morning at school, when I would look out at the sea of heavy jackets and try to spot her hair. No more talking about deeply philosophical things late at night. No more making out after we talked about the deeply philosophical things. No more deeply philosophical things at all. Goddamn it, R.E.M. We were over.

"Just . . . uggg . . ." I opened the door and stomped out into the snow.

The first thing you realize when you step outside in the middle of a January night in Wisconsin is that you're stupid. It was cold. Not cold in the sense that something in your freezer is cold but cold in the sense that there is no God. Negative-twenty-degree cold. It was snowing just a bit, drifting down in little flakes of death.

The upper part of Palmer Park was really just a forest with a parking lot. Oh, sure, there was a swing set in there somewhere, and if you fell down the hill you'd eventually end up in a frozen kiddie pool, but apparently the people of Janesville just gave up on this part. They probably had better things to do. Like fighting for their daily survival since they'd stupidly decided to settle in a frozen wasteland where the only food available was cheese curds.

We were up on the hill, and the dark trees around me were all bare. Their trunks were black in the night, in contrast to the foot of white snow that lay on the ground like a dream.

When it's below zero degrees, the air stings. It felt like a million little lumberjacks were chopping away at my exposed skin, probably because I was wearing a stupid coat that wasn't even all that warm, and had somehow abandoned the hat Amy had given me.

I stumbled away from the car, my tennis shoes punching through the upper crust of the snow and sinking into the loose freezing drift beneath.

Please follow me. Please follow me.

I should not have left the hat in the car. That was dumb. I am dumb.

I weighed the possible results of my action:

1. Death.
2. She runs after me and admits she was wrong, and we go back in the car and make out more and pretend this never happened.
3. She runs after me and admits she was wrong, and it is too late because I have already frozen to death.
4. She runs after me in order to admit she was wrong, and she ironically freezes to death before she can reach me.
5. Yetis eat me.

"Craig!" she yelled.

Bingo.

"Get back in the car! It's cold as hell as out here!"

"No!"

Stopping just long enough to put on her giant red mittens

that looked like feminine lobster claws, Amy got out of the car. Amy was dressed far more sensibly for the cold since she was far more sensible than me. She had her green fuzzy parka thing, her mittens, and a bluish hat that smelled like her hair and was probably the greatest thing in the universe. I had no hat, no gloves, and my jeans had holes in the knees.

"Goddamn it, it's cold!" she shrieked.

"I know! *What was wrong with the people who settled here?!*"

The other thing about cold this wretched is that it swallows sound, which was one of the many reasons I was shouting. Fun fact.

And then she was right next to me, hugging me like we were giant toddlers in snowsuits.

"I'm so sorry," she said. Her hair smelled like sunshine, and I let myself hug her back.

I have no girlfriend echoed through my mind. It was especially awful, since Amy was the only girlfriend I'd ever had, the only girl I'd ever kissed, and the only girl I'd ever fallen in love with.

And now we were apart again, even though we were standing as close as possible in the dark, freezing, bitter awfulness that is Wisconsin in January. I stayed there for two or three seconds, which is about the amount of time before frostbite sets in. My tears, if I'd had any, would have frozen on my face.

She pushed the hat back into my hands.

"I'm gonna need a ride home," I said.

TWO

An Incident from My Childhood That Explains This Nonsense

It was my ninth birthday party, which I shared with my sister, Kaitlyn, who also happened to have the same birthday.

We're twins, although, as you probably figured out, not identical ones. She definitely got the better deal in the genetic lottery. For most of my life I was scrawny, undersized, and had an unfortunate cowlick that looked as if some part of my brown hair had to jump for joy all the time. In middle school I took a pair of scissors to it in what has come to be known as *the hair incident*. I had a year-round tan and was all of five foot one until my sophomore year of high school. Kaitlyn, on the other hand, figured out the mysteries of hair care early on. Her auburn hair had a natural wave to it, like undulating sea-foam fanned by water nymphs. All of my friends thought she was hot. She was naturally athletic, like she had transplanted genes from an antelope or something—she was a star forward for the soccer team and ran track in the spring. She was also the devil.

It's kind of awful having a twin sister who's a hundred times cooler than you, and even worse is the period of time from age nine to fourteen or so when she's taller than you and can kick your ass. (Granted, even in high school, she could still kick my ass on account of her innate fierceness, but at least I was taller.)

The conflict between us probably started in utero (somehow I imagine her fetus forming a middle finger very early on), but it really began with our pets. Actually, it began with her pets.

I don't know who cursed our family, but from a very early stage it was clear that someone had stolen an unholy amulet from a sarcophagus or something and called doom upon us.

First, I killed her sea monkeys. Then I killed two or three jars of lightning bugs we'd collected in the summer (although that might have been the result of not putting air holes in the jars, but she never wasted an opportunity to blame me for the carnage). Even the pets I didn't directly slaughter met horrible ends. Things got bad when we got guinea pigs. Kaitlyn went through four of them: Muffin, Bo-Dag, Son of Bo-Dag, and Bo-Dag Three. Son of Bo-Dag escaped from his guinea-pig hutch and was not discovered until five days later when his corpse began to send off quite strong smells from our basement. He had gotten trapped behind our couch, which was unhappily situated on a hot air vent. Son of Bo-Dag had baked to death in furry terror. That was the worst pet death until I accidentally sat on Bo-Dag Three after a particularly brutal game of Sorry. I wasn't looking, and he had been let out of his home for a breath of fresh air only to find my butt descending on him, crushing him like a tiny, furry éclair.

She also had a hamster named Giggles that committed suicide. He put his little head in his hamster wheel and pushed.

And then there was Stephen.

We never should've got Stephen. My parents should've realized we were cursed and declared that no pet was safe.

But Kaitlyn was unstoppable when she wanted a pet. She made posters. She sang songs. She cut out pictures from magazines and made detailed presentations to Mom and Dad. And when I say she sang songs about getting a pet, I mean she continuously sang songs for three or four hours at a time. It was enough to make a hamster commit suicide.

Anyway, Stephen was a Persian cat we got from the Humane Society. He was a big white fluff ball. You could only see his little smashed-up face if you looked directly at him; otherwise, he looked like a snowball had grown little legs and was wandering around, pissed off.

If you've ever met a Persian cat, you know what I'm talking about. They're assholes.

Kaitlyn loved everything about Stephen. She loved the low growling sound he made whenever I came near him. She loved the way he'd let you pet him for three or four seconds before biting the crap out of your hand and trying to claw you apart.

She was also extremely protective of him—especially with me, as she blamed me for the slaughter of every animal she had ever loved, even the ones I didn't sit on or suffocate. (Although, to be fair, sea monkeys are not animals. They're shrimp, and they are also the lamest "pet" ever.)

Anyway, all of this is to set the scene for our ninth birthday party, which was fated to be the last birthday party we'd have together.

In previous years, our mom had managed to get us to agree to gender-neutral themes like "Muppets" or "balloon fun," but this year we were irreconcilable. I had chosen *The Hobbit* as my theme, which drove my mom into a worrying stress spiral, not least for the fact that I had demanded giant spider decorations. Kaitlyn, for her part, had chosen the exact opposite: Barbie.

As you can imagine, there was no universe in which Barbie and hobbits coexisted. (Either Barbie would be put on the front lines to be eaten by the giant spiders, or the hobbits would get new, snazzy outfits—either way it made no sense.) My parents had tried—well, actually, my mom had tried. My dad had thrown up his hands and offered "lions" as a possible solution, which was to say, he was going to take us to the zoo and feed us to lions if we couldn't compromise. His plan failed because we were at least half-sure he was joking. So there was a dividing line in our backyard—on one side, the denizens of Middle-earth, and the other side, totally unrealistic plastic women.

"They can't even stand," I said to her.

"Shut up," said Kaitlyn. "Go play with your dwarves."

"Hobbits. Dwarves are a different race."

"There is something wrong with you. Really wrong."

We had each invited the same number of people, but I had three acquaintances show up, and she had about thirty-seven girls there. From orbit, you could tell the difference between our parties. What's worse is that my friends, sensing that something like the plague was affecting my side of the yard, had gravitated over to the Barbie side because they were traitors.

"Let's put the parties together," offered my mom. "I feel like there's room for magic in the Barbie universe."

We both rolled our eyes at that.

Kaitlyn offered no concessions to my side of the yard, and went out of her way to show just how much more fun she was having than me. Equally horrible was the fact that each person at the party brought a present for one of us, all of which were now located on a "present table" that was 90 percent pink. It was all going horribly wrong.

This is where Stephen comes in.

All my life I have been afflicted by a lack of common sense, and it was particularly noticeable on this day. Here was my thought process:

I need to get girls to come over here. What do girls like? Cats. We have a cat. I'll bring him outside and carry him around. Then all will be well and we can play pin the scale on the dragon.

I found Stephen in his usual place, sitting under my parents' bed, pissed off and hating the world. I crawled on my stomach, fended off his claws, and managed to grab his back. He emitted the low, mournful growl that was his way of saying *Hello—please get the hell away from me.*

But I was undeterred, and managed to scramble out from under the bed and scoop Stephen into my arms like a white, puffy ball of evil.

Stephen was an indoor cat; my dad had long argued that he was an animal and needed to hunt, but he had been overruled by the fact that Stephen showed no inclination to ever go outside or do anything to acquire food for himself. He was pretty useless as a cat.

I brought him outside, feeling his furry body tremble in rage and panic.

"Look what I've got over here," I said in a singsong voice from my abandoned hobbit side of the yard.

Bringing something cute and fluffy into a group of thirty third-grade girls is a recipe for a stampede. Just as I imagined, they dropped their Barbie activities and rushed me.

Stephen's evil cat eyes went wide when he spotted the flood of girls. He braced his back claws against my sternum, tore through my shirt, and sprang away from me like he had been fired from one of my dad's guns. He shot to the ground and raced through the gaggle of girls like a thunderbolt. I had never seen him move that fast in his life.

He shot around the house and headed for the street.

I know what you're thinking. *A car ran him over, didn't it?*

Nope.

There was no car, but there was a giant German shepherd puppy that spotted a lightning-fast ball of white fur and thought it looked like a super-fun chew toy. By the time we reached the front yard, there was blood and fur and an adorable German shepherd being restrained by its horrified owner.

Death had come to our ninth birthday party. J. R. R. Tolkien would have been proud.

In my mind, I think of Stephen like the eternal pessimist. Every day I bet he thought, *I'm going to die today. I hate these people.* And at last, he was right.

Anyway, that was me in a nutshell. Trying to impress people the wrong way, only to have it end in horrible tragedy.

THREE

Breakup Number Five

April 15, 1994.
9:07 p.m.
My basement.

As I got older, I slowly conquered the entire basement of our house. At some point, it had been imagined as a family rec room, but the creeping tide of my nerdishness forced the rest of the family out due to sheer embarrassment. The fact that Kaitlyn and I had been largely at war for the past eight years had something to do with it as well. The faux-wood paneling my dad had installed in the late '70s was perfect for tacking up posters of dragons and aliens. I had transformed one of the old coffee tables into a diorama, which was complete with metal miniatures of wizards and dwarves. I had even found a couple of crappy old bookshelves and had filled them with an endless supply of fantasy novels. In short, it was a space designed to repulse females.

And yet I had brought Amy into it, and, miraculously, she hadn't run for the hills. She didn't mind sitting on the couch; she didn't mind the faint smell of death that still hung in the air from Son of Bo-Dag's immolation. She was cool with all of it.

We had set up an old television down there and spent much of the last month watching movies while buried beneath blankets. It was an exercise in escapism, of course, as both of our lives were in the process of falling apart. Hers was collapsing, while mine was merely deteriorating, and like good Wisconsin people we had both made the unspoken pledge not to talk about any of it and watch horror films instead.

Should we talk about our feelings regarding the ongoing tragedies in our lives? Oh look, Critters 3 *is on. I sure hope that will answer all the unresolved questions from both* Critters 1 *and* 2.

It wasn't a perfect system, and where there had once been long, deeply philosophical talks that lasted all night, there was now a sinister cloud of silence. It wasn't the best way to run a relationship, but it was a model that seemed to work for everyone's parents, so we were giving it a shot.

Anyway, we had just finished *Hellraiser II*, which was a lot worse than the original *Hellraiser*, so it was a lot more fun to watch. I had mastered the art of making funny voices during the entire movie (or at least, I thought I had mastered it; I probably annoyed the hell out of her, which might have been one of the reasons for the breakup, but who knows?), and I was on a particular roll that evening.

If you're not familiar with the Hellraiser series of movies, congratulations. Basically it's about a weird guy who wears black leather and has pins in his face. Like, three hundred pins in his face. He's named, surprisingly enough, Pinhead. Pinhead is summoned by demons every once in a while and sends people to hell, where they don't have a good time. Every once in a while he says, *We have such sights to show you.*

I had a great time imagining alternate employment options for Pinhead.

"What if he was, like, a tour guide?" and

"Wouldn't it be awesome if Disney bought the rights to this and put him in Disney World?" and

"Wouldn't it be great if he used the pins for storage? Like, hooked hot dogs to himself?"

So we were sitting there having a great time, and I had her hand in mine. She had fingers like a bird; they were pale and white and a little bony, but I loved them.

I suppose I haven't really described Amy. This is usually the point where the hero says that the heroine was beautiful and perfect and had eyes like moonbeams or whatever. And, yes, all that was true about her. She was way more attractive than me. I had no business being with this girl.

She also walked a little bit like a duck. Not in a stupid way. But she just ever so slightly shuffled a bit when she walked. She had a weird thing where her hips were double-jointed, which sounds totally awesome but kind of had no effect other than to make her capable of standing straight up and twisting her feet around to face about forty-five degrees behind her. Weird, right?

All that is to say she wasn't very athletic, and when she ran it was a bit awkward, which was just perfect for me, since I sucked at all things related to sports except for watching other people play them.

So, at this point in time, once *Hellraiser II* had finished, she let go of my hand and shuffled over to the backpack she had dropped at the foot of the stairs. She took a deep breath, like she was mentally preparing for something.

After having been dumped four times, I was especially sensitive to Amy's body language. If she sneezed, I felt my heart twinge. If she took too long to respond to a question like *How are you doing?* a feeling of cold, tingly terror would race up my spine. When she opened the backpack and took out a letter, I felt my stomach drop.

"What's that?" I asked.

"Um . . ." She looked down at her hands.

Shit.

"So I wrote you a letter."

"Great."

No response.

"Is it a nice letter?"

Silence. *It is not a nice letter. It is a letter of doom.*

"I've been thinking about things," she said finally.

"Nice things?"

Silence.

Then she started to pace. This was new. I hadn't been dumped with pacing before. She had the letter in her hands, was looking down at it, and was shuffling a bit back and forth. "I wrote down some things that I want to tell you . . . but every time we talk I can't seem to make them come out, so . . ." she said finally.

"What do you want to tell me?"

"That's why I wrote you the letter. To avoid actually having to say the things. . . ."

"What's the gist of it?"

She looked down at her hands and made a little noise like "Hurm." *Oh, that behavior I recognize. That's the universal sign for* I must crush you now.

I got up from the couch and started following her pacing. "You can talk to me," I said. "I know that I have been stupid in the past, and I am working on my own idiocy, and—"

"It's not about what you're doing," she said. "It's about what I'm doing."

"Are you breaking up with me again? Is that what you're doing?"

She looked down and made the terrifying "Hurm" noise again.

"You can't break up with me in a letter," I protested. "Letters are for good things. We've established this. We have a pattern!"

She tried a new tactic. "You're going to find somebody so much better than me."

"What? No, I'm not! Look at me! Are you insane?"

"You're a great guy; there are probably a lot of other girls you could be going out with, so I feel like I'm preventing you from finding them right now." Of all the lies Amy ever told me, this one was probably the most ridiculous.

"I don't like anybody else! I'm finding you! I found you! We found each other!"

"But I can't be found right now, Craig. That's what I'm trying to tell you."

"Why not?"

"I wrote it in the letter!" she said, her voice rising just a bit. She shook it back and forth in her hand.

"Tell me. Talk to me. What did I do wrong?"

"Ugh!" She looked at the ceiling. "You didn't do anything wrong! We do things wrong together."

Kaitlyn emerged from the stairwell with a bowl of potato chips. She crunched one into her mouth and stood there, watching us.

"Do you mind?" I yelled.

"You want one?" she asked, popping another potato chip in her mouth.

"We're in the middle of something here."

She turned to look at us, as if she hadn't heard the telltale sounds of Amy stomping my heart into dust yet again. "Oh crap," she gasped. "Are you dumping him again?"

"Can you leave, please?" I said.

"What is it this time?" she said. "Is it the commentary during movies, 'cause that's annoying as hell, right?"

"Would you get out of here?"

She put her hands up, starting to back her way up the stairs. "Don't blame me. I tried to adjust your personality and you didn't listen." She got about two steps up before she turned. "Hey, Amy, we should hang out sometime."

Amy twitched. "Uh . . ."

I picked up the nearest foam sword and threw it at her. Foam swords are not especially aerodynamic, so it glided harmlessly through the air and dropped to the ground about ten feet away from her.

"All right, whatever. I'll be upstairs if you need me."

Amy and I stood there for a moment, a few feet apart. I could hear my parents talking upstairs, as if everything was normal and I wasn't getting crushed once again. The air turned cold.

"Please read the letter, Craig." She shoved it into my hands, which were losing all feeling.

I tried a joke. "Does it say 'Just kidding'?"

But it didn't. She had put it in an envelope, and from the weight of it, it felt like half a novel.

"I think I preferred it when you dumped me in the middle of the woods."

Amy gave a halfhearted smile, like she appreciated my attempt at humor and was duly sorry that I was not terribly funny.

I tried to keep going, even though it felt like I was swimming through mud. "Actually, I prefer it when you don't dump me at all. Those are the best days. You know this isn't going to stick, right? You've already dumped me four times—"

"Three times."

"I think it's four."

"Three."

"I'm counting the thing two and a half weeks ago. Fine, three, whatever. You've dumped me three times and it hasn't stuck yet. So that's . . . that's just . . . you obviously are addicted to me like some kind of heroin addict . . . whatever it is I got"—I spread my arms out in a feeble show of bravado; I was highly conscious of the fact that I was in a dingy basement. With a crappy TV, faux-wood paneling, and an embarrassing collection of little monster figurines—"you can't get enough."

I paused. One eyelid stopped working. *This is a stroke. I think I'm having a stroke. Maybe if I die she'll change her mind. That's stupid, Craig. Why would she change her mind if you're dead? Then she can't go out with you at all.*

"Are you okay?" she asked.

"What?"

"You seem a little messed up."

"I'm getting dumped! And I'm probably having an aneurysm or something."

"I'm sorry."

"I would appreciate it in the future if you would stop breaking up with me." The words spilled out of my mouth like an avalanche of stupid. What did I think she was going to say to that?

Then she hugged me. The hug of death. The hug that meant *you're-such-a-great-guy-but-I'm-afraid-this-battle-station-will-be-fully-operational-by-the-time-your-friends-arrive.*

I held on. She patted my back like she was settling down an animal. I kept holding on.

"Craig."

"This sucks," I said.

"I know."

She let me go to arm's length and looked into my eyes. Her eyes were mostly blue, but not entirely blue; they faded to a kind of amber color near the edges. I used to think I would be looking into those eyes forever.

The world rocked a bit and went fuzzy at the edges. "Please read the letter," she said, and kissed me on the forehead.

Hours later, after she left, I took it out of the envelope. It was four pages long, on some kind of artisan paper that still contained tree bark and could only be found in specialty stationery shops in rural Maine. Her blue writing filled up the spaces like a long, spidery trail of doom. Amy was pretty seriously dyslexic, so misspellings abounded, but each one just reminded me how much I loved her. I read about two lines and then set it down as my world fell apart for the fifth time.

FOUR

What I Saw in Her

At this point, you're probably wondering what I saw in her, as she seems like a demon beast from hell. But most of the time she wasn't anything like a demon beast from hell, not even a little.

During our relationships, those periods of calm and joy between the inevitable periods of disaster and doom that followed, things were awesome. At least in the beginning.

My parents had a strict "no phone calls after nine p.m." policy, which was enforced as if the mere ringing of a phone after nine would bring about the apocalypse. Kaitlyn and I didn't really have curfews; we weren't really expected to do a lot of chores around the house; basically nothing was expected of us as human beings except for one thing: no damn calls after nine o' clock. At precisely nine, my parents would retreat to their parental safe zone not to be seen again until morning, unless it so happened that my dad would emerge, clad solely in horrifying bikini-style 1970s briefs, hunting for a beer.

It was tough on all of us.

The first time one of my friends called after nine was in sixth grade.

"Craig is not available," said my dad.

"Why not?" said my friend, unaware that he was poking the lion.

"He is not available," repeated my dad, his voice sounding low like the gears of a doomsday device.

"Can you tell him that—"

"I am telling him nothing," said my dad, hanging up. Later I was threatened with a week's grounding if the phone rang after nine, and he made a point of explaining to Kaitlyn that if any boys called after nine he owned many, many guns.

We had one phone line because my parents were cheap. We didn't even have call waiting. Kaitlyn would monopolize the phone line until well after nine. (Side note: Not only did Kaitlyn have boyfriends, she also had actual friends, so she had a lot to talk about apparently. My friends, who I will describe in just a bit, had learned their lesson about calling after nine, and didn't believe in phone communication anyway. They mostly just showed up at my house in the middle of the night and ate my food.)

Anyway, this is all a roundabout way of saying that I was always the one who called Amy. And my point is that this is part of what made our relationship awesome.

I'd wait until ten or so, when I was sure Kaitlyn was off the phone. Then I'd stare at the phone on my bedside table like it was a portal to another world. It didn't matter how many times I called her, I was always nervous. My stomach lurched. Little bears clawed their way up my esophagus. My throat went dry and I temporarily lost the ability to speak intelligently. Luckily, I had written out topics of conversation in advance. Tonight's discussion: November 16, "The Love Song of J. Alfred Prufrock." (For reference: this is twelve days after we got together the first time and five days after we read "The Love Song of J. Alfred Prufrock" in AP English.) And then, before I could think better of it, I was dialing her number.

"Hi," she said.

I froze up. How does one respond to this? I had forgotten.

"Craig?"

"I mean, is Amy there?" Why was I asking? What was wrong with me? One second into our conversation and I was already stupid.

"Do you think I sound like my brother?"

"No, I just, um . . . How are you?"

"Good." And for some amazing reason, I could hear her smile through the phone.

I tried to imagine what she was doing. She had a butterfly chair in her room—made out of white canvas, it was one of those fragile things that looked like it had floated in from Scandinavia and yet was somehow both sturdy and environmentally conscious. I imagined her sitting in it, the phone against her skin.

I was lying on my stomach with my face against my pillow and my eyes closed. I held the receiver as close as I could to my cheek, as if I could somehow feel Amy through the phone line. I tried to sense the warmth of her skin; the way the light from her reading lamp made her glow like the surface of the moon.

"Don't you think so?" she said.

"Hmm?" I said, snapping back to reality.

"That we're in a perpetual cycle of becoming someone else?"

"Oh, definitely."

"But I think it's important that you embrace the fact that you're becoming a new person. That's life, you know? I'm not who I was last year."

"Who were you last year?"

"I was scared. I was shy. I was more concerned about what people thought of me. But now, you know, it's like, I'm feeling like I'm shedding that."

"Like a dog?" I was so deep.

"I have a theory about that. It's like a snake. You have to shed your skin to grow. You never see a snake regretting its old skin."

"Snakes don't really talk, so maybe they're just consumed with regret all the time and we just don't know. Maybe that's why they don't even walk. They're just like, *Oh, man, that skin was great and now it's gone and I'm just gonna lay here and slither.*"

She laughed. "You know what I mean."

"Yeah. I think. Probably."

"Over the summer I had a huge blowup with some of my so-called friends. And I realized, you know, I don't need these people. I don't need to be the person they want me to be. I kept thinking I've got one more year until college, and then I can be my true self, and then I was like, why am I waiting? Let me be my true self now."

"I have no idea what I'm going to do about college. I just wrote my admissions essay."

The essay question had been *What famous figure from history do you think is a good role model?*, and I had picked Fyodor Dostoevsky because I was an idiot. I'm sure other people had written about inventors of vaccines or Mother Teresa, and I had picked a crazy-ass Russian dude with a gambling problem who lived in a basement and wrote things like "Suffering is the sole origin of consciousness." Good job, Craig. I'm sure there was an admissions officer somewhere laughing his ass off at my essay and showing it to his admissions officer friends like, *Check out this dumbass.*

She laughed again. "You know what I'm saying?"

"Sure," I said, realizing I had zoned out again and she had probably said something important. "It's just like . . . 'The Love Song of J. Alfred Prufrock.' By T. S. Eliot."

"Well, yes, but I think that's more about alienation than anything else, and what I'm talking about is acceptance. Like,

Prufrock can't accept that he's changed and the world is becoming different, you know?"

"Yup," I said, crossing it off in my notebook. *Shit.*

You're probably beginning to understand why I wrote down things to talk about.

"I think my favorite line," I said, looking down at the rest of my notes, "is 'I have heard the mermaids singing, each to each. I do not think that they will sing to me.'"

"Aww," she said. "Why?

I smiled into my pillow. I hoped she could see it too. "Because that's how I used to feel before I met you."

"I'm singing to you," Amy said into the phone. "Except I really suck at singing."

"I think the singing is metaphorical."

"Maybe they're like the Sirens. Luring lonely poets to their doom. And really they've got teeth like knives and will rip you to shreds if you come too close."

"That pretty accurately describes my love life up to this point."

"I'm sure it's not that bad."

"It's pretty bad."

"Oh come on."

Amy was my first girlfriend. Well, okay, there was Jessica Southern, my junior year, who I went out with for nine days. We kissed once, and then she decided that the whole thing was a misunderstanding. Which it probably was. So, twelve days into my first relationship with Amy, we had already lasted exactly

33 percent more than my previous record (yes, I had done the math).

"Tell me about your first kiss," she said.

"No," I said.

"Come on. I'll tell you about mine first."

"All right."

She paused for a bit. "I was in sixth grade. It was after school with a guy named Brent Preston."

"He sounds dreamy."

"He was! Shut up. I was really tall, and he was the only boy in class who was almost as tall as me, and his friend gave me one of those notes with a check box on it? Like, do you like Brent, check yes or no. So I knew that was a trap, so I had one of my friends send a note back saying, 'Which box do you want Amy to check?'"

"That's like James Bond–level thinking."

"I know! Strategy. And he checked that yes, he wanted me to check yes. So we met up after school by the monkey bars . . . for some monkey business."

I laughed. "That's amazing."

"I know. We did not fall in love, though. All right, your turn!"

"No, I want to hear more about Brent! Did he have gorgeous eyes? What were his abs like? I want the whole romance-novel version."

"There is no romance-novel version! It was awkward and weird, and that's about it. Brent is unimportant. You're telling me about yours now."

"Fine. It was eighth grade," I said.

"Wow."

"I was a late bloomer."

"Go on."

"Okay, so we were on a field trip somewhere, and I didn't have a lot of friends, so there was no one next to me on the bus. And this girl Megan D'Angelo comes over and sits right next to me and she's like, 'You are so cute, I think we should kiss right now.'"

"Damn!"

"So I do what any guy would do in that circumstance, I say to myself, *Yes, it's finally happening! We are now boyfriend and girlfriend.* So we kiss."

"Was it magical?"

"It was slightly less than magical. It was like touching lips."

Amy laughed. "That's what a kiss is."

"I know! That's all it was. We touched lips. And then she's like, 'I'm coming over to your house every day in the summer and you're never going to be able to stop me,' and I'm like, *Whoa, this relationship just got really intense and I'm in, like, way over my head now, I need to slow down*—I don't know if I thought my mojo was really working or whatever, but . . . So I said, 'This is how AIDS starts,' which made no sense. And she laughed and she's like, 'You're so funny,' and she starts mussing my hair, and then she goes back to sit with her friends."

"A whirlwind romance."

"And then later I found out her friends had bet her a dollar if she could kiss the ugliest boy on the bus."

Amy was quiet for a second. I had never told anyone that story before.

"Oh. That's pretty shitty," she said.

"It's fine."

"And I'm sure you weren't the ugliest boy on the bus."

"'Cause some kids were really hideous in middle school," I joked.

"No, 'cause you're cute now. I'm sure you were cute then. Pre-blooming."

"Thanks."

And we talked and talked long into the night, and long past the time when my dad emerged searching for a beer, until I'd finally exhausted my notebook. The next day I'd start writing it again.

FIVE

My Weird Friends

Now is probably the time to introduce a few more characters to the story. You know, for context. Just so you understand exactly why there were zero mermaids singing to me. Or if the mermaids were singing to me, they were only doing so because their mean mermaid friends were paying them.

My friends consisted solely of a few weirdos that I had met in middle school. We played Dungeons & Dragons together and had bonded over our mutual awkwardness. It was kind of a symbiotic relationship—we embraced our oddity, and as a result grew stranger and stranger. First up, a kid named Groash.

Paul Groashnewski went by Groash because it sounded like *gross*—even though he wasn't especially gross. He was tall and rail thin, and resembled an overgrown spider with a concave chest. Nearly every day he wore the same T-shirt with the word SLIMEBALLS on it, which had at one point been black but had slowly evolved into gray through countless washings since middle school. He also sported a strange pair of what he called *activity pants*, which weren't sweatpants or jeans, but something that occupied the strange hinterland between the two. Throw in a pair of black combat boots, a safety pin for an earring, and a dirty-blond Mohawk and you'll understand why my dad referred to him as "that weird kid."

My other friends included Brian Nguyen, who wasn't even cool enough to aspire to the trench coat or safety-pin earring, and Elizabeth, who was a girl and yet somehow still hung out with us.

Elizabeth was about an inch taller than me and had a mop of curly brown hair that sat on top of her head like a lost animal. She was still cute, even though she wore baggy painter's jeans and tended to dress in shapeless sweatshirts. She was the kind of girl who kept a wallet on a chain and was the first one in our school to get her nose pierced. She was big into computer programming, and occasionally Elizabeth and Groash would hang out with skate punks, who terrified the hell out of me and Brian. Brian was in the formative stages of rebellion, and had grown his black hair just long enough so that it covered his eyebrows. He wore nifty John Lennon glasses that he had acquired somewhere, and showed an alarming lack of fashion sense. All of them had managed to escape any connection to after-school activities, athletics, or church functions with the exception of Brian, who wrote nihilistic news articles for the school newspaper. (Example:

He called the school's new ban on hats a "pointless exercise in social engineering destined to fail.")

I'm not going to explain Dungeons & Dragons. Let's just say we were hopped up on caffeine, sat around a table, pretended to be elves and dwarves and wizards, and fought monsters. Brian was our Dungeon Master, which was kind of like a mix between referee and storyteller. His job was to invent a whole bunch of weird-ass stuff that would fight us, and then we'd roll a bunch of dice and have an awesome time and make lots of noise so that Kaitlyn would be mortified enough to leave the house to go have sex with someone or get drunk.

So, anyway, to set the scene, the four of us hung out in my basement a lot because Groash's family was a wreck, Brian didn't want us at his house, and Elizabeth's mom was an honest-to-God witch. With spells and everything. It was way cool, but she was also a sometime nudist with biker friends, so going over there was something of a terrifying crapshoot.

Every Saturday night, the four of us would gather with a case of Mountain Dew, a basket of puppy chow trail mix, and three boxes of Little Debbie brownies, which were made out of materials not native to Earth, and we'd play Dungeons & Dragons. At some point we'd order pizzas and Groash would steal an entire pie and devour it by himself in the corner while the rest of us looked on with shock and horror.

"It's probably not healthy to eat that fast," said Brian, observing this mad ritual for the thirtieth time.

Groash said nothing because he had folded two pieces of pizza together and was maneuvering them into his mouth.

"You guys act like it's some kind of primal war to get the most food," said Elizabeth.

"It is," managed Groash. "And I'm winning."

"Animals," grumbled Elizabeth.

"Speaking of which," snickered Brian, rolling some dice behind his Dungeon Master's Screen. (Which was basically a tri-fold with pictures of monsters on one side and dozens of complicated charts on the other. It was an essential tool of any Dungeon Master seeking to prevent the players from learning devious secrets or reading the module.) "Speaking of which . . . you hear a slurping noise from the water behind you, and before you can react, a giant crayfish leaps out of the water and stabs you in the back with its pincers."

"Son-of-a-bitch," howled Groash, taking two more pieces of pizza.

You get the general idea.

"What the hell do you guys do down there?" Kaitlyn would ask. "Are you summoning demons?"

"No."

"It sounds like you're summoning demons."

"We're not. We're adventuring."

"Oh God. You need to stop. Just stop."

She'd raise her hand like I had just dropped a dead possum on the ground in front of her and she had to shield her eyes from the sight of it. And then she'd steel herself and put her hands on my shoulders like she was being really helpful and say, "This is why no one will ever love you."

And you know what? She was kind of right, as Kaitlyn often was. She really had her finger on the pulse of the mermaids, being one herself. But I figured it was better to embrace who you truly are rather than pretend to be something else. I had my friends. I didn't care if people thought we were summoning demons.

"So you are summoning demons."

"No, Kaitlyn, if we were summoning demons, we would have already succeeded, and you would be disemboweled by now."

"The only reason you know a word like *disemboweled* is from Dungeons & Dragons. Your entire vocabulary is a nightmare."

"Whatever."

"Whatever you."

And then we kept doing that for a while.

SIX

How Amy and Craig Met

If this were a romantic comedy, this would be called the meet-cute. The meet-cute is an event that happens about five minutes into the movie where the heroes meet in a contrived, yet adorable way, in which they mysteriously hate each other, or there's some kind of stupid misunderstanding that will come back to haunt them later on. Then they eventually solve it and kiss and get married, and then nothing interesting ever happens again, because everyone knows that once you get married all comedy and romance end. But I'm getting ahead of myself.

If I was writing this movie, there were a number of ways it could've gone down:

1. Car accident. My car slides on the ice into hers. She gets out of her car and hits me in the face with an ice scraper. I start bleeding and cry like a baby and lose

consciousness. She has to look through my wallet to go call an ambulance and discovers both that I am more buff than she thought and that my buttocks are entrancing. *Probability of happening in real life: 10 percent.* (I would need to borrow Kaitlyn's *Buns of Steel* video for a few weeks before this would happen; also, we'd need to meet when it was icy in Wisconsin—so between September and May.)

2. We spot each other across a crowded room. Why? Who knows? We're at a party (that's the first implausibility— that I would be invited to a party—but let's just say I'm there). She glances in my direction. Our eyes meet. She notices that my eyes are dark and full of mystery. *Who is that sexy boy in the dark, wool trench coat? He almost resembles Dostoevsky.* (In my mind, girls are attracted to Dostoevsky. Perhaps that's why I chose him as a role model, even though he resembled a homeless dude who ate rats. Fun fact: Dostoevsky probably did eat rats, because he was imprisoned in Siberia.) *I must speak with him, but not here. Anywhere but here.* I casually pick up a rat and take a bite out of it. She thinks that's awesome. *Probability of happening in real life: 2 percent.*

3. I stalk the hell out of her in a non-threatening, family-friendly way. I memorize where her classes are. I make sure I'm in the hallways in her passing period so that I can walk past her, make eye contact, and give

a wry little smile like *Hey, what's up?* I find out her phone number and call her to ask about homework in classes we don't even have together. I find a way to have Brian interview her for the school newspaper. Just a feature on Amy. Like, a random-hot-girl profile on Amy. *Probability of happening in real life: 87 percent.* (I put the probability that high because I had already tried method three on two separate occasions: my three-years-long crush on Jessica in grades six, seven, and nine (I took a break during eighth grade, don't ask), and my unfortunate obsession with Megan in the spring of my sophomore year. Both crushes ended in nightmarish disasters that may have involved writing bad poetry and, in the case of Megan, a poorly constructed bust made out of modeling clay.)

But it wasn't any of those things. Instead, the meet-cute began with the announcements.

"Youth in Government is looking for people to sign up," said the monotonous voice of our vice principal, who managed to turn every announcement into a death march of troubled grammar and awkward pauses.

Ha, I scoffed. *Those people sound like dorks.* I went back to sketching a picture of Rothgar, my thirteenth-level dwarven paladin.

"So if you're . . . interested in government, I guess . . . or are a youth, Youth in Government might be the club for you. Here to talk about it more is Youth in Government president, Amy Carlson."

"Hi, everyone! We meet every Wednesday night at the YMCA; and it's way cool, and we get to go on a field trip to Madison after Thanksgiving. I'm serious; it's really fun. We've also got a pool table. So . . . um . . . if you're interested, just swing by the Y at seven this Wednesday."

My ears perked up. A superhot girl had announced that she just happened to be president of a highly nerdy activity. A nerdy activity that required no skill or experience or ability whatsoever—you could just show up and hang out with her. At the YMCA. Which was probably the scene of any number of ill-advised romantic hookups.

Did I have a chance?

Normally, the answer would be no. Amy Carlson was no ordinary hot chick. She was president of everything. She wasn't just senior class president and in charge of Youth in Government; people actually started clubs to get her to be in charge of them. It was stunning. She was almost certainly going to be our valedictorian, and despite the fact that she walked just a bit like a duck, if aliens descended on our school and demanded a specimen of human perfection, she'd be the first one sucked up by the tractor beam. Of course I knew about Amy. We had gone to different middle schools, but in high school it was impossible to miss her. The principal probably called her up at night and asked her for advice.

People like me did not hook up with people like her.

And yet, maybe this was it. Maybe she was different than I thought. Maybe she was just the kind of amazing, high-functioning nerd who would appreciate a guy in a trench coat with a dwarven paladin. Perhaps she would be impressed that my character had a lot of hit points and a really low armor class. Perhaps I shouldn't mention that.

My first accomplice was Groash. I cornered him in the hallway after first period.

"Dude," he said. "Youth in Government?" He shouldered the ugly blue duffel bag that contained half of his worldly possessions and adjusted the new safety pin in his left ear. "Do I look like I'd go to Youth in Government?"

"I need somebody to go with me."

"Take Brian; he's smart."

The thought of bringing Brian with his dungeon-mastering snorts filled me with dread. "I need someone kind of normal." I paused for a second and thought about Groash's safety-pin earring and Slimeballs shirt. "Like, passable as a human being."

"It sounds like school after school, dude. Why the hell would we do more school at night? That doesn't make any sense."

"They have a pool table." I could count on the fact that this would be news to Groash despite the fact that it was on the announcements.

"They have a pool table?" he asked, suspecting a trick.

"Yes. It's free pool. You don't even have to do anything. You just get free pool."

"Do they have food there?"

"How would I know that?"

"I thought you knew about this shit."

"I need you come to Youth in Government."

"It sounds awful. Youth? Who uses the word *youth*?"

"Please?"

"Ten bucks."

"What?"

"I'll try it one time for ten bucks."

"I'm your friend!"

"If you were my friend you wouldn't try to get me to do things."

I eventually got him to go after negotiating him down to $7.50, which was ridiculous since I was the one picking his ass up and driving him downtown to the Y anyway. When I say "downtown," I am referring to downtown Janesville. If you've never heard of Janesville, you are not alone.

Janesville had the benefit of not being a suburb and not being a city, so it did have an actual downtown, with buildings that were actually three or four stories tall. One of these was the YMCA, which had mutated over the years. It used to be a home for indigent young men tramping about the country on trains and sleeping on cots. Now it was basically a gym.

The lounge where we met had been a smoking lounge for about seventy-five years, so it smelled like failure. The carpet was mostly stains; the floor creaked; and there were probably mutant rats hiding in the walls, plotting our doom. It also had a pool table.

"Sweet," said Groash, whose nose didn't register smells like a normal human nose would. This was because of his living situation. His house smelled like dead raccoons. Because there were dead raccoons under it.

But there was Amy—and some other people, whom I'm not going to bother to describe because they are not important to this story. Also present was the college representative, a girl named Amanda, who was a little chubby and had her hair spiked up, like she used to be a rock star or something. Amanda wore a leather jacket and didn't give a shit.

"All right, listen up," said Amanda when we got there. "My name's Amanda, and I don't give a shit."

Groash clapped once and stopped when I elbowed him in the ribs.

"I don't really know what you guys do here, but the Y's paying me minimum wage to hang out and make sure you don't burn the place down. Whatever. I don't really care. I'm going to go play pool."

Then she did that.

Amy took over. "Great. Thank you, Amanda." Amanda gave a thumbs-up as she racked the billiard balls. "Um . . . hi!" Amy gave a little wave and rocked forward on her toes a bit. She was wearing light blue sneakers, faded blue jeans, and a magical white sweater that seemed like it was formed from an adorable sheep that had sacrificed itself just to be near her. Her blond hair fell in a majestic wave over her shoulders.

"I'm Amy and this is our VP, Chelsea." She gestured to a petite girl in a debate letter jacket with five pounds of fluffy brown hair.

"Hee-eyy." She waved. "I'm Amy's right-hand woman, so . . ." She looked over at Groash and shook her head slightly. "So yeah."

Amy smiled. "So, um . . . this is Youth in Government. Yay! You're probably not into the yay-ing yet, but it's really fun. Like if you have interest in government, this is a great way to learn about civic institutions."

I nodded. *Yes. I am here to learn about civic institutions.*

"Basically we're going to assume roles as state representatives and senators and participate in a mock legislature. So, um . . . that is a lot more fun than it sounds."

"Yes," I said audibly.

"What?" she said.

"I'm sorry?" I said.

"You said something?"

"I was agreeing with you. I'm just—you know—the mock legislature sounds really fun." A little voice inside me, the one that had steered me wrong for seventeen years, whispered . . . *Now is your chance. Be funny. Be funny now.* "Can we mock the mock legislature? Like, heyyy, you're not a real legislature?"

Silence in the room. Very quietly, Groash made the low whistle of a bomb dropping.

Then Amy smiled. "That's funny."

"I've got more material if you're interested."

"Please no," said Chelsea.

Later, we split up to think about legislation. The aim was for us to write bills and then try to shepherd them through the congress just like the real Congress would do, although we would probably do it with a lot less political grandstanding and backroom deals.

Writing legislation is the most sensual of all the legislative arts. This is why so many people in the Senate fall in love with each other. Well, at least in the high school senate they do. I figured it would be easy to come up with a mock law. Imagine something I didn't like and then outlaw it. But I didn't exactly want to be the jackass in the group (I was hoping Groash would fill that role naturally), because I sensed that was not the way into Amy's heart. So I had to come up with something good.

I drew a blank. Nothing came to mind. I normally considered myself to be a pretty smart guy, when it came to things that didn't involve human interaction. I took the fact that I never had to try in any of my classes as clear evidence that I was an undiscovered genius and was just biding my time. I prided myself on not starting any research papers until the night before they were due and writing them as fast as possible and still getting a B plus. (Brian had taken this to a new level and wrote most of his term papers during lunch, which was both infuriating and inspiring.)

So, anyway, I had nothing. I stared at the wood table in the

Y's rec room. Someone had carved the word *dick* an inch deep with a knife. Whoever carved that had more ideas than I did.

"Hey, guys," said Chelsea, after she'd seen a few proposed bills. "How about no more laws legalizing marijuana?"

Groash groaned from where he was playing pool with Amanda. "I thought this was supposed to be fun!"

Amy spotted me with my head in my hands and came over.

"How's it going?" She smiled.

I looked down at the word *dick* carved meticulously into the desk. "Um . . ." I put my hand over it. "Good. Totally good. Brilliant, in fact."

"Great," she said. "Do you have any ideas?"

"So many. Just . . . so many it's hard to pick one," I lied.

"That's always my problem, I'm always like . . . aah! Where to start?"

"Exactly!"

"So I just chuck everything out the window and start with health-care reform."

"Oh yeah. Oh totally. Health care is sweet."

"My mom's a cancer survivor, so . . ."

I am a dumb person. I am not smart. Why do I say things?

"But that gets really complicated really fast!" She laughed.

"I know! So screw it."

Her eyelid twitched a bit. So did mine. *Did I just say screw health-care reform to a girl whose mother had cancer?*

She managed a smile. "So what's one of your ideas?"

"Um . . . well I'm having trouble framing it, you know?"

"All you do is just identify the problem," she said, putting one hand on the table and leaning down just a bit. I could see the fluorescent lights through the waterfall of blond hair that fell off her shoulder. *I want to put my face there*, I thought. Somewhere, I imagined I heard a chorus of woodland creatures breaking into song. (Or YMCA creatures, which were most likely rats.) "Like, is there a problem that you see?"

"What?"

"A problem."

"What's the problem?"

"The problem you're trying to solve with the law. That you're writing. Right now."

It was excruciating. It was like watching a car wreck in slow motion, where the dummy is ejected from the driver's seat and smashes his smooth white head into the windshield. *Must concentrate so as not to look like a dumbass.*

"Um . . . leaves. There's . . . um . . . like a leaf problem. In the fall. They fall down."

What was I talking about? Was I going to ban leaves falling off trees? Was that my proposed legislation? If I could've kicked my brain in the balls at that moment, I would've. *Wake the hell up and get on your game.*

"Oh," she said, her hair shimmering like a golden flood of awesomeness. "Yeah, I mean you could do something about the leaves falling down. Like, what is your solution to the leaves?"

Superglue. On all the trees.

"Superglue." And then I realized I had said what I was thinking out loud, which was a real problem when communicating with girls.

"What?"

"We superglue the leaves. To all the trees."

Have you ever had a lawn mower that you have to start with one of those pull cords? And you pull on it, and the engine goes a little bit? And you pull again and kick the damn thing, and it doesn't work? And then, finally, you pull as hard as you can, and it starts (sometimes)? My brain finally started.

"I'm kidding," I said. "You totally thought my bill was about supergluing leaves to trees!"

"Yeah, that's what you said. That's why I thought that."

"Yeah, no, it's about um . . . mulching. How leaves in garbage bags contribute to the . . . uh . . . landfill problem and how we should make people either mulch their leaves or . . . um . . . shred them." I was doing pretty well until the "shred them." What the hell was that? Make everyone buy a leaf shredder? Actually, in Wisconsin, I could've just said that we should shoot the leaf piles with shotguns to break them up. That would've worked.

"Oh, that's a good idea," she said, and I could actually see a wave of relief wash over her as she came to the conclusion that I wasn't an alien masquerading as a human.

So that's how we met. Talking about mulching leaves.

Cue the romantic music.

SEVEN

Craig and Amy Get Together in a Romantic Sense; Hot Damn

Every Wednesday, we'd go to the Y; Groash would play pool, and I would work on my bills. There was the mulching bill. There was my proposed bill to lower the drinking age back to eighteen.

"Please, no more of those," said Chelsea, putting her face in her hands.

I wrote a bill preserving forestland from development, which Amy kind of liked. And then I wrote something about raising taxes on rich people to pay for homeless animal shelters, which she liked even more. Basically, my entire legislative philosophy was to figure out what Amy liked and then write that into law. If she liked My Little Pony, I would've written a bill taxing the hell out of rich people to pay for My Little Pony statues all over the state.

Pretty much anytime a guy does something in front of a girl (provided he is attracted to girls), his basic aim is to seduce that girl by being great at it. *If only I can put this spherical ball through* the hoop, she will love me. If I make this pool shot, she will realize I am the guy for her. For me, it took this form: If I craft perfect legislation, Amy will fall for me.

This is probably why men become actual senators in the first place. I realize this does not explain female senators. I believe female senators exist because they are trying to, you know, improve things.

So I tried. Unlike Groash, whose only bill was banning visible back hair (after the first three bills legalizing marijuana had been shot down).

Even though she was only a junior, Chelsea had the thankless task of trying to mold Groash into a model of a future elected representative. It was difficult because, let's face it, he was barely housebroken. Most nights she left the Y in an exasperated stupor.

"You can't sit like that," she would say.

"Dude. This is how I sit."

"That's how you sit when you don't give a shit. If you want to have people actually listen to you, you have to sit up straight."

"You're like my new dad."

But they became kind of friends, and Amy and I sort of hit it off, even though we traveled in completely different social circles. I mean, she was the class president of everything, and I was, at most, the lieutenant of not much at all except dorkishness. However, I happily discovered that there was also a deep vein of weirdness to Amy that manifested itself in her laugh, which was kind of a high-pitched honk. It sounded a little like a chipper seal clapping its flippers together and made her seem a little less perfect, which I loved. So I wrote my bills, and we talked, and every time I saw her my heart leaped into my throat and crushed my windpipe like an aluminum can.

This went on until Wednesday, November 3.

Groash was on a periodic vacation from his house. Basically, every so often he would leave without telling his mother where he was going and would crash at somebody else's house for three or four days until the friend got sick of him. In the pantheon of moms, Groash's mom was somewhere just above hamster. She didn't eat Groash right after he was born, but she didn't do a whole hell of a lot after that. She usually didn't notice much when he was gone.

But he wasn't coming to YIG (that's what we called Youth in Government; we used an acronym because we were so damn cool). Chelsea had contracted some kind of avian flu (I assumed Groash was probably the carrier of the disease), and the other couple of people who were part of our team didn't show up; so it was just me and Amy and Amanda.

"All right, whatever, I'm leaving," said Amanda. She probably had things to do, like get high.

So it was me and Amy. Alone. Amy was wearing a white shirt with the words CHANGE IS GOOD written in small print over the chest. Her hair was back in a ponytail, and she was in the middle of throwing up her hands in frustration.

"Dang it," she said. "I guess we can work on doing more bills, or we can just cancel."

"My sister's not coming to pick me up till nine."

"Oh."

That comment hung in the air for a minute, and I was acutely aware of the room. The old, beat-up pool table. The ancient wooden desks emblazoned with profanity. The musty smell from the sweat of countless generations of young men. My face started tingling. In every situation like this in my life I had gotten scared, I had fled the room, I had found an excuse not to take a chance. But . . . change is good, right? I felt my pulse throbbing in my temples. *I should do something. I should be funny. I should—*

"Well, we should do something fun, then," she said with a quirky smile.

"Yes!" I shouted. Or maybe not shouted. Maybe I whispered that huskily while brushing my bangs out of my eyes. Maybe I always did push-ups before I went to Youth in Government to make me look ever-so-slightly more buff.

"You want to go for a walk?"

I will walk with you into hell and back.

"Sure," I said, trying to sound casual as my soul caught fire and exploded with joy.

It was one of those rare evenings in early November when it was actually warm enough to be outside. And when I say "warm enough," I mean that you could still see your breath, but it wasn't so cold that you were a shivering mass of ice.

We walked through downtown, which was largely deserted because most of the businesses had moved out by the interstate. So we walked through empty parking lots and past vacant buildings and the random insurance agency and lonely coffee shop with one customer. There was no one else on the sidewalks, and the light from the streetlamps was yellowish and dim.

Amy skipped ahead of me most of the time, shuffling a bit, then hopping up on the occasional parking barrier. The whole area near the river had been paved over long ago, but the cement was cracking now, and there were areas where chunks of the sidewalk were missing.

"I want to show you something," she said.

I hustled after her as she crossed one of the busier streets. Past that, the concrete gave out and we were in a group of sparse, overgrown weeds that I guess could be considered trees.

"Come on," she said, picking her way through the trees to an old railroad bridge.

In the distant past, trains used to go through downtown and carried things like cars and the circus, but these days the tracks were largely unused. There was a small hill of loose rock leading up to the bridge, and Amy clambered over it like a very attractive goat. I mean, okay, she didn't look like a goat. That was a poor choice of words, but she was goatlike in her climbing abilities. I stumbled after her, starting a small avalanche, but succeeded in not dying or otherwise embarrassing myself.

She stopped about halfway across the bridge and looked out over the river. The light from the nearby buildings bounced off the black water, glinting and shimmering.

IT WAS ROMANTIC.

"I wonder if there's any organized crime in Janesville," I said. "And if they killed people, maybe they would dump them in here."

She honked a laugh.

"I like how your mind is always on crime," she said. "It really tells me a lot about you."

"I have a disturbing past."

"Do you?"

"There have been a lot of . . . unfortunate accidents around me." My mind drifted back to Son of Bo-Dag and his accusing, squashed little guinea pig eyes.

"That doesn't surprise me."

I laughed. "Have you ever killed a man?"

"A man? No." She elbowed me in the ribs. "Not lately. 'Course if I did want to kill a man, this would probably be the place."

Mist was sinking over the river. It felt clammy and cold, like the spirit of the town was conspiring to drive me out. I edged a little closer to Amy. She was wearing her green fuzzy parka thing.

"You know, I come out here sometimes," she said.

"Really?"

"Yeah. It's cool. I mean it's nice to just be by myself sometimes."

"That's like a nineteenth-century-poet thing," I said.

"To look out at a river?"

"Yeah. Like you're thinking deep thoughts."

She turned to me, with one eyebrow half-raised. "You'd be surprised."

She was close, and I could see the reflection of the distant streetlights in her eyes. My breathing got shallow.

"If you kill me now," I whispered, "the leaf-mulching bill will die with me."

She honked again and elbowed me in the ribs. "I think that's probably a good idea. First of all, in order to manufacture all the superglue you're going to need, you'll have to clear-cut all the forests for glue factories."

"I'm cool with that. Price of progress."

"And then where are you going to get all that glue?"

"Probably have to kill all the horses."

This time she bumped into me with her shoulder, *which was awesome.*

"Right," she said, "but to get all those horses, you're going to have to steal them from people, so you'll probably have to institute martial law to get them—and, of course, once you've got martial law, then you'll have a dictatorship. And then after you become a dictator, you'll start murdering your political rivals. But the leaves will stay on the trees."

"Like I said, it's a small price to pay."

The mist intensified. The railing in front of us was slick, and I gripped it with my hands, looking down at the black water below us. *Don't die. Life is just getting good.*

"This is much better than working on our bills," I said. "And it's not like we're going to be politicians anyway."

"You have too many dark secrets."

"Exactly. And what about you? Do you have any dark secrets?"

Her eyes sparkled just a bit. "Sure. But I'm not going to be a politician either. I don't know what I'm going to do with my life, but not that."

"That's okay. You're only seventeen."

"Eighteen."

"Ooh. You're an older woman. Nice."

"I got held back in second grade." She said it in offhand way, like *I killed a man in Reno.*

"You got held back?" *Amy Carlson got held back? The president of everything got held back?*

"Yep."

"Wow."

"I couldn't spell. I mean, seriously, I hated school. As soon as we started having spelling tests, they put me in Remedial English. I mean, nobody even bothered testing me for dyslexia at the time, so they just assumed I was stupid and made me repeat second grade."

"That sucks."

"Yeah. I didn't even get diagnosed until eighth grade. I just always assumed I was kind of dumb. Everything that was easy for everyone else was really difficult for me. I got my driver's license when I was a sophomore, though, so that was cool. Suddenly I had a whole bunch of new friends who used me for rides." She made a little "hurm" sound.

And then we were walking again, this time on the other bank of the river, where there was a stone wall to keep people from jumping in (not that anyone would jump in). As we were going along, I felt her hand slip into mine. I tried to keep walking and concentrated on making sure my feet were going one in front of the other, but mostly what I was doing was mentally hyperventilating.

Sheisholdingmyhand! Sheisholdingmyhand! Sheisholdingmyhand!

We did manage a conversation, even though I was still trying my hardest to concentrate on putting one foot in front of another.

"I've got a theory," she said. "You have to embrace chaos. I mean, I guess it's weird for the girl at the top of the class to say that, you know? But that's what life is about. It's about making peace with uncertainty."

"Change is good," I said.

She smiled. "Change is good."

"Unless you're a werewolf."

"Sometimes change is bad."

We kept going. Youth in Government normally lasted for two

hours, and we spent all of it just walking around. Every so often the wind would whip up, and the edges of my eyes would water— when I was little everyone made fun of me for crying all the time when it got cold, and since it was Wisconsin, I was basically leaking 24/7. I wanted to tell Amy everything. About how I'd never felt comfortable in my own skin, how I couldn't seem to figure out how to "be" around other people, how everything that came so easily for my sister was so difficult for me. I wanted to tell her how I needed to get out of Janesville, how I wanted to see the world or at least find someplace where I didn't feel like an alien all the time. I imagined there was some better version of me just waiting to emerge, like you could open up my ribs like a pair of wings and there would be the beautiful, hopeful person that I thought I was.

I wanted to tell her that was going to be me someday. But mostly I listened.

"There's a patch of forest behind my house," she said. "My dad bought it when he bought the house—twenty acres or something. And it's all unspoiled, you know? When I was a kid, when I was feeling miserable, which was pretty much all the time, I'd go out there. You know when we talked about Emerson and those guys in English class? That's what I'd do. Just go out and open my eyes as wide as I could and take it in, you know? Every little detail, every little scrap of beauty. That was God."

"Do you still do that?"

"Not as much." She looked far away for a bit. "I don't have the time."

We were back at the Y, standing on the street. Kaitlyn would be here any minute to pick me up, driving the car we shared. I had held Amy's hand for an hour, even when it made no sense. Even when we were going up and down stairs, when it looked like we were a pair of convicts who escaped from a maximum security prison.

So now she stood there, about to return to the real world. *What do I do? Do I try to kiss her?* What if she had been holding my hand by accident and then felt too embarrassed to drop it? *Whoops, I thought you were mentally slow and needed some guidance, that's why I held your hand for the last hour or so.* Would my sister get there on time? I should—

And then her face was right in front of mine, and she was kissing me. The cool tip of her nose touched mine and it was a hell of a lot better than smashing lips together.

Thus began the greatest time of my life.

Soon to be squashed, of course. By the dark secrets.

EIGHT

The Way Out

When I was growing up, I figured it was only a matter of time before I developed mutant powers. Sure, a steady diet of comic books may have produced unrealistic expectations of how life was going to go (maybe I'd die a few times, only to be resurrected in an alien body, maybe I'd turn evil for a spell, maybe I'd get cloned—who knows?), but I thought that my outcast status was a sure sign I was chosen for greatness and/or mutation.

In fifth grade, we took a tour of the local GM plant. It was a vast, cavernous space that smelled like acid and metal. Skeletal sections of massive trucks, Suburbans, slowly jerked their way down conveyor belts, occasionally tended by guys with beer bellies and unfortunate haircuts. We were forced into a long, snaking, single-file line and marched through the place for two or three weeks, up and down staircases, and into and out of hell itself. A lot of our fathers worked there (mine didn't—he was at the Parker Pen plant, which was another kind of hellish factory, except they made, you know, *pens* instead of huge trucks).

"It's tough when you start out," said our guide. "But once you build up seniority they move you to the easier jobs." He laughed and gulped from his can of Shasta soda. "Bob over there has been here thirty years—now he just taps on the windshields." Bob waved, holding up his tiny rubber hammer.

My classmates nodded. Some of them joked. Some of them were seeing their futures. Working on the line, tapping on windshields, and drinking low-grade soda. (Shasta? Seriously? What the hell?)

I watched as Kaitlyn and her friends giggled and clustered together, perfectly at ease. Some of the boys were running around despite the continuous shouts of "No running! Hey, I meant no running! Damn it. Quit your running! Shit. Whoops, I mean shoot." I stood in the back, watching.

I didn't know how they did it. And even though Brian had joined our class fairly recently, we weren't close friends yet. I didn't have any close friends, actually. I didn't know how to make it work. It was like everyone else knew how to swim, and I was waiting on the edge of the water, terrified to drop into it, certain I would drown.

Even in fifth grade I knew that I didn't belong. I didn't belong in this factory, spending my days tapping on windshields, but I didn't belong with the other kids either. I imagined something more, but I wasn't exactly clear on what "more" was.

When I get my mutant powers, I'm so fucking out of here.

My mutant powers, sadly, were late in development, and at ten, I probably wouldn't have used the f-word, but you get the general idea.

My plan was to get out. If that required joining a super-team of misunderstood crimefighters, so be it.

Actually, the above story probably would have done better as my college admissions essay than my eventual paper on Dostoevsky, which contained phrases like "Dostoevsky sensed the ugliness and the beauty of human suffering." I was big into beauty and suffering.

But the way out arrived the summer after my sophomore year. It was my first piece of college mail, a glossy, high-quality pamphlet showing a bucolic campus filled with a group of very attractive, racially diverse students smiling and holding their books. They were laughing—clearly life was very humorous on this campus. Here, finally, might be the place where I would belong. It looked like everyone belonged. I should note that none of the people in the photos were wearing a dark, woolen trench coat, but still, it looked amazing.

It said Oberlin College but might as well have said THIS IS A MORE REALISTIC FUTURE THAN BECOMING A MUTANT.

"No," said Dad when he saw that one. "Absolutely not. Under no circumstances. That place is for hippies."

So I put that one in the "maybe" pile.

The mail kept coming. Sometimes two or three a day. By the end of my junior year I had amassed a stack of pamphlets two feet thick. Some of them were offering fancy things like computers or trees or a pack of druids roaming campus.

Kaitlyn was getting the mail too, but early on she had settled on UW-Madison. Madison was a good school, but I didn't want to go there because it just seemed like a vaster, more intense version of high school. Plus, my sister would be there. I needed something smaller. I decided to list it as a "safety" school and then focused on picking the kind of schools that would send my dad into epileptic fits.

This one costs a billion dollars? Awesome. Apply.

This one requires everyone to become a vegetarian and wear beads? Done.

Co-ed dorms? On it.

This one encourages students to howl at the moon during finals? Perfect.

Anywhere that seemed to have a small number of students, a large number of trees, and a safe distance from home fit the bill. Now all that was left was to winnow down the list, find a place to visit, and apply.

And I was all set to do that until I kissed Amy, at which point my priorities shifted radically.

———

"I need three hundred dollars," I said, a week after the magical day in front of the YMCA.

It was dinner, and, like most dinners Mom made, it sucked. Usually, we had breaded cutlets of some kind of unidentifiable fish product. Nobody complained, because the alternative (my dad cooking) was worse. There was a time when she ceded responsibility of the cooking to my dad, but after our sixth consecutive meal of burned meat sculpture, we went back to Mom.

"I need three hundred dollars," I repeated.

Dad looked at me. "Is this for drugs?"

Yes, Dad. You've hit the nail on the head. I've got a shipment of heroin coming in from Colombia, and I need to pay my dealers.

"Craig's not cool enough to buy drugs," said Kaitlyn.

"What does that mean?" asked Mom.

"He wouldn't even know where to get drugs."

"I know where to get drugs!" I didn't know where to get drugs actually, but I wasn't about to let Kaitlyn be right about anything.

"Craig!" cried Mom.

"Where, then?" Kaitlyn demanded. "Where do you get drugs?"

"I know people," I said.

"Craig!"

"You're such a liar."

Mom turned to Kaitlyn. "Do you know where to get drugs?"

"Of course. I'm not socially illiterate."

"I hate it when you talk like this," said Mom, eating her fish.

"Can we get back to my pressing need for three hundred dollars, please?" I tried to hand Dad the little handout Amy had made explaining our need for a crap-ton of cash.

"What is this for?"

"It's Youth in Government. We're going to take a field trip to Madison in December. We go to the capitol and hang out and pass bills and stuff."

"It's drugs," said Kaitlyn. "'Youth in Government' is new slang for cocaine."

"Shut up!"

Dad scrutinized the handout and tried to determine if this was, in fact, code for white gold.

"It's good for my college application!" I stammered, hoping that would convince him.

"Well, son," he said finally, springing his trap, "I think I can find the money . . . if you go deer hunting with me this year."

Wisconsin doesn't really celebrate Thanksgiving as much as it gives thanks that it's time to send the menfolk into the woods with guns. 'Cause there are deer in them there hills, and they are asking for it, prancing around with their little hooves, eating stuff, and looking very shootable. At least, I suppose that's the logic that draws five hundred thousand men with guns, decked out in silly orange vests and hats with earflaps, into the woods. During deer hunting season, Wisconsin has the third-largest standing army in the world. I am not making this up.

I hated hunting.

Kaitlyn was never forced to go, because she was a girl, which, despite the many inequities of the patriarchy, at least gave you a free escape from hunting. I had been dragged along exactly once—when I was eleven. I guess my dad figured my ability to kill our pets could best be utilized killing deer in the wild.

"You know, I've just got so much on my schedule right now," I lied.

"Like what?"

For the last six years, I had gone through every conceivable excuse. I had faked illnesses. I had hidden in the basement. I had performed an exquisitely choreographed mental breakdown. Anything. Each time my dad would finally surrender and say, "Next year you're coming for sure." But this time, the hunting trip would interrupt my new relationship with Amy—what if she forgot about me when I went into the woods? What if I forgot about her? Could we survive being apart for half a week?

"There's a lot of reading I need to get to—in preparation for—"

My dad interrupted. "You can do that on your own time after we're done hunting. You'll like it. It'll make you a man."

"I'm pretty sure that's just a biological process, Dad. It's probably inevitable—"

"Craig—"

"He should go," chipped in Kaitlyn, eager to see me suffer.

There was no way out. If I wanted three hundred bucks I was

going to have to sit in the woods and murder Bambi the way God intended. And then I realized I had one last chance—

"College visit! I need to go on a college visit. So sorry. So very sorry. Can't make it this year."

Dad's scalp wrinkled in annoyance. Victory.

"I know," said my mom, grinning. "You can do a college visit right after hunting! So you can have more time together."

Damn it.

"Fine," I said. "But I'm not killing anything. Intentionally."

So that's how I ended up deciding to visit a college named GACK.

Okay, it wasn't actually named Gack. It was actually GAC, but that doesn't sound as funny.

That's just an acronym, though, for Gustavus Adolphus College, which was apparently named for a Swedish dude with a luxurious mustache. It was located in bustling Saint Peter, Minnesota, which was a quaint collection of houses that had no business calling itself a town. It was close enough that we could drive there, and far enough that it didn't feel like home.

"This one, huh?" said my dad, examining the pamphlet like he was deciphering hieroglyphics.

"Yeah," I said.

"This is the one," he repeated, smoothing out his mustache.

"Sure."

"Okay then. Okay." He took a deep breath. "They got a price tag on here?"

"It's probably like a million dollars." I watched as his soul cracked a little bit. "I'm kidding. It's probably slightly less than that."

Dad dropped the pamphlet on my bed and stood there for a second, looking around. "Maybe we can sell some of these comic books." He retreated to the door. "But, uh . . . if that's what you want to do, then we'll go check it out. Okay?"

"Okay."

"I mean, what the hell is the point of me working all the time if you can't go to school, right?"

"Thanks."

I have to admit, it wasn't what I expected from him. But there was still the matter of deer hunting, which was going to occur immediately before our trip to Minnesota. If only there was some way to get out of the hunting portion. I had developed a new plan: convert to Buddhism. I had the conversation ready in my mind:

ME: Dad, I have to tell you something.

DAD: What is it, son? And might I remind you that before we visit that fruity college in Minnesota you will become a man.

ME: Right. Well, I need to tell you something. I'm a Buddhist now.

DAD: The hell you say?

ME: I no longer believe in hell. I'm a Buddhist.

MOM (shouting from somewhere else in the house): What's Craig saying?

DAD: He's got a butt fetish!

ME: Buddhist, Dad. Buddhist.

DAD: Oh.

ME: I'm following the noble eightfold path to enlightenment.

DAD: Shit. Well, you're still going hunting.

ME: I'm spiritually conflicted about that.

DAD: I'm not.

Even in my imagination, the plan failed.

Honestly, though, I couldn't even get into it. I was too wrapped up in Amy. We didn't have any classes together. But we talked every night on the phone, and I felt like I had been granted entrance to an entirely separate universe that existed parallel to my own. A universe that had always been there, side by side with mine, and yet was totally foreign. We made out all the time. Pretty much, whenever anyone left the room, we were sucking face. I won't go into too much detail about it except to say that a lightbulb popped over my head, and I realized that this must be what everyone else is doing with their lives all the time. Like, everyone was just waiting for me to leave the room and then leaping on each other in the most glorious party imaginable. And until this point, I had never been invited. Maybe I had just never felt like I had permission to join the party.

My fantasies spun into the future; what Christmas would be like, what would we do on spring break, the amazing night we would have together at prom when she would glide down the stairs in some kind of shimmering dress and I would spontaneously learn how to dance. My whole senior year lit up like a glowing map.

Life was great.

Until the father-son trip of death.

NINE

Father-Son Bondage
Oh God, Stop It

PART 1: The Hunting Trip of Death.
PART 2: The College Visit of Death.
PART 3: The Ride Home of Death.
PART 1.5: The Brief Stop at the Truck Stop of Death.

I realize "hunting trip of death" is a little bit redundant, as the entire purpose of hunting is to cause death. It's like saying the road trip of driving or something.

Anyway, as the day of our trip grew nearer, I began feeling claustrophobic and started sweating at inappropriate times. I was distracted in class; instead of taking notes (or secretly writing Amy's name, like, four hundred times because I was an idiot), I started drawing pictures of deer with little captions, like "Don't kill me, please" or "Strike me down and I will become more powerful than you can possibly imagine" or "Just try it, mofo." I wrote a lot of things from the deer's perspective.

There's a concept in Wisconsin called deer widows, which is basically when all the menfolk leave town to go on their trips and the women are left behind, bewildered and confused, to do whatever it is women do without men. (Celebrate.)

We set off on a Monday for the north woods; my dad had packed the car with supplies from the secret gun room, including thirty-four pounds of beef jerky, which would provide for the bulk of our sustenance. I brought along a rat-eared copy of *The Brothers Karamazov* and some stationery.

"You're not gonna need any of that," my dad said, shaking his head.

"We don't read or write while hunting?"

Dad's eyes narrowed, and I'm sure the thought of *Where did I go wrong?* reverberated through his mind (like usual). This was going to be a tough week for him.

We had worked through seven pounds of beef jerky by the time we reached the cabin that would be our new home without womenfolk. My dad liked to hunt with a cadre of ex-military bastards whom I will now painstakingly describe, as I spent three days with these creatures in a tiny cabin in the north woods.

1. Chester. I didn't catch Chester's last name. Chester smoked Marlboro reds and wore a giant puffy coat and spat a lot. He spoke in a mumble, and no one could understand him. He was generally perceived to be the smartest and nicest human of the group.

2. Buck. I am not making this up. The guy's name was Buck, and he was hunting for bucks. Buck's favorite words were *god damn it*, and sometimes he could create entire sentences out of only that sentiment.

3. Uncle Jim. Uncle Jim was seventy-six years old, as thin as a cardboard box, and had a mustache like a giant caterpillar had died below his nose. He could barely see, which was a really helpful quality for a person wandering through the woods with a rifle. Uncle Jim took a shine to me right away.

4. Poole Tom. Why was he called Poole Tom? You would have to ask Poole Tom's mother. It was also possible that Poole Tom had no mother and was, instead, an Italian sausage that had been struck by lightning or had fallen into a vat of mysterious chemicals. Poole Tom was 272 pounds of solid fat, Green Bay Packers trivia, and bratwurst. Poole Tom was everything you imagine Wisconsin to be, wrapped up into a greasy package and equipped with enough firepower to break into Fort Knox.

And, of course, me and my dad. They called my dad "Handy" for some reason that I did not want to understand. My dad went all in on the whole hunting ensemble. He looked resplendent in his puffy orange coat, as if someone had coated the Michelin Man in Cheez-Its and popped a Green Bay Packers hat on its head. The hat covered up his gleaming bald dome, which was normally his most pronounced feature, but he made up for it with a powerful reddish mustache. I guess you could call his mustache auburn, if that color were ever applied to mustaches. The rest of him was wiry and tough; he had smoked for most of his adult life (he quit shortly after the last of our pets died, which made him cranky), and the years of nicotine had sunk into his skin.

Let's talk about how awful deer hunting is for a minute.

Imagine it is twenty-six degrees outside. There's a light freezing drizzle in the air, the kind that gets inside your clothes and makes you feel like a corpse. You are in the woods. That part is kind of nice. Your objective is to remain completely still as long as possible.

So you're there, crouching, because you must crouch; you have to pee; your thighs—which were never terribly strong to begin with since you don't do a lot of exercise—are burning with the heat of a thousand suns; and the cold drizzle is sneaking down the back of your spine and finding its way to your crotch region, which is only making the need to pee worse. In your hands is a rifle. Why is there a rifle in your hands? Because your objective is to wait until beautiful nature creeps into view and SHOOT THE HELL OUT OF IT.

This is what our forefathers did, I imagine my dad saying.

Our forefathers also had no teeth, painted themselves blue, and danced naked in the woods.

Then, after twelve or fourteen or nine thousand hours of this, you go back to a "shack," which is a marginally heated cabin in the woods in which you all sleep in the same room for camaraderie or some other insanity. You bring along giant industrial sleeping bags meant to keep people warm on Mars, and then you lie down on the floor in a big room where Poole Tom falls asleep first. Do you think an animated Italian sausage named Poole Tom snores? Would you like to take a guess? Just take one little guess.

THE MAN SNORES LIKE AN ATOMIC BOMB GOING OFF EVERY SEVEN SECONDS.

Oh, and, hey, do you think it smells nice in there?

"You don't want to shower on these trips," said Uncle Jim. (He's not my uncle, by the way. I don't know why he was called Uncle Jim.) "Deer can smell soap from a mile away. And that fruity dandruff-shampoo shit? Fuck that." Uncle Jim was a sweet old man who dripped death from his fingertips.

All right. I'm calming down. I must remind you that people are doing this for fun. They look forward to it all year. Like, the rest of the year they're just sleeping in their pansy-ass beds, and using their pansy-ass shampoo, and just dreaming of the day when they can leave that all behind.

I imagine Uncle Jim, retired, sitting around and looking at the sunset with his wife. "This November, Martha, I'm gonna sit around in the woods and not shower."

And she's probably thinking, *Don't come back.*

Day one. Dad and I were in the woods. It seemed like my dad's enthusiasm for the trip had been blunted by the realization that he had to go on the trip with me. He'd been a little glum the whole time.

"You're gonna like this," said Dad, smoothing out his mustache. On deer hunting trips he never shaved, so the rest of his face had begun to grow a salt-and-chili-powder sea of stubble.

"I'm not gonna shoot my gun," I said. "If I see a deer, I'm not going to kill it. I'll give it a massage."

"When the time comes, you'll know what to do." My dad had a lot of faith that I would spontaneously mutate into a Man, and he was pretty sure it was going to happen on this trip.

"I know what I'm gonna do. I'm not gonna shoot. That's what I'm gonna do."

"All right, son," he said, clapping me on the shoulder. "You think that now, but when you see a deer . . . you'll know what to do."

"Pretty sure I won't."

"Pretty sure you will."

"Pretty sure I won't." *Seriously, Dad, I can do this all day long. The deer will hear this stupid conversation and stay the hell away.*

"Let me tell you something," he said, trying a different tactic. He crouched kind of low, his back against one of the pine trees. "I've been coming to this cabin with these guys for twenty-three years. I have not missed a time. When your mom was nine months pregnant with you and your sister, you know what I did?"

"You went hunting?"

"I went hunting."

"Was Mom pissed?"

"Women get pissed about all kinds of things. It's best not to even think about it. Now, normally, I would tell you not to use the word *pissed*. But we're in the woods, and we're men. And we can use the word *pissed*."

"Can I use the word *fuck*?"

"Can your mom hear you?"

"I don't think so."

"Well, there's your answer then. Out here in the woods we will swear like men." I have to admit that Hunting Dad was a lot more relaxed than Regular Dad. "Anyway. Twenty-three years. You know how many deer I've shot in twenty-three years?"

I knew.

"Zero," he said, putting his gloved fingers up to make a zero. "You know how many times I've fired my gun? Nineteen. I've missed every time. But I took the shot."

"Is there some kind of life lesson here, Dad? 'Cause I'm missing it."

"You gotta keep shooting. Even if you miss." He nodded sagely, staring off into the woods.

We saw no deer on day one, so we didn't need to shoot. The reason we saw no deer might have been that I was purposefully jumping up and down, waving my arms, snapping twigs, and playing a game of "Nobody kills Bambi on my watch." That might have had something to do with it.

———

Day two. Dad and I were in the woods again. The other guys had heard about what happened on day one and stayed away from us.

The weather was horrible. It warmed up a bit, which was the bane of all deer hunters, because it meant that it would be raining and not snowing. The rain fell in huge, icy drops, slapping the undergrowth like a squadron of bombers.

My wool coat was less than useless in the rain, and it soaked up the ice water like a sponge. I shifted back and forth like I needed to pee, my hands shoved deep into my pockets. The rifle was pinned between my arm and my chest, which was a damn stupid way to hold a rifle.

"Hey, Dad, maybe we're going to get pneumonia."

"We're not getting pneumonia. That's an old wives' tale." Dad had no time for fancy diseases when there was killing to be done.

"I'm freezing out here."

"Maybe you shouldn't have worn that dumb-ass coat. I told ya."

"I know."

"You want to look like a poet, you're gonna suffer like a poet."

"Thanks."

"Our ancestors survived weather like this. They didn't complain, either."

"Our ancestors are all dead. Probably from pneumonia. Maybe I'll write a poem about it."

My dad cracked a smile. Maybe the first one the whole trip.

"Maybe that's what I could major in. Poetry writing. Hey, that's where your money could go. Sending your son to school to study fruity pneumonia poems."

"You're killing me." He chuckled. "Ah, shit, Craig. Study what you want. I mean, I'm pretty sure you've got no future working with your hands. I figured that out when you were about six and you sat on that guinea pig. So you better be able to work with your brain."

"Yeah."

"Better that way, anyway. Used to be . . . I started working at Parker Pen out of high school. You could get a decent job then without a college education. Get benefits, pension, the whole bit. But, uh . . . it's not that way anymore. It's never gonna be that way again, so . . . so maybe there's a future in poetry, what the hell do I know? Not much." His eyes drifted off into the woods. "You think you know how something's supposed to work. How life's supposed to go and then . . . then things change."

Change is good, I thought. But I didn't say it.

We saw no deer on day two.

When we got back to the hut, Buck had got a buck. It was worth fifteen points. It took me a long time to figure out that the points system only referred to the number of points that were on the buck's antlers, which made sense, I guess. I had always figured that there was some giant scoreboard somewhere.

"Goddamn it!" he shouted, apparently happy. "God-damn-it."

"Wow," said Dad, trying not to be jealous.

"Goddamn it," said Buck, thoughtfully.

When you kill a deer, you strap it to the top of your car, and you go home, laughing and crying and confident in your manliness. The rest of us stayed on.

The last day. There was an odd look in Dad's eyes today. I would call it defeat. There had been twenty-three years without deer. He had only managed to bring his son hunting twice in that time, and here I was, acting like a complete donkey out in the woods. I had my reasons, of course, namely that I was responsible for the death of enough innocent animals and didn't want to be the cause of any more.

So, anyway, before we went out at dawn (oh, that reminds me of another reason hunting sucks: you need to go out just before the sun comes up), I heard him in the other room talking with Uncle Jim. I only heard the last line of the conversation when Uncle Jim said, "I'll fall on that grenade."

Then Uncle Jim came over and told me I was going out in the woods with him today.

Being with Uncle Jim was slightly less fun than being with my dad, which is to say that it was negative fun. Uncle Jim was all business all morning long, but after it became clear that the deer had learned to stay away from the moron in the trench coat, things lightened up a bit.

"Craig," he said, after we'd had our daily lunch of beef jerky.

"Yeah?"

He ran his hand over his big, fluffy mustache.

"Are ya gay?"

"I don't think so."

"Everybody's a little bit gay?"

"Maybe ten percent then?" I was just ballparking that. I was probably 0 percent gay, but I didn't want to contradict him.

Uncle Jim nodded. "You going to college next year?"

"Yeah."

"Gonna be a gay college?"

"I'm not sure they actually have gay colleges, but I'm open to the possibility."

Uncle Jim set down his gun. "You got a girlfriend?"

"Pretty sure."

His mustache curled around a little bit, which I guess indicated a smile. "Well, you better find out. Let me tell ya something, though. Shit. That first girlfriend? That's all the gold in Fort Knox, kid. All the gold in Fort Knox."

"Yeah." I think Uncle Jim was trying to be wistful here, but I'm not sure it was working.

"After that first one? Shit. Fuck it."

"Yeah." I nodded, not really sure what he meant.

He patted my knee. "Know what I'm saying?"

"Yes," I lied.

"Fort Knox. All the best in life is right there for you, right now. *Savor* it."

"Okay."

"'Cause before you know it"—he smiled again—"you're just an asshole sitting in the woods talking to a kid, and ain't nobody gonna love you again." Then he got up and took his gun and walked away. I sat there for a minute, watching him and trying to think of what he must have been like as a teenager.

TEN

The College Visit of Death

We stopped at a truck stop to shower. I want you to let that statement sink in for a second. *We stopped at a truck stop to shower.* If you've never been to a shower at a truck stop in central Wisconsin during hunting season, you are missing one of life's grandest adventures. Let's just say that cleaning was not a priority for either the workers at the truck stop or the voluminous naked dudes who were hanging out and chatting.

I'm not going to try to explain why men raised before 1960 or so feel perfectly comfortable letting it all hang out, but there it was. I seriously saw a guy wearing a shirt, and socks, and shoes, and *nothing else* standing in front of a mirror and shaving. What is this thought process? How does one make the decisions that lead you into this? *Socks? Check. Shoes? Check. Underwear? Who needs it?*

I'm sorry. I need to move on. I really need to move on.

Gustavus Adolphus was about a five-hour drive from the hunting spot and allowed us to engage in the scintillating father-son conversation that was a hallmark of our relationship.

"There are some hills in western Wisconsin."

"Yes. Yes, there are hills."

"Not something you see every day. Hills."

"Nope."

"Not quite mountains. But definitely hills."

"Definitely."

"Trees on 'em."

Kill me. Please, God, kill me.

I gave up on the conversation and focused on the thing that had occupied my brain for most of the past two weeks: Amy. What was she was doing right now? Was she crafting legislation? (I had weird fantasies, I admit it.) *I have a girlfriend* reverberated in my brain like a happy background radiation. I could endure hunting, I could even make it through the college visit, if I focused on that.

Dad drove in silence most of the way, which was better than the talking. And I'm not sure whether it was the complete failure of deer hunting, or the thought of his son going to college, but his mind seemed far away too.

When we crossed the border into Minnesota my stomach started churning and my skin buzzed. It felt like I had swallowed a series of moles and they were busy gnawing at my insides. You know, my typical reaction to new social situations. But I thought of Amy again, and maybe it wasn't so bad this time.

Gustavus Adolphus is a perfectly nice place. It's like a college, only smaller and more adorable. Brandeen, our tour guide, who sported rainbow-colored hair and a shirt that said GOD LOVES LESBIANS, happily escorted us around campus while my dad disintegrated.

Every once in a while he would make a comment from the back of the group like "So what kind of jobs do people from this college get?"

Then she'd say something like, "Getting a job isn't really the point of going to college; instead it's more important to grow intellectually and discover your own truth."

He turned a bit yellow. It was like Superman was chained to a liberal arts college made entirely of kryptonite. *If I had to go hunting, you have to go through this college visit.*

But the tour was great, and I sat in on a class, which was also great, and then I had a meal in the cafeteria, which was not great but still okay, and then the shit hit the fan.

That's when I met Jonas, my host student for the night. My dad had gone to Best Western to recover and pray for deliverance or financial aid, and I was left to spend the night on campus with this guy.

Jonas was tall and thin, with a sweep of black hair and beady little eyes like a rodent. He had the collar turned up on his polo shirt and wore cool pants that he had acquired from a thrift store somewhere. We were on the third floor of a dorm named Co-Ed, which kind of gave away that it was a co-ed dorm. The tour guide had helpfully explained that it was once named Norelius, but that was hard to say, so they went with Co-Ed instead.

I stood there for a second.

He stood there for a second.

"Hey . . . My name's Craig, I'm a prospective student," I managed. The moles in my stomach started drumming on my intestines.

His beady little eyes focused on me for a second and then unfocused. "Shit," he said. "I totally fucking forgot about this. Um . . . fuck."

I nodded. "Yeah." This was starting out great.

Jonas went to his dresser and spritzed himself with cologne. "Son-of-a-bitch, man. Um . . . you want to sit down or whatever?" He gestured vaguely to a couch the color of a corpse. "Don't sit on that. I'm telling you."

"Okay," I said, standing in the dead center of his dorm room. Jonas opened a tiny fridge that nestled next to his bed and took out a bottle of Pig's Eye, which was a special Minnesotan brand of beer famed for its cheapness.

"You want a beer?"

"No, I'm cool. I'm trying to cut back."

"No doubt. No doubt. Fuck!" He kicked his bed. "I'm so sorry, man. I wish I had something planned for you. Tell you what? We're gonna have an awesome time, okay?" He tipped the bottom of the bottle up to the ceiling and proceeded to down the entire beer in one gulp. Afterward he gasped for breath and declared, "Shit."

Silence descended again. I tried to make small talk. "So do you like it here?"

He squinted. "What are you even talking about?"

"At the college?"

"Do I like it at the college?"

"Yeah. I guess that was my question."

"Fuck. Um . . ." He ran a hand through his hair. "Look, dude, I'm not really the person you should be asking questions to, right? Like . . . I don't fucking know if I like it here. How would I know?"

"Huh." I nodded. *This is nice.*

Things got worse in a hurry. Jonas spent the next ten minutes calling his friends and saying things like "I know. Shit. I know. Right. Damn it," which was apparently some kind of language that they used to communicate. We crossed campus to look for a "party" at another dorm, then crossed to a second dorm to find a second "party," and then finally made it to a third dorm where we found the actual party.

The party was stuffed into a near pitch-black lounge, which had all its windows open to let in the freezing Minnesota air. This was needed to counteract the effect of seventy people stuffed into a room the size of a minivan. A large guy with a full beard ran a keg out of the corner, and he was mobbed like he was a celebrity. I got separated from Jonas almost immediately; he squeezed through a scrum of flannel-clad longhairs and disappeared.

I tried to follow, but the wall of humanity closed up behind him. Something wet crashed into me from behind—a burly football player with four cups of beer, the contents of which were now sliding down my back. The wave of people surged toward me, moving somewhat rhythmically to music—Prince—but of course no one could really dance because there was no room.

Huh, this bears a striking resemblance to a few nightmares I've had. How interesting.

I knew no one. The worst part was trying to figure out where to look. I couldn't make eye contact with anyone, obviously. So I tried to stare at the floor and make myself as small as possible. I was also acutely aware that I was in the dead center of the room—it was impossible to squeeze my way to the walls, where I might be able to find some safety by leaning against something and looking nonchalant. Instead, I stood there, buffeted from every side, surrounded by people having a much, much better time.

I clearly would never escape. Most likely I would die here.

PROSPECTIVE STUDENT FOUND SQUISHED TO DEATH IN FOUL-SMELLING BEER-DRENCHED MESS! THIRD DEATH THIS WEEK!

About thirty hours later, Jonas reemerged, somewhat energized and more than a little drunk.

"Shit," he said, when he saw me. "What the hell have you been doing?"

Standing here, paralyzed by anxiety. "Um . . . you know . . . stuff."

"This place is lame, man, you want to get out of here?"

Somehow we ended up in the basement of another dorm, in the room of a guy named Cutter, who was growing dreadlocks and lived entirely by blacklight. He had various posters of Jimi Hendrix on the walls, which were illuminated by Christmas lights. All the standard-issue furniture had been moved out and replaced with shapeless, amoeba-like things that sucked you in and wouldn't let go.

Jonas riffled through his cool pants and produced a large baggie of marijuana.

Oh yay, I thought. *This gets better.*

Pink Floyd was on, an album called *Animals* that had a song with a lot of pigs oinking on it. I'm not making this up. Other denizens of this subterranean world appeared once the smoking began—they had a little pipe shaped like a snake that they passed around.

A cold, prickling sensation began in my stomach and surged up into my lungs. *This is when the cops get me. This is when they break down the door or smash through the windows and cart us off to prison. Or I'll be initiated into "the gang." They'll take out a cow's heart and I'll have to take a bite out of it to prove my loyalty to the cause.*

These people are criminals. I'm in a room with criminals.

This was not on the brochure.

I started sweating. The music got louder. The smoke collected near the ceiling, only slightly counteracted by the bundle of incense they were burning.

Not cool not cool not cool.

In short, I was not reacting well. I was getting all the paranoia and none of the mellow groovy feeling. If this was college, I wanted no part of it.

"Oh shit, man," said Jonas, seeing me huddled in the corner, rocking back and forth. "You cool?"

"Oh, yes. Most cool," I lied.

"You want some?" I looked hard for the cow's heart, but he was only offering the pipe.

"Nope, I'm good. Super good. Just taking in the ambiance."

"You wanna bail?"

Please, God, yes. Let us bail. Let us bail like no one has ever bailed before.

"Sure," I said, trying not to sound too eager.

"'Cause I know another party that's ridiculous," he said.

We tromped back across campus. Jonas regaled me with a tale of a mythical horse tranquilizer.

"So if you smoke it, you need someone else there, because you don't move afterward." He giggled, super excited about this for some reason.

"Probably because you're tranquilized," I said.

"I know! Fuck! We're on the same wavelength!"

I stank like beer and pot. I was pretty sure that if I attended GAC I would be dead by the end of the first semester.

"All right, check it," said Jonas. "This other party is downtown in an apartment, and these guys are serious."

I longed to go back to deer hunting.

"I'm just gonna head back to my room to resupply and we'll be out of here," he said.

I stopped walking and let him get ahead of me.

Maybe I'll just camp out here on campus and no one will notice.

It was getting cold, below freezing now, and I was in an open spot away from the trees. The clouds had cleared, and the moon was bright like a searchlight looking for a kid that had fallen into a stream. There were a few people standing outside the dorms, wearing heavy coats, and pointing up.

I looked up too, and I saw them.

The northern lights.

When they show the northern lights on television or in pictures it looks like a little colorful worm undulating close to the horizon. Like, *Hey, I'm just a weird-ass snake made of shimmering light and I'm just going to wave back and forth over here.*

That's not what they look like at all. I had grown up in Wisconsin and never seen them before in person.

It was more like cascading waves of blue and green light, and they raced across the ENTIRE SKY. It was like the whole dark sky had been shattered, and pink and purple arcs of light were cracking open everywhere.

And I could *hear* them. There was a little popping sound as each wave raced over my head.

I stood there, head craned to the sky. My eyes were watering from the cold air, and I could feel tears streaming down my cheeks. I wasn't crying, but, you know, it probably looked that way.

For a moment I felt the tension ease out of my body. I realized I had been freaking out for about five consecutive days—from the misery of the hunting trip to the insanity of the night's parties; my soul had curled into a ball and was rocking back and forth in the corner. *This is not my future. This is not my future.* And now—somehow—this was what I wanted to see. *The world is bigger than this.*

I took a deep breath. *It's going to be okay.*

I looked around at the other people staring at the sky. They weren't the denizens of the underworld. They weren't a raving band of drunks and stoners. There were people who looked like they could be my friends. Others were joking and laughing. I also noticed a high percentage of girls. This could be all right.

"Hey," said a girl near me. "Are you Jonas's prospie?"

"I'm trying not to be."

"If you want to ditch him, you should totally come with us."

"No, I'm resigned to my lot in life and . . ." I stopped, hearing myself. "You're not having a wild drug-addled party, are you?"

"No."

"Then I will totally hang out with you."

Her name was Melanie and she was tall and had a mane of waist-long curly brown hair that could be used to house a squad of birds. She lived on Jonas's floor, in a triple with two other girls who seemed to be the foundation of the secret resistance, if the resistance were composed of cute girls who lived in a world of potpourri and upscale home furnishings. Tori Amos was playing on CD. There was a hot pot.

It was great.

"This is Craig, he's Jonas's prospie."

The other two girls groaned in sympathy. "Oh my God," said one of them, who kind of resembled John Lennon. "I'm so sorry about that."

"He's like a plague on this floor," said a tiny black girl. "He keeps getting prospies and no one knows how this is happening."

"The last prospie he had puked in the lounge."

"It was a nightmare."

"Seriously," said Melanie. "That guy is a total asshole."

"I was kind of discovering that," I said.

"You're safe now."

"You're safe."

About an hour later, we were having a great time. Popcorn had been made. Incense had been lit, which was driving away the smell of booze and marijuana that clung to me like a cloud of evil.

I had settled into an armchair (they had actual furniture that you could sit on!) and was listening to the rattle and pop of the radiator. The nervousness that had coagulated in my stomach was gone. I felt like . . . I felt like myself.

"You want some tea?" asked Melanie.

"Hell yes I do."

I will add that at this point I had never had tea in my life. I don't know what was wrong with my family (scratch that, I do know what was wrong with my family, and tea was probably not high on my dad's list of acceptable manly beverages) but tea was not something that we aspired to.

Melanie gave me a mug of hot water and Nina (John Lennon) handed me something that looked like a tiny ball and chain, vaguely reminiscent of a morning star (which is a medieval weapon with a spiked ball on the end of a chain that can be used in melee combat—yes, that's right, I knew a lot more about medieval weaponry than tea). Inside the ball was a mass of green foliage.

I stared at it and the thought occurred to me: *I do not know what I am doing.*

I looked around, then I pried open the ball and dropped the mass of green stuff into the water. It settled to the bottom of my mug and lay there, mocking me. I didn't know a lot about tea, but I knew enough to realize that I had just made a terrible mistake. The tea leaves looked up at me and I imagined a tiny, high-pitched tea-leaf voice saying, *You have failed.*

"Some guys, you know. They're just not cut out for high school," said Marketa (the tiny girl). "You're probably more of a college guy."

That was probably the greatest thing anyone had ever said to me.

Only slightly undercut by the fact that I seemed to be a guy not cut out for tea.

"Sure," I said, not sure whether to sip the tea or not. It was not changing colors. I tried it. It tasted like hot water with leaves in it.

"Have you thought about what you might want to major in?" asked Nina.

"Um . . . I don't know yet." *Definitely not beverages.* "What are you majoring in?"

"I haven't declared yet, but probably Russian literature."

A shot of electricity went through me. "You don't say. . . ."

Half an hour later, after we had talked through *Notes from Underground* (It's about a delusional guy who lives underground and hates humanity. Super fun. He also writes notes, hence the title), Melanie unrolled a sleeping bag on the ground. "You're staying here tonight. Chances are Jonas isn't going to make it back anyway."

"He probably doesn't remember you exist," said Nina.

"That's a good thing," I said.

"Just remember," said Marketa, "you don't have to hang

out with that guy if you come here. You get to make your own choices."

"That seems wise," I said.

"You pick your own future," said Marketa. "You get to be who you want to be."

Who did I want to be?

I wanted to be the kind of guy who writes his girlfriend a letter at one thirty in the morning. So that's what I did.

ELEVEN

Craig's First Letter to Amy

November 20, 1993.
1:28 a.m.

Dear Amy,

Greetings from GAC! (It sounds like a cat is puking up a hairball.)

It's almost one thirty in the morning (I suppose you probably figured that out since you can read my helpful time stamp thingie at the top of this letter), and I am sitting in a dorm room after a harrowing and crazy evening spent ditching lunatics and hiding in bathrooms. College seems like it's going to be a lot of fun. Terrifying fun. But it's all good, and I'm still alive, which is a bonus. I'll tell you all about it when I get home on Sunday. Actually, I might be home before you get this letter, so if I've already told you about it, *you already know what I'm talking about, in which case this will no longer seem that interesting.*

Anyway, I wanted to write you because I wanted to put my thoughts on paper and what better way to do that than to write a letter to my awesome girlfriend?

By the way, it's crazy, but I miss you. I know I've been away for five days, but I missed talking to you tonight. Maybe this letter is a way of talking to you. I kept on imagining walking around campus and wondering what you would think of it. Like, I had a tiny Amy hanging out on top of my head, riding me like one of those people who rides elephants on a hookah. Howdah. Howdah. Riding a hookah would be a different thing. Also, I realized I just wrote that you would be riding on top of my head and that sounded very weird but please forgive me, it's very late and my brain is not firing on all cylinders.

But it's amazing here. I mean, the class I went to was all about this theory of structuralism, which is basically how every story is kind of the same when it comes down to the bare bones of it. It's pretty amazing to think that human beings have been telling the same kinds of stories for thousands of years. I'm sure you would have some theories on that. It was like, "Oh, this is what learning is supposed to be. Huh. I wondered. Are there going to be any multiple-choice questions on this?"

And the campus is beautiful. Some of the trees still have their leaves on them, so it's like this golden and scarlet paradise. There were teams of Canada geese flying overhead and honking. I wish I could show it to you. (The AP English in me is like, nice use of sensory language, Craig, it really gives you a sense of place.) It even smelled nice. Like the day before winter.

By the way, I'm in a room with three girls at the moment. (Oh wait, they are women. I have been instructed that in college these are now women, not girls.) And one of them has said that my letter-writing

Hi. My name is Marketa and I'm stealing Craig's letter for a moment to let you know that Craig is very cool.

This is Melanie and I'm stealing this from Marketa and I wanted to let you know that you've found one of the good ones. Seriously. Men are assholes. Almost all of them. And this guy seems all right.

I'm back. I didn't pay them to write that. They are genuinely moved by my bizarre decision to write you a letter at two in the morning. Clearly, I am a keeper.

I'll tell you about the hunting trip when I get back, but at the moment I am blocking it from my mind because of its horribleness. Just know that I did not kill any deer, and I probably saved a few deer's lives by being loud and obnoxious in the woods. Am I a hero? Probably.

I should sleep.

In conclusion, it's pretty great here, but not as great as you.

I've got your senior picture in my wallet, and I take it out and look at it, which is really dorky and probably a little stalkerish, I guess. But I love looking at it. You have really pretty blue eyes, and they made you tilt your head just a bit to the side, like you were listening to the ground. But I still like that because I imagine you're looking at me.

So I like your eyes. And I like your hair. And I love the way you kind of dance with your hands out when you're listening to music. But, mostly, I like the way you think. I love thinking with you. And I hope we get to do a lot more of it.

Kind of a weird way to end a letter, I admit, but I'm officially out of good ideas.

I can't wait to see you and talk to you again.

Craig.

TWELVE

The Ride Home of Death

About an hour into the ride, the conversation began.

"So what are you thinking?" he said.

"I don't know. What are you thinking?"

Dad turned the radio station to country music. Someone was singing about drinking beer by the riverbank in the moonlight. I believe there was also a mention of pretty girls in there too.

"So . . . did you like, um . . . that college?"

"GAC?"

"That can't be its name."

"Gustavus Adolphus."

"Yeah. That. With the girl and the shirt."

"Yeah, actually. Um . . . I mean, I think it's at the top of my list."

Dad sighed audibly. Like a giant, my-son-is-a-dumbass-and-is-going-to-ruin-my-life sigh. "You know I've always had a policy of letting you make your own mistakes."

I smiled. "I'm pretty sure it's not a mistake."

"Right. Of course. Sure. Well . . . it's your life. If you decide that . . . a place like that is where you want to spend four years of your life, then . . . then we will try to make that happen."

"Great."

"Good."

An uncomfortable silence sank in. Dad turned off the radio.

"It's just . . . okay, um . . . it's a lot of money."

"Yeah. Definitely."

"A lot of money. More than your sister is getting to go to UW, so . . ."

"Well, I can apply for financial aid. And there's our college savings, so we should be able to do it, right?"

Dad looked down.

"I don't know, Craig. I don't know."

And then something very strange began to happen to my dad. From an outside observer, it would appear that he was experiencing . . . emotions. I had seen emotions in other humans before, particularly my mom, but they hadn't made much of an appearance in my dad's life before.

"So I need to tell you something," he sighed. "And I haven't told your mother this yet, but . . . there's going to be layoffs in December. And . . . I have been told—nothing is final yet—but I have been told . . . that . . ."

He stopped there. His hand went up to his chin and scratched his face.

It felt like we were driving through a tunnel. The light faded out a bit. What did this mean? My dad had worked at Parker Pen since he had gotten out of high school. He'd been there forever. He was a senior manager or something. I couldn't imagine him without a place to go every day.

"So . . . so things might um . . . be changing here."

He stretched out his hand and gripped my shoulder. "I'm gonna try my best, okay? I'm gonna make sure we find that money somewhere, but . . . I just want to prepare you in case we have to adjust plans."

"Okay," I said.

"So . . . so that's it."

I tried to think of anything, anything to say. "You'll get a new job. I mean, if you do get laid off, there'll be another place," I managed.

He nodded. "Sure. I'll probably um . . . I'll go over to GM and see if they need anybody, and . . . look around." He exhaled.

I looked back at my dad. His eyes were watching the road, but they were far away. The clouds passed by the sun and it seemed like he faded a bit. I imagined my dad in that factory, walking up and down those steps every day. A piece of me wilted inside.

"But if I don't get a job there," he said, "it might mean, um . . . we might have to move."

We went back to silence for the rest of the way, and for a brief moment I thought life was pretty bad, but I didn't realize I was only a week away from . . .

THIRTEEN

Breakup Number One

November 27, 1993.
9:30 p.m.
Her room.

Of all the times she dumped me, this one probably hurt the most. I know it's weird to say it, because I wasn't officially "in love" with her yet, but all that means is that I hadn't told her that I was in love with her. I was still in love with her. No doubt about it.

It didn't have anything to do with the letter.

It also had nothing to do with the fact that Amy had expressed an interest in playing Dungeons & Dragons with us.

"What?" said Brian, when I told him, two days prior to the actual event. "Are you kidding me?" If I was awkward around other people, Brian was downright petrified. He was most comfortable communicating through a series of fiendish traps and monsters designed to destroy our characters. The whole social part of existence gave him hives.

"She wants to check it out," I said.

"Who does?" asked Brian.

"Dude," said Groash. "Amy Freaking Carlson."

A hush went through the room.

"That's my girlfriend," I said casually, like I-have-just-landed-on-the-moon, that's-right-you-heard-that-correctly, the-motherfucking-moon. "I told her what we do over here and she wants to check it out."

Brian rubbed his eyes. "What do you mean, check it out? You mean play? She wants to play?"

Elizabeth groaned. "No. This is what always happens with you guys, you fall in love with some chick, and then you bring them over here and they annoy the hell out of everyone."

"This is like my first girlfriend ever," I said.

"I've never had a girlfriend," said Brian.

"All right, Groash does it, then. There was that freshman you brought over." We all nodded. "There was that other freshman." We all nodded again. Those were unfortunate episodes.

"Amy's not like the losers Groash dated," I said. "She's cool."

"Hey!"

I looked at him. "Come on."

"All right. But dude—she likes you now, right? If she sees this, she's not gonna like you anymore. I know women."

Elizabeth rolled her eyes.

"Dude, I do. Whatever. They're not that difficult."

"You're an idiot," she said.

"Are you sure you're actually going out with her?" said Brian. "This doesn't sound realistic. You could be having an extended delusion."

"It's not an extended delusion."

Groash jumped in. "I heard there's like this horse tranquilizer—if you smoke it, you trip for days."

Was there some kind of stoner message board that I was missing out on? Notice: new horse tranquilizer makes you trip for days. Pass it around.

"It's not— Guys," I sputtered. "She just wants to meet you. Check you out."

Brian made a little snorting sound.

Elizabeth put a hand on my shoulder. "Are you sure that's wise?"

"She's already met Groash," I said. "How much lower could her opinion of me go?"

"This is not going to happen," said Brian. "Are you kidding me? She doesn't know how to play, I can tell you that much. And then we're going to have to *explain* everything to her; and that will slow everything down, and I want to get to the fight with the Association of Darkness before Christmas."

"I still don't think they should be called the Association of Darkness," said Elizabeth. "That seems like a lame name for an evil cult."

"They didn't ask you!"

Elizabeth kept going. "Like, who came up with that name? I hereby call this meeting of evil priests to order. We'll be taking suggestions for our name. Yes, you in the back. How about the Fraternity of Unpleasant People? No thanks. You, over there. The Corporation for Public Evil? That doesn't even make any sense."

"No girls," said Brian finally. "They're critical."

Elizabeth put up her hands. "If there were more women in the Association of Darkness, they would've come up with a better name."

"Can I just make this point?" I said. "I have the choice next Saturday of hanging out with you guys or hanging out with my superhot girlfriend. Which do you think I'm going to choose?"

Brian collapsed. "Fine. But she's playing a fighter."

"Hey, can I bring a chick again?" asked Groash.

But Amy didn't come over the next Saturday to play Dungeons & Dragons. She was busy breaking my heart.

It was the first time I went over to her house.

"Okay," she said while we were in the car on the way over. "I need to prepare you for this."

"Your parents are aliens."

"No."

"Your parents are cannibals."

"Craig."

"Your parents are Wookiees."

"That's also an alien. Um . . . my parents are old. My dad is sixty-four, and my mom is sixty-one."

I did some quick mental calculations. "Wow."

"I'm adopted. Both me and my brother are adopted."

"Oh, that's cool." There was obviously a lot I didn't know about Amy. "Was it like a big secret or anything?"

"Um . . . no. My parents told me when I was, like, six. We had my brother by then, so it was pretty clear that we were not, you know, blood related."

"Oh."

"Either that or my mom had a much more interesting life than she let on. Glenn's African American."

"Oh. Very cool." The entire black population of Janesville could fit inside a minivan. Well, maybe not one minivan. Maybe, like, two minivans or a charter bus. Anyway, we were in the running for the Whitest Town in the Universe. "So, um . . . have you ever wanted to find your birth mom?"

Amy smiled. "That's always the first question."

"Sorry."

"No, it's not just you. Everyone asks that. Like that's supposed to be the happy ending, you know? You get reunited with your birth mom. That you're somehow unfinished or empty without her—sometimes they say 'real mom.' I *have* a real mom."

"Yeah."

"And she's a piece of work. But . . . of course I've wondered about it. When things aren't going well with your parents you kind of . . . you think about it. Maybe there would be a connection there. Anyway, that's not what I needed to prepare you for. My mom is . . . uh . . . she's very sweet and also . . . um . . . demanding. You'll see."

And that's how we got to the interrogation of Craig as performed by Amy's mother.

Amy's mom was stationed, as she usually was, in the kitchen. Her dad had taken his usual spot on the La-Z-Boy. Her dad, by the way, was a fairly large guy with a broad, smiling face and a full head of snow-white hair. He had huge hands and looked like he could've been in a Flintstones cartoon.

Amy's mom was petite, with the twinkly features of a renegade Swedish elf. She had white hair that was pulled back in a smart ponytail, and she bore a rather strange resemblance to Amy. (Which was odd, because they weren't genetically related.)

"So who's this? Who's this?" she asked with her thick Wisconsin accent. You have to imagine all her *o*'s were the size of beach balls.

"This is my friend Craig; we're actually going to do some studying in my room," said Amy, trying to run the gauntlet as fast as she could.

"Oh, no. You don't get away that easily."

"She's gonna talk to you now," called her dad from the other room. "Better buckle up! It's coming down on ya."

"Oh, you are the worst, Dan. He's the worst." She grabbed one of the chairs by the kitchen table and pulled it out. "Sit, sit, sit. Tell me about your college plans."

"Mom."

"I bet you have college plans. You look like you have college plans."

"Well I, uh . . . I just visited a liberal arts college in Minnesota. Gustavus Adolphus."

Amy's mom rocked with glee. "Oh, that's a good school. That is a good school. You know he's Swedish?"

"I do, actually. I researched him and saw pictures of his luxurious mustache."

She laughed, which was a kind of musical honking. "You are funny! This one's funny. He's dead, ya know. He's been dead for a long time. King of Sweden."

"Yeah."

"I wish this one would go closer to home." She jabbed a finger at Amy. "She's going to Australia next year."

"No I'm not!"

"Might as well be Australia. UCLA."

"That's in California," called her dad from the living room.

"They know it's in California, hon. They're not dumb."

My heart sank when I heard that. I knew it wasn't even December. I knew we had been going out for about four weeks, but the thought of her traveling so far away next year felt like someone was ripping my insides apart with a claw hammer. She had mentioned UCLA, but I didn't know it was a done deal. I decided that as soon as I got home, I was going to apply to UCLA, which was idiotic. (Not that going to UCLA was idiotic, but changing your entire life plan based on a one-month relationship ranks pretty high up there on the stupid-things-to-screw-up-your-life list.)

Her mom tapped the table. "Of course, she could always go closer to home."

"Mom—"

"She doesn't want to do that. She doesn't feel the need to be close to us. It's fine. It's all fine." She chortled. "We'll manage without her. Somehow."

"Anyway, we've got a lot to do," said Amy, trying to escape.

"What are you gonna major in? You probably haven't thought that far ahead, have you? Oh, I am so sorry. Sometimes I just talk and they all want me to be quiet, but I'm gonna do it anyway!" She paused for a second. "So have you thought about it?"

"I don't know. Maybe English?"

Amy's mom smiled wide. "Oh that's great. I love English."

"'Cause it's always coming out of her mouth," called her dad.

She laughed. "You're a hoot, Dan. He tried standup comedy once."

"I did not."

"He did. 1971. We were in Milwaukee. He gets up to tell his jokes. You know what happens? Nobody laughs. They were all thinking, *Who is this lug?* So I get up and I just start yelling, 'LAUGH!' Everybody laughed."

Amy tried to pull me toward her room. "So anyway—"

"What do your parents do?"

"Complain a lot," I said.

Amy's mom laughed. "You should do comedy. What does your dad do when he's not complaining?"

"He's working at Parker Pen," I said, stumbling over that a bit.

"Fred Sewickley works at Parker. Does your dad know Fred?"

How does one answer this question? "I really don't know."

"Mom. Please," said Amy.

Amy's mom had a cheerfully brilliant way of ignoring her daughter. She would give her just the slightest wink and then barrel forward like a Swedish steamroller. (I guess that would probably be a Zamboni.) "Does your mom work?"

"She teaches science at the middle school."

"Oooooh," she exclaimed.

"We really have a lot of work to do," said Amy.

"Oh, sure. Sure ya do. Don't want to talk to Mom anymore. That's fine. I'll just stay in my place, then. Okay. You want cookies?"

"No thanks, Mom."

"What kind of cookies?" I asked.

———

They were snickerdoodles, and they were lovely. The way she said the word *snickerdoodle* was practically a parade for the Wisconsin accent.

So that's how I arrived in Amy's room for the first time. With cookies.

I would leave with no cookies.

Amy's room looked like the room of an adult. (Okay, yes, technically, she *was* an adult and I was obviously a child, but still . . .) It was nothing like my room. There was nothing embarrassing about it. She didn't even have a bed. She had a futon. She didn't have stupid posters or other embarrassing things on the wall, she had, like, art—framed Georgia O'Keeffe portraits of rather suggestive-looking flowers, and Ansel Adams prints. She had a bookshelf. She had a desk with actual photographs in actual picture frames. It was ridiculous. My first thought was, *Oh, this is how a real person lives.* Her books were even cool-looking. I had a grimy bookshelf in my room that was covered with ratty, enormous Russian paperbacks (that I had actually read). Her bookshelf had hardcover books that looked like they had been handcrafted by artisan monks. The only nod to childhood was a gigantic stuffed bear slumped in the corner like it was recovering from an all-night bender.

I looked around for tea, hoping it wouldn't come to that.

Also interesting: Amy closed the door. At my house, if my parents were home, this would not have flown. Kaitlyn was never allowed to be in her room with a boy with the door closed. My dad had too many guns for that. But I guess Amy's parents were so friendly that they didn't even care or own guns. Very cool.

She sat on the edge of her futon and patted the side of it.

Holy God, I love you went through my mind as I sat next to her, but I didn't say that. I kept it together.

"This is really nice," I said. "It's like an alpine retreat or something." Not that I knew what an alpine retreat looked like, but it sure sounded classy.

"I'm so sorry about my mom."

"She seems nice, actually."

Amy shook her head. "She can be totally nice. But she's also . . . relentless. On the surface she'll say nice things to you, and then behind your back, she'll send you things like this." She got up and plucked a book off the bookshelf.

"*The Ten Stupid Things Women Do to Screw Up Their Lives*," I read. "Yeah, I can't imagine parents giving their kids something like this." I chuckled.

"It's really lame," said Amy. "It's all about self-sabotage and letting a man control you and everything."

"Yeah," I said. "I mean, who would do that?"

"Right. It's like, don't you have enough respect for me to know that I wouldn't do these things? Don't you know who I am?"

"Sure."

There's a thing that nerds do when they spot another nerd's books. It's kind of like when two dogs meet each other and sniff each other's butts—like, *What did you eat today?* And, despite all appearances to the contrary, the books on Amy's bookshelf revealed her true nature: nerd. (High-functioning, passing-as-normal nerd, but still nerd.) There was the quintessential *Mists of Avalon*, the Virginia Woolf, the entire Joseph Campbell set. She had cool books.

"You ever read *The Tao of Pooh*?" she said, showing me a little hardbound book with a picture of Winnie-the-Pooh on it.

Did it have tortured Russians in it? Nope, then of course I hadn't read it.

"Have you read the *Tao Te Ching*?" The girl had a copy of the *Tao Te Ching* on her shelf.

"Not recently. I mean I probably absorbed that when I was six or seven, but I put that in my kids' book section."

"Well, I haven't read all of it either."

"What the hell is wrong with you? You can't even begin to understand it until the last chapter or two," I joked.

"I don't think it has chapters. It has verses."

"That's what I meant. Probably." We were sitting shoulder to shoulder on her futon, and she had the Pooh book in her hands. She was wearing the white fuzzy sweater that was probably the most comfortable thing ever designed by humans. I was wearing something else. Seriously, I didn't really care what I was wearing. If you put your fingers over my eyes right now and asked me what I was wearing, I couldn't tell you.

"The thing about Winnie-the-Pooh: He just is, you know? Like, Piglet and Eeyore, they're always stressed-out or depressed or whatever, but Pooh is content to be what he is. Pooh is, like, effortless, you know? He just is. And that's basically how you should live your life."

"Like Pooh. Like a piece of Pooh."

When she got mad at me she usually tickled me, and that was pretty awesome. So the tickling began.

"You are infuriating," she said as she stabbed me with her long fingers. "I'm saying that I want to live my life without worrying about what other people think of me. Like my friends, I don't know, they're very judgmental. Everything has to be perfect with them. And I used to care, right? Like *Oh, no, Debbie's pissed at me* or *Tricia's gonna hate those earrings,* and now I'm like, 'Screw it. Why do I care what they think?'"

"Maybe they're not really your friends," I said.

"Maybe not. I've been hanging out with Chelsea more this year, anyway. It's just . . . better."

"I guess that's the benefit of hanging out with a bunch of weirdos." I smiled.

"You don't care what they think?" she said.

"I'm not sure they do a lot of thinking about me. At least not my clothes. I mean you've seen Groash and the Slimeballs shirt."

"Yeah."

"But I think about you a lot," I managed.

"I think about you too," she said.

This was about the time we would normally start kissing, but we didn't. We kept talking and looking at more books, and she told me about how she had been feeling like she was compensating for her struggles in elementary school by trying to win everything in high school. But she was tired of doing that. ("Hey, you can slum with me," I suggested.) And now she was trying to find a new way, but it was always hard. And I told her about my dreams and the trip to GM and the way the northern lights revealed the hugeness of reality.

And maybe that's when we should have kissed.

But we didn't.

I started to feel like something was wrong. Little by little, things began to fall apart. The conversation had more pauses and more gaps. Then Amy would start looking away from me, and I couldn't quite figure out what was going on.

We were supposed to go back to my house to play D&D at nine, and it was almost time to go. We had been talking for over two hours.

I was holding her hand. She was sitting right next to me.

Sometimes Amy had her hair up in one of those little evil-clam-looking things. But this time she had it down, and when she looked down and away from me, I couldn't see her face. I could just see the curtain of blond hair. She had pulled my right hand into her lap; she was holding my hand with both of hers now. I could feel her thumbs nervously rubbing my palm.

"Are you all right?" I asked.

Amy didn't say anything. She kept rubbing my hand.

"It's okay," I said, trying to kiss the side of her head, but that didn't really work. She was hunching up a bit now, staring down. I pulled away a strand of her hair and tucked it behind her ear. Her nose was red; she was crying.

"What's wrong?" I said.

"I really like you," she managed to say, rubbing my hand so hard it started to hurt.

"I really like you too," I said, totally confused.

She turned just a bit to look at me with her bloodshot blue eyes and then looked away again. "I didn't really want to do this with you," she said.

I felt like I had swallowed a brick. What did *that* mean?

"What is it?"

Then she was really crying, so much that she could barely speak. I tried to get closer to her. I wanted to put my arm around her, but she wasn't letting go of my hand. "I didn't think . . . this was gonna . . . happen, and you're . . . such a great . . . guy . . . and I love talking to you."

The brick increased in size. Little lumberjacks were starting to chop away at the back of my neck.

"I have to tell you something . . . and it's okay . . . if you hate me."

"I'm not gonna hate you. I'm not." At this point, I could see the train coming. I was getting dumped. Somehow, in some way, this was going to end, and *I* was the one comforting *her* while she did it.

"You're gonna hate me."

"I'm not."

There was a brutal silence, and then she said, "I have a boyfriend."

FOURTEEN

Breakup Number One (Part Two)

Still November 27, 1993.
Still 9:30 p.m. (about).
Still her room.

It felt like someone had punched me in the face.

What. The. Hell?

Suddenly, everything for the past four weeks went spinning through my mind. She had a boyfriend? How was that even possible? I had seen her nearly every day. I had written her the Letter; we had kissed on the bridge; we had talked to each other all the time. I met her in the hallways in between class. We had talked on the phone for hours. What the hell?

And that's when I saw the picture on her desk.

It was a guy. In a heart-shaped frame.

Amy still clutched my hand, and she was sobbing now. Her huge, choking sobs were probably loud enough that they could be heard outside the room. She was a mess; she had her head down and was pulling Kleenex out of the box like a machine. There was a drifting rain of crumpled Kleenexes falling from her face. And every time she dropped one, she went right back to my hand like it was a life preserver.

A normal person probably would have pulled away. (Hey, look, a metaphor for our entire relationship. How convenient!) A normal person probably would have stormed around the room or, at least, reacted in a negative way of some kind. It's possible that this theoretical normal person would have used poor language at this moment in time and cursed her out. But as we've established, I was not a normal person. I was me. I kept holding her hand.

Finally, Amy was able to tell her part of the story.

"He's older. His name's Chad; he's in college. . . . We started dating at the end of junior year, so not that many people really knew about it. . . . I'm so sorry, Craig. I didn't mean to do this. . . . I didn't. . . . I just . . . I don't know what I'm doing. I don't know what I'm doing. . . . I wasn't even thinking about him when we went for that walk . . . and then the next thing I knew I kissed you—and I was thinking the whole time that I didn't want to hurt you, and I needed to tell you. But I didn't. I didn't tell you, and the next day I saw you again and I liked you so much; and I was going to tell you then, but then . . . You probably hate me. It's okay if you hate me."

The whole room was sliding away from me. I felt the futon

underneath me, and I tried to hold on to it even though I was sitting down. Amy had fallen apart again.

"Well?" she asked me, expecting some kind of outburst.

I didn't say anything. I hadn't cried yet, but, holy God, it hurt. Everything that I had thought about her had just been ripped apart; everything I imagined we were going to be for each other had been set on fire. It felt like waves of ice were sliding up and down my skin.

I let go of her hand and got to my feet.

"Did you tell him about us?" I managed to say.

Amy looked up at me, tears streaming from her eyes. "Craig, there isn't going to be an us."

"I want there to be an us," I said, and I got about halfway through that sentence before I burst into tears too.

And then Amy was hugging me.

"Will you take care of me?" she whispered.

The breath caught in my throat. *What the hell did that mean?*

". . . Yes," I said.

She clutched me, still crying, and I stood there like a statue that had broken loose from its base.

FIFTEEN

Misery

If only I had become an actual Buddhist, things would have been much better. Or if I had followed the Tao of Pooh and just been pooh. I didn't have the benefit of either of those Eastern philosophies, though, so I took the American way: lying around and moaning.

A huge snowstorm had blown through shortly after Amy broke my heart, and I was thrilled when school got canceled. I couldn't imagine seeing her again after what happened. It would probably be best if I went through the rest of my days with a bag over my head, or crept beneath the school into the boiler room like the Phantom of the Opera. I resolved to get myself a little half-mask and learn how to sing really well after I recovered from my earth-shattering misery.

"Everybody Hurts" by R.E.M. was on the radio. I didn't even think it was ironic.

I lay on my bed, staring at the ceiling. Outside the snow continued to pile up.

"Uhhhhhh," I moaned.

Kaitlyn was standing in my doorway with the expression she always had when she entered my room: bewildered disgust.

"Did she dump you?"

"I don't want to talk about it."

"My twin sense was tingling. I could sense your pain." Kaitlyn tentatively took one step into my room, fearful that the décor might come to life and attack her or infect her with geekery or something.

"Thanks."

"Also, you're moaning really loud and it's really annoying."

"I don't think my life has any meaning anymore," I whined.

She sat down on the side of my bed and patted my shoulder. "Oh, come on. It didn't have any meaning before."

"You're really good at cheering me up."

"I'm not trying to cheer you up. I'm trying to get you to stop moaning. I'm working on my AP History paper. Did you finish yours?"

I rolled over and grunted into my pillow.

"Well, you should get it done," she said. "Mr. Bo is going to be ten times meaner to you than I am. So at least you have that to look forward to." She got up and stopped to look at a poster of a girl in a chain-mail bikini on the back of my door. "Can I just say something, as a human being and a woman? This is ridiculous. There have been studies. This is causing you psychological damage."

"*You're* causing me psychological damage," I groaned.

"Suit yourself," she said. "I'm sure you'll be very happy with chain-mail-bikini girl." She stopped in the doorway and sighed. "It's not the end of the world, Craig. It's just close."

Oddly enough, my sister didn't manage to cheer me up. But I did move from my room to the living room, where I was able to lie on the couch, hugging a pillow for warmth. It may have been slightly pathetic. I might have reduced the volume on my sad-sounding moans, but I'm pretty sure they were still coming out of my mouth. I'm not proud of these moments.

"Oh, sweetheart," said my mom, settling in next to me and patting my knee. "You want to talk about it?"

"No," I moaned, hugging the pillow.

"What was her name?"

"Amy."

"Amy," she said. "You know if you had brought her over here, I would've known her name. Next girlfriend, you need to make sure we meet her, okay?"

I nodded.

"And there will be another girlfriend, don't you worry. You are a very attractive boy. I was at the grocery store the other night and I ran into Mrs. Williamson, your second-grade teacher, and she remembered you. She said, 'He was always so cute.' And I said, 'You should see him now.'"

"I'm not sure this is appropriate, Mom."

"I'm your mother, I don't have to be appropriate. Appropriate is for other people."

I hugged the pillow tighter.

She ruffled my hair. "You know what I do when I feel bad? I make little wishes. Not big ones. Just like, 'I wish it would be sunny today,' or 'I wish there was an air freshener in the doctor's office.' That helps. Does that make you feel better?"

"Not really."

"Because you haven't tried the wishing yet. And remember, there are other girls out there. Your father went through a bunch of slutty tramps before he found me. A whole bunch. Just a whole squad of them. And that turned out all right. Okay? You want a hug?"

I nodded and she hugged me. "Little wishes," she said.

I wish that wolves would eat Chad.

I did feel a little better.

The first day I went back to school was a disaster. I wandered the halls between classes, sure that any moment Amy would come from around the corner and I'd see her.

The worst was AP History. It was usually my favorite class because I was sure to see her pass by the door. She was in band, which did terrible and confusing things to her schedule, and around her lunchtime her class got out while my class was . . . It was confusing. I just knew that I would see her pass by the door about halfway through.

AP History was taught by a big, ruddy guy named Mr. Bollig, whom everyone called Mr. Bo. Mr. Bo was huge and had hands like bear paws. In his spare time he coached football and reminisced about Vietnam. He had beady eyes, and occasionally he'd stare at you for an uncomfortably long period of time, as if he was sizing up whether or not you were a threat and he'd be forced to choke the life out of you. AP History was super fun.

I sat in the back, watching the door like a dog with its paws over its nose. Then I saw her walk by. I felt my chest cave in when I saw her, as if a moose had kicked me in the ribs and crushed my sternum. Then it break-danced on my flattened body. It didn't help that there was sunlight streaming into the hall, and it caught her just right, setting her blond hair and fuzzy sweater aglow like an angel.

I stared toward the front of the room, but she was everywhere I looked.

It occurred to me that now we were going to have to pretend we didn't know each other. We couldn't make eye contact in the halls. We couldn't talk to each other on the phone. We had to pretend all of that was a mistake. I guessed it was. It's funny how someone can go from being your whole world to someone you can't look at.

"Isn't that right, Craig?" Mr. Bo had sauntered down the aisle and was looming over me.

"Yes," I said.

His face darkened. "Really?"

I blinked, not sure what he was talking about.

"Craig?" said Mr. Bo. "You agree with that?"

A hush seemed to be falling over the class. Brian had turned to look at me, shock on his face. "Shut up, dude," he hissed.

Mr. Bo turned on Brian. "Did you say something, Brian?"

"I don't think Craig heard the question, sir," he explained.

"Oh, he heard it. Craig here thinks that the plot to blow up federal buildings in protest of Vietnam was a good idea."

"I said what?" I said.

I spent most of the day like that. Stumbling around in a zombi-fied daze. I felt like my skull was a cantaloupe that someone had hollowed out with a melon-baller. Everything about me hurt. My neck, my arms, my stomach. All of my muscles were wringing themselves out.

My friends did their best to cheer me up.

"Just think," said Groash. "In thirty years she probably won't even be that hot anymore. She might still be kinda hot. She might be dirty. You know what I mean? Like, sometimes older women have done some crazy shit."

Groash wasn't very good at it.

"She's making a big mistake," said Elizabeth, putting her arm through mine to steady me. "The best thing to do now is just be yourself."

"What?" said Brian. "That doesn't make any sense. Be better than yourself. Being yourself is what got you dumped."

I have to add at this moment that I hadn't told anyone that Amy had dumped me because she had a boyfriend. Why? In a twisted way, I thought it reflected badly on her, and I didn't want to hurt her image with my friends. Like I said, I didn't make a whole lot of sense as a human.

"Live your life," said Elizabeth. "Be who you are and then girls will like you."

"Dude," said Groash. "What the hell are you telling him?"

"I'm giving him good advice."

"Craig has been himself for a long time," said Brian. "And it hasn't worked."

"Hey," I blurted.

"Except for this one time," he said. "And I think we can all agree this was a total anomaly."

"She went temporarily insane or something," said Groash. "No, dude. Nobody likes me when I'm myself either. That's why I've got a whole thing where I pretend to be an orphan."

Somehow I got roped into going to Elizabeth's house after school. Apparently my friends determined that I was unfit to be left alone, or with my sister.

"I'd be alone with your sister," said Groash. "I'd be alone with her so much."

"Please stop."

Groash had left to go be with some of his skate-punk friends, and his house wasn't exactly suitable for human habitation anyway. There was no way we were going over to Brian's house ("No," he said. "Trust me."), which left Elizabeth's house as the only viable alternative.

She and her mom lived close to downtown, in a little duplex. I'd been there exactly once, and it had been a disturbing experience.

The snowstorm had dumped about ten inches of snow on the town, and the wind that whipped up had blown some of it into huge three- or four-foot drifts. It was the kind of day where the little kids went sledding until their noses turned purple. The sidewalks to her house were half-shoveled. Some enterprising citizens had taken their shovels or snowblowers and cleared off part of the sidewalks. Other people, probably the more sensible ones, said screw it and stayed inside.

We'd walk easily enough for a block or so, and then it was like we were trudging through the ice planet Hoth. Except I had no boots because I was stupid, and my tennis shoes sank in the snow up to my calves. It sucked.

It exactly mirrored how I felt. An icy wasteland, half-cleared.

Elizabeth walked arm in arm with me, as if I needed steadying. I probably did. When we got to an unshoveled section of the sidewalk we'd struggle through like toddlers in snowsuits.

"Dude," said Brian. "You don't need to hold him. He's not going to fall over."

"He might fall over," said Elizabeth.

"Craig," he said. I looked at him. "You're not going to fall over, are you?"

"I'm all right," I said.

"Fine," said Elizabeth, and she let go of me. "You're free. Fly, little bird."

Right next to me was a three-foot snowdrift. I spread my arms wide and fell face-first into it.

My body made a *poof* sound when I hit the snow. I lay totally still. *I wonder how long I can stay here? Ow, this kind of hurts my face. Snow looks like it's comfortable, but it's actually cold and prickly. I should've worn boots today.*

I heard Elizabeth behind me.

"You think he's dead?"

"Not yet," said Brian.

I'll say this about Elizabeth's house. It was the best-smelling place on earth. It was probably the result of some mysterious incense that was burning somewhere, but the whole house smelled awesome, like if cinnamon and chocolate had a baby or something. It was great. (Actually, the whole house didn't smell awesome, the half of the house that Elizabeth and her mom occupied smelled great. The rest of the duplex probably smelled like failure.)

Elizabeth's house was what happened if there was no illusion of adult supervision. There were purple and red tapestries hanging from the walls. There were puzzles of dragons and wizards glued together and framed like paintings. There were about half a dozen fertility statues. And that was the stuff I could identify. The rest of the place was festooned with chimes, pagan symbols, and the occasional Calvin and Hobbes poster.

"This is basically the opposite of my house," said Brian as he fondled two fertility statues simultaneously.

"That one's supposed to be a penis," said Elizabeth.

Brian set it down. Then he stole a glance at it. "I think these statues are giving you unrealistic ideas."

Elizabeth smirked. "You never know." She turned to me. "Here's what we do. We play some video games until our thumbs bleed and listen to the Violent Femmes. Does that sound good?"

"Sure," I said.

She looked at me like I was a lost puppy. "You're gonna be okay. I'm gonna get some cider—we don't have anything else."

There was a beaded curtain to the kitchen, because of course there was, and before Elizabeth could slide through it to get the cider, her mom appeared.

She was wearing clothes. Thank God it was winter. Elizabeth's mom was a hippie in the '60s, and instead of growing up and selling out like the rest of her generation, she had just continued to get weirder with time. Her hair was waist length, with the same curl as Elizabeth's, except even wilder and thicker. She probably had twenty pounds of hair. She wore a kimono, and more beaded necklaces than a craft fair. Her arms glittered with silvery bangles. Instead of walking, she floated, tinkling and sparkling. She was like an enormous crazy-ass fairy.

"Hey, Mom," said Elizabeth.

"What's up?" she said.

"We're gonna play some vids. Do we have any cider?"

"What do you want cider for?"

"To drink it."

"Oh. I suppose we have some, then."

I had collapsed onto what passed for a couch, which was really just a strange collection of giant tufted pillows that contained two or three cats. She looked down at me.

"Billy."

"Craig."

"Oh yeah. Craig." She studied me with a bemused smirk on her face. "I know you."

"He just got dumped," added Brian helpfully. "It was brutal."

"I'm fine," I lied. "It's no big deal."

"He almost died on the way over here. Fell in the snow." He re-created me face-planting into the snow with his hands.

Elizabeth's mom put two fingers together in front of her mouth, deep in thought. "Hmm . . . and now you're here for my wisdom."

"Um . . . actually, no . . . I don't need wisdom. . . . We're just gonna geek out with some games."

"He probably needs wisdom," said Brian, his eyes sparkling. "He's rudderless actually. Like a lost bird."

She drew closer. "I think you need coral."

"I don't know that a piece of coral is going to solve my problems," I said.

"Of course not," she said. "It focuses your mind."

"Oh."

"And hones your sexuality. You have to remember that your most important sexual organ is your mind."

I shifted uncomfortably in the pillow collection, keenly aware of the fertility statues looming over me.

"You have such power in you," she said, drawing nearer, in a shimmering tinkle of musical bangles. She was like Obi-Wan Kenobi if Obi-Wan was a witch in a duplex. "Can you feel it? All you have to do is find it in your heart . . . and unleash it. Right now you're all stopped up."

"Mom," said Elizabeth, returning with cider. "Craig didn't really come over here to receive coral—"

"Shhh." She waved her away. "This is my gift." Elizabeth's mom patted me on the chest. "Pain is a blessing because it means you're alive. The more love, the more pain. Close your eyes and embrace it. Love it."

And, strangely enough, I listened to her. I closed my eyes. And there, in my mind, was Amy—the moment we had held hands on the bridge with the lights from the city glittering on the dark river. It felt like an ice pick through the chest.

"And now for you," she said, turning to Brian. Brian went pale and nearly dropped his glasses.

"Mom, please stop."

"So much sexual fire in there," she rumbled. "What makes you sing, little bird?"

"Maybe we should go to my house," managed Brian.

It was a long walk to Brian's house. The sun had gone down—in early December the sun sets in Wisconsin shortly after it comes up, like a groundhog seeing its shadow. Plows crackled up and down the streets, occasionally sending an avalanche of dirty snow tumbling in our direction. We walked with our hands buried in the bottoms of our pockets, hunched against the bitter wind. I could've really used a hat.

"You tried, right? You tried. That's cool," said Brian, shivering.

"And got flattened."

He shrugged. "But you did it. I mean, you kissed Amy Carlson. Like—are you kidding me? So what if it didn't work out? You tried something." He skipped over a drift of snow and darted to the other side of the street.

This probably was the moment I should've told him what really happened. *Yes, I tried something, but she was actually going out with another guy at the time, so it was an unmitigated disaster.*

I crossed the street and Brian's eyes were far away. "I mean, I give you shit, but I admire that. It took courage. I don't ever . . . I don't know."

"You don't ever what?"

"Go for it."

"Well, if I'm any indication of what happens when you go for it, maybe you're making the right decision."

He shook his head and smiled weakly. "No."

I'd been friends with Brian since the fourth grade, when he was the new kid at my elementary school. There weren't a lot of Asians in Janesville. There weren't a lot of anybody except for Germans and Polish people. Brian's family had escaped the war in Vietnam on boats and arrived in America in 1975, just after he was born.

We'd been put in a group together—we were supposed to create a skit about advertising something, and I had protested. I'd said, "Americans and Chinese don't mix." He'd replied, "I'm Vietnamese." My teacher was having none of my casual racism and put us together anyway. After that, we found out we had an affinity for monsters, weird science fiction, and comic books.

I thought about that first comment a lot. I'd apologized for it over the years, of course, but it felt like a stain on my soul—like a little racist mushroom growing in the dark cellar of my brain. If I could give my nine-year-old self the benefit of the doubt, maybe I just really wanted to be in a group with someone else and didn't want to be with the new kid. Maybe I'd heard it from someone else, but still, what a dickish thing to say. It was only the tip of the iceberg for him, though. He was teased relentlessly in school; first for being Vietnamese and then for being a nerd. In seventh grade people had spelled out "go home freak" on his front yard with plastic forks. I had been, in some small way, a part of that.

We walked side by side, which was hard, since some people had scraped a suggestion of a path through the snow rather than clear the whole sidewalk. The headlights of passing cars sent frosty blue shadows dancing around us.

"If I look on the bright side," I said, "suffering is probably good for me. According to Dostoevsky." Damn, if only I could've written that college essay now.

Brian shook his head. "This is what my mom tells me: You think you know what suffering is? Try riding in the hold of a cargo ship for two weeks with a newborn. Then talk to me about suffering."

"Yeah, that sounds a little worse than what I'm going through."

"Gives you some perspective, doesn't it? They literally tell me that every time I complain about anything. I'm like, 'I don't want to do the dishes,' and my mom's like, 'Oh, it's too difficult for you? You know what's actually difficult? Breastfeeding you in a refugee camp, that's what's difficult.' So I end up doing the dishes a lot."

I walked in silence a bit.

"Thanks," I said.

"You kissed the girl of your dreams, dude," he said. "Some of us haven't gotten there yet."

I felt the chunk of coral in my pocket.

"You know what?" I took it out and handed it to him. "You should have this."

"It's not even a gemstone, dude."

"Yeah."

He took it anyway.

"Actually, if you want to learn about true suffering, just wait until you go up against the Association of Darkness. That's gonna take real courage. You have no idea. No idea what's coming at you."

That was true in more ways than one.

SIXTEEN

Sex;
In Which No Sex Happens

First of all, there is no sex in this chapter, but there is sex in chapter eighteen. So you can skip to that if you're only in this for the dirty parts, but, of course, you'll miss all the very, very crucial context.

My dad did indeed get laid off in December, and by the time March rolled around he still hadn't found a new job. Things were getting a bit tense, but it was alleviated by the fact that Amy and I had gotten back together. (Okay, we had broken up two more times, but at this point in time, we were together again and all was right and good with the universe.)

We were in the basement on a Saturday night, right before spring break.

"All right, Blutus, your turn," said Brian, dripping contempt from his protected perch behind the wall of screens. Blutus was the name of Amy's character, who was a ninth-level fighter that had just joined our adventuring party. Blutus had a giant battle-ax and was pretty incompetent.

Amy looked down at the table like she was trying to read Chinese.

"Okay, so I roll . . ."

"The twenty," I said, handing her a twenty-sided die.

She held it like a small grenade and then dropped it on the table.

"Fourteen," she said, turning to look at her inscrutable character-record sheet. "Do I hit?"

"Well, you hit last time with a twelve, so that would probably be a yes," said Brian. "Roll damage."

I handed her two regular D6 (that means a six-sided die, or the standard die that is used in playing Monopoly, Trivial Pursuit, and determining if the United States is going to invade somewhere). She dropped them carefully on the table while Groash and Elizabeth looked on in dumbstruck boredom.

There's a delicate ecology to the nerd society that is Dungeons & Dragons. Like a finely honed machine, it requires that everyone be on the same page. There are, I'm not kidding you, something like eight hundred pages of rules to be digested and memorized. We seriously took the rule books home and read them for fun. Well, at least I did. Elizabeth didn't really subscribe to this total immersion in geekdom philosophy because she had something resembling a life.

But Brian, Groash, and I were total lifers. We'd played since elementary school. I had gotten hooked when my dad accidentally bought a Basic D&D set in third grade for Christmas, and Groash had shoplifted tons of stuff because his mom had no money. Brian's parents were not exactly enthralled with the prospect of their firstborn son spending his time battling monsters and dragons in a fanciful imaginary world, but somehow he had convinced them that it would look amazing on college applications. Brian was great at bullshit.

Anyway, we were a finely tuned geek machine. And Amy was destroying it in every way imaginable.

"Okay, seven," she said.

"Add your bonuses," I said, trying not to talk to her like she was a toddler.

Amy looked at the arcane list of numbers snaking up and down the papers. This was harder than calculus. "Okay, so let's see, plus four and plus nine and plus . . ."

Brian snapped. "It's not that hard! You have a magical weapon bonus, a strength bonus, a specialization bonus, and a preferred enemy bonus—plus seventeen. You do twenty-four points of damage!"

"She gets another attack," I said.

"So which die do I use again?" Amy asked.

A big vein was popping out on Brian's head. "This is killing us!"

"Dude," said Groash. "Chill."

"Sorry," said Amy. "Is there like an easier version we could play?"

Brian took off his glasses and clutched his face to prevent it from melting. "No . . . there is no 'easier' version."

Elizabeth chimed in. "I think she should just concentrate on role-playing. You know, the guys get so obsessed with the numbers they don't even bother with actual role-playing."

"Bullshit," said Groash. "I role-play all the time."

"Your character is *exactly* like you."

"Yeah. He's awesome."

"O-kay," said Elizabeth, making a big okay sign with her fingers as sarcastically as possible.

The door opened and Kaitlyn was there, staring at us.

"What the hell," she said. She was clearly dressed for going out, with her frosted jean jacket and bangly bracelet things that she had taken to wearing. She looked like a visitor from the popular planet.

"Oh great, there's another one," said Brian. "Are you gonna play too? Are we gonna have all the girls play now?"

Kaitlyn's mouth opened in horrified, disgusted shock.

"I want to let you know," she said, her eyes withering with contempt as she adjusted the bangles on her wrist, "that I am going out, and Mom and Dad said that no one was supposed to be over here."

Mom and Dad had gone to the casino. We had canceled

our family vacation to Florida because plane tickets were too expensive, so instead of that they decided on going on their own vacation to the casino for two days. Seriously. This is what they did. Kaitlyn had suggested that maybe gambling away all our college money was not the best plan, but Mom had said, "Oh, we don't gamble when we go to the casino," which confused us just long enough for them to get out the door.

"So what do you think they're doing?" I'd asked Kaitlyn later.

She'd rolled her eyes majestically. "What do you think they're doing?"

"I don't know."

"They're going to a hotel resort for two days and not inviting us. What do you think they're doing?" She said the last part very slowly.

Realization dawned over me like a horrible sunrise. "Oh shit," I said.

"Yeah."

Anyway, back in the present, Kaitlyn gestured her bangly arm dismissively. "So your weirdo friends need to get out."

"Why do you care?" I said.

"I care because Mom and Dad put me in charge. So there."

"That's a lie—"

"JUST GO," she declared.

"What's up?" replied Groash, nodding his head ever so slightly.

"We have a lot scheduled for tonight," said Brian. "And it's hard enough trying to get through it while there are certain distractions."

Kaitlyn looked at Amy, confused. "God, you're doing this now?" You could tell that something inside her brain was being reordered. Like, they were both hot girls; they both spoke a certain secret hot-girl language; and I'm sure she had no idea why Amy was going out with me. Not only that, here she was, dwelling in a basement with a bunch of nerds and dice and dragon figurines. Kaitlyn's understanding of the universe was collapsing.

"It's fun," lied Amy.

"Um . . . it's not *fun*," protested Brian. "It's thrilling."

"Oh God," said Kaitlyn. "Make it stop."

"All right, all right, we'll cancel the game," I said, reluctantly getting up from the couch. "Where are you going, anyway?"

"None of your business."

"If Mom and Dad call, what am I supposed to tell them?"

"Tell them I'm in the bathroom."

"I'm not gonna lie for you."

"Yes, you are." She stared at me like she was using a Jedi mind trick. "Because I'm telling you, brother, there's going to be a time when you need me to lie for you. I have a long memory, and I am vindictive as hell."

"Okay," I said in a quiet voice.

"All right, get out of here. Git."

"Lame," said Groash on his way out. "So what are you doing later?"

"Get the hell away from me."

"So that's a maybe?"

Elizabeth, Brian, and Groash left, with Elizabeth driving her Cutlass Ciera, which was the size of a boat and spun out in circles whenever the roads got slick. Then Kaitlyn left to go to whatever party she was going to, which left just . . .

Me and Amy.

In the house.

With no parents until Sunday night.

Which led to . . .

SEVENTEEN

Breakup Number Four
Aargh!

March 25, 1994.
1:13 a.m.
All over my stupid house.

This seems like a good time to talk about my bedroom. Even
though I largely existed in my basement, I did, in fact, have a bedroom on the first floor of my house. Unfortunately, it had been
decorated by an idiot: me. At this point, Amy and I had gone out
on four separate occasions for a grand total of eleven weeks or
so, and she had never been to my room. Ever. She was probably
thinking that I had a dead body stashed in there. The reality was
worse.

Before I describe this room, I want you to imagine that you
harbor romantic feelings for me. Let's say you thought I was
cute, somehow enjoyed looking at my dark, woolen trench coat,
and appreciated the fact that my hair, though not perfect, was

still a reassuring shade of brown. And even though I had the physique of a twelve-year-old Albanian girl, you still found me attractive. Furthermore, let's imagine that the knowledge that I played Dungeons & Dragons didn't cause you to implode from embarrassment. You're fine with all that.

You would not be fine with my room.

I decorated it when I was thirteen. Let's put that out there. And what I had done, with my tiny thirteen-year-old brain, was take the covers off all my favorite comic books (of which I had hundreds and hundreds) and staple them to the walls of my room. It took me a week, and every so often, Kaitlyn would enter and shake her head. Or my dad would come in and say, "I don't think this is a good idea. But it's your room. You just have to live here." In the hallway I'd hear my mom say, "He has to make his own mistakes, dear." So my room was floor-to-ceiling comic-book covers. It was as if wallpaper had mutated into hundreds of costumed, heavily muscled maniacs.

I'm not done.

That's the background. I had also hung quite a few pictures on the walls, over the comic books: pictures of M. C. Escher prints and weird monsters torn from magazines and, yes, the aforementioned poster of a girl in a chain-mail bikini. I had meant to take that down. Honestly. I also went through a glow-in-the-dark-skulls-are-cool phase, which had resulted in three of them clustering on my desk leering at us.

So, yes, my room was a nightmare.

After everyone left, Amy and I were downstairs on the couch, when she said, "It's pretty tough at my house right now, so I don't really want to go home."

"I know."

"Can we go to your room?"

And I stupidly said, "Sure."

And when we got there, she said, "What the hell is this?"

"Um . . . I'm not normal."

She smiled and touched me on the chest and said, "I don't want normal."

Then she kissed my neck and wrapped her arms around me. "Maybe you should turn out the light." And I was just about to do that when she said, "What's going on with that poster?"

Contrary to popular belief, the poster of a scantily clad lady on your wall does not produce similar results in actual females. Quite the opposite, in fact.

"Oh, um . . . shit. That's not mine. That's like . . . uh . . . robbers came in here."

"Robbers?"

"Yeah. And they put that up. As they were leaving. Sort of an apology for robbing me."

"You're a dork."

"I'm going to take it down, now that you mention it." I took hold of it and realized that my stapling method of attaching things to the walls was yet another poor choice in an entire room of them. I was trying to remove it delicately, but it wasn't working.

"That's okay," she said. "I'm going to put like thirty posters of shirtless lumberjacks in my room."

"Really? Lumberjacks? That's your dream occupation for your man?"

"Clearly that girl has a PhD."

I had wedged my fingernails in the staples, but I couldn't pull them out. "She's probably a scientist actually."

"Did you read that in her profile? What are her turnoffs? Staples? Sexist men ogling her? Clothes?" Amy poked me as I continued to struggle with it. "Here," she said, grabbing a Post-it note off my desk. She scrawled STOP SEXISM NOW on it in broad black letters and slapped it right over the girl's boobs. "That's better."

I turned out the light. The glow-in-the-dark skulls grinned.

THIS IS THE DIRTY PART

Before I had started going out with Amy, my entire experience with kissing involved that unfortunate bet on the bus. And that wasn't much of a kiss, it was more like being pecked by a salamander. A salamander that skittered away to its friends, collected its money, and laughed at you. So I was extremely self-conscious about the whole affair.

But that didn't matter.

Besides the glowing skulls, the only light came from the streetlight outside, which shone through the cracks in my blinds and sent slashes of yellow light glancing around the room. I had never been like this with her before, with no one home. My window was open a crack, and I could hear the crickets chirping outside and felt the soft breeze of the cool night air.

This was what I had been waiting for my whole life. My heart was thrumming in my chest as she kissed me; I wanted to tell her I loved her, I wanted to compose sonnets on the fly, I wanted to be able to give voice to the things that were breaking loose inside of me. All the time I spent as a picked-on little kid, being teased, being an outcast, with the feeling that no one really liked me—it was all cracking open and vanishing.

That's what I wanted to say. Our actual conversation went like this:

ME: Okay.

HER: What?

ME: Did you say something?

HER: No.

ME: Oh. Did you want to say something?

HER: I don't think so.

ME: Okay.

HER: What?

ME: Did you say what?

So we kept kissing. And the thought occurred to me: *We're going to have sex.*

And then the next thought:

Does she want to have sex? Would that be taking advantage of her emotionally in this circumstance? But maybe sex will make her feel better. If we do it right. Shit. I'm overthinking this. Get it together, Craig. Should I say something? Maybe I should make words with my mouth. No, that seems too complicated. I'll just keep doing what I'm doing.

That's a dumb idea. I'm stupid. Is that Captain America *issue #314 up there? Why did I put that on the ceiling? Are the skulls watching me?*

We kept going. The clock ticked away. The breeze turned colder, but we didn't notice. Clothes were removed.

It took about three hours of making out to get to the point where I could actually make the words come out of my mouth.

"So do you want . . . to . . . ?"

"Want . . . to . . . what?" she said, kissing my neck.

"Have . . . the . . . thing . . . where . . . we . . . try to . . . do the sex?"

She looked me in the eyes. Her pupils were huge and black in the dim light. "Okay."

"Is that a yes? That's a yes, right?"

"Yes."

"Yes?"

"Yes."

If there was a cheering section in my brain, it was going wild.

There was one slight problem.

There's no other way to put this but . . . my manhood was asleep. In a manner of speaking.

Remember, we had been making out for three hours. Most of that time, I had been working fine, but I wasn't an athlete like my sister. There were limits to my physical abilities. Quite a lot of them, actually, but that's neither here nor there. So before you get all judgey-laughey about this, let me remind you that three hours is a long-ass time. So anyway . . . so . . . um . . . things were not functioning properly. We got fully naked and then . . . nothing.

Nothing at all.

I'm gonna take another time-out here.

Since puberty, there had been exactly one goal in my life. Yes, I know I wanted to go to college and fit in and find my voice, but really there was just one goal. I wouldn't get out of bed in the mornings if there were not some way to advance toward that goal. For about six consecutive years, I had spent nearly every waking minute thinking about this specific moment, and now . . . now it was here, and I DID NOT WORK.

I may have broken down a little bit. It's true. I may have had some harsh words for my penis or the superheroes on the walls. There might have been tears.

Anyway, twenty minutes later, after a dismal and awkward failure, we had our clothes on again.

The breeze from outside had grown colder. Amy sat on the edge of the bed, brushing out her hair with her fingers. I sat on the other edge of the bed, a million miles away, washed in a cloud of failure and shame.

"So I guess I need to go home," she said.

I could barely make out the comic books. The words on the covers rearranged themselves.

Avengers #275: Disaster!

The Uncanny X-Men #216: Nightmare world!

Fantastic Four #306: A Monster once more!

Wolverine #2: The erectile dysfunction issue!

"It's okay, Craig," said Amy.

I didn't say anything.

"Are you all right?"

"I am never going to be all right again," I said.

"That doesn't really make me feel good."

"I'm not blaming you."

"I'd hope not. I didn't do anything wrong."

I gritted my teeth. "Next time it's gonna be great, I promise. I'll study or something. Calisthenics, maybe." I was hoping for a laugh or something, but she just sighed.

"This was probably a stupid idea. We don't have to have sex."

"Yes, we do!"

In retrospect, I realize I made a series of mistakes in this conversation. She was trying to steer things back in the right direction, but I was not listening. So, please, enjoy the upcoming verbal carnage.

"I just don't think we were . . . ready, you know?" said Amy. "Like, we haven't gotten to this point yet in our relationship, and I just . . . Let's just take it slow."

"Did you get to this point with Chad?" I asked.

Boom. There it was. *Oh, Craig, you are a fucking idiot.*

"Yes," she said. "I did."

"I figured."

"Oh. You figured? Why did you figure that?"

"I don't know."

"You don't know? Is that why you thought we should have sex tonight?"

"Well, you did it with him."

Of the first six breakups with Amy, this one was the most my fault. You can see it coming, right?

I'm going to spare you the apocalypse that followed that last comment and fast-forward to about an hour later when she was finished tearing me a new asshole. I believe her last words were "Fuck you!" and she was out the door.

Just as Kaitlyn was pulling into the driveway.

EIGHTEEN

The Apology

"Karma," said Kaitlyn.

It was two in the morning, about an hour after Amy left. I was languishing in the kitchen. My rib cage felt like someone had taken a baseball bat to my heart. My hands ached. The evil fluorescent lights gleamed maliciously. Kaitlyn was leaning against the fridge with a can of Coke.

"This is karma coming back to bite you in the butt."

I could barely find the energy to speak. I wanted to crawl in a hole. "What karma?"

"You're taunting the universe with this whole Amy Carlson thing, and the universe is striking back."

"What are you talking about?"

"The universe hates you. Therefore, Amy Carlson is dumping your ass over and over again. It makes perfect sense to me. This is intensely gratifying to watch."

"Shouldn't you be, like, consoling me right now?"

"Nope. Not at all. You suck."

I put my head down on the counter. We had a little island-type thing in the kitchen with these horrifically uncomfortable barstools. Mom had gone on a redecorating kick at the end of the '80s and had made a series of poor choices. The counter felt cold and plastic, like the surface of some alien spaceship.

I felt tears brimming.

"Oh God," said Kaitlyn. "Seriously, stop it. Stop what you're doing." She let out a huge sigh. "Fine. What happened?"

I told her.

"God, you're dumb," she said. "You think she owes you?"

"I didn't say she owed me—"

"You acted like it. Like, as soon as she has sex with somebody, then she's required to have sex with everybody else? That's basically what you said to her."

I was quiet. Kaitlyn kept going.

"What she did with another guy doesn't change how she feels about you. Otherwise you're going to be competing with every guy she's ever been with, you dumbass."

"How many guys do you think she's been with?"

"WHO CARES?" Kaitlyn rapped on my forehead with her knuckle. "She's not with them now, is she? She's with you. She wants to be with you for some reason. If you want to have sex, you need to be adult enough to handle sex. Period. And part of that, moron, is realizing that you don't own her past and you don't get to retroactively make her feel bad for everything she's done before she met you. 'Cause you know what that makes you? If you're going to make her feel bad about stuff she can't control now? That makes you a dick."

She sipped her Coke in triumph and leaned back again.

". . . Yeah," I said, not feeling any better.

"What was that?"

"You're right," I said.

"Thank you. You know what I would do if I was you—"

"If I *were* you."

"What?"

"It's 'if I were you.'"

"What are you talking about?"

"It's the subjective mood. You can't say 'if I was you.'"

Kaitlyn blinked thirty or forty times. "Holy shit."

"Okay, fine, sorry, what would you do?"

"I think you know."

It was time for the Grand Gesture.

In romantic comedies, the Grand Gesture is the moment near the end of the movie where the hero or heroine, who is just about to lose the love of their life forever, must do something outrageous to ensure the happily-ever-after all the audience has come for. It's the moment in *Say Anything . . .* when Lloyd Dobler lifts the boom box over the top of his head. It's the moment when someone is running through the airport to catch someone at that instant before the person gets on the plane. When someone is running down the street in his or her underwear, or bicycling, or driving, or racing, that's it. There's usually a lot of running.

And get this: the Grand Gesture always works. Always. And then it's roll credits.

I snatched the keys to Mom's car off the island, and I grabbed my coat.

"Where the hell are you going?" asked Kaitlyn.

"I'm gonna make history," I said.

"That's not what I was suggesting," she called out. "I was going to say give up!" But I didn't hear her because I was already out the door.

It was nearly two thirty in the morning when I reached Amy's house. A light mist had crept up from the cornfields and the roads were a little slick. But I drove like a madman because I needed to make this a big moment. I couldn't lose her. Not like this. There had to be a way to win her back. On the way there, my mind was racing. What possible gesture could I make?

POSSIBLE GRAND GESTURES

1. Boom box over head. Already been done. I also had no boom box. Plus, it was two thirty in the morning. I had to be quiet.

2. Show up in a Winnie-the-Pooh costume. This idea was terrible. But I was brainstorming, trying not to throw anything out.

3. Break into her house? This seemed the most plausible, but what would I do when I succeeded at that?

4. Compose a poem on the way to her house. I tried this. But I am no good at poems, and it sucked.

5. Wing it.

I ended up choosing method number five because I was already in her driveway. Then I thought better of parking in her driveway, so I put my car in reverse and parked three houses down. Then I got out, dashed over the grass, crispy with frost, and found myself staring up at her window on the second floor. Her light was off.

The whole house was dark and silent. The bare branches of the trees in her backyard loomed overhead. My breath escaped in puffs of steam.

I danced around for a bit, trying to keep my brain alive and think of something. When I failed at that, I picked up a small stone, held it in my hand for a moment, then tossed it at her window. I missed. I missed the whole house actually.

I should've tried harder in gym class.

Luckily, there were more stones nearby, and my aim gradually improved. The hard part was calibrating the right amount of force. I started out way too light; I wouldn't have woken up anybody. But then again there was also a large terrifying German shepherd named Bear in the house. Bear could probably break through a window, chase me down, and eat me on the front lawn before I could scream. So I didn't want to wake him up. Her parents were another issue, although they were old. The other issue was her little brother, whose bedroom was right next to hers.

Whap. Whap. Whap. Nothing. *Whap! Whap! Whap!* Then I missed the house again. I really sucked at throwing rocks.

WHACK!

I waited.

WHACK!

The light came on.

I raised my arms in a gesture of love or surrender or, even more likely, *Don't shoot me.*

"I'm sorry," I whispered as loud as I could after she had opened the window to see what the hell was going on.

"What do you want?" said Amy, her voice still choked with tears.

I spread my arms out wide.

Think of something. Think of something now.

You are not thinking of anything. You have serious problems.

Amy waited.

Then an idea occurred to me. I dropped my coat to the ground. Then I pulled my sweater off. I had a little trouble with that, actually, 'cause I was trying to maintain eye contact with her while I did it, so one arm got caught, and, okay . . . I flung my sweater to the cold grass. Then I took a deep breath and pulled my shirt up over my head.

"What are you doing?" hissed Amy as I grabbed my belt.

"I really don't know!" I hissed back. I unloosened my belt and dropped my pants.

At this point I had forgotten to take off my shoes so my pants basically ended up around my calves.

So I stood there, in my jungle-scene boxer shorts with little cartoon animals on them. The air was biting my skin and goose pimples were popping up all over me, but I took hold of my waistband.

"Okay," I said, huffing. "I just wanted to let you know that I am really sorry and I am really vulnerable right now and—"

"Would you put your damn clothes on?" She laughed.

"I haven't really thought this out past this point, to be honest with you, and I realize this seems kind of stalkerish and I apologize for that," I called back. "But maybe I could come inside before I freeze to death?" Two minutes later, I was in her room and fully clothed. My Grand Gesture had continued with a rambling, nonsensical monologue in which I was crying quite a bit, but at least I managed to keep my clothes on. I won't bore you with an entire transcript of what I said, but it was something like this:

"I am so sorry. I was an idiot. I don't know what's wrong with me. I probably wasn't raised right, and I never meant to get all jealous like that. That was so stupid, and I realize that I don't control your past and I can't judge you for anything you've done before, and there's, like, a horrible double-standard thing and I don't even want to get into that right now, but it's okay, and of course it's okay. You've done things and that's completely fine—it's great actually, it's great, and I think the important thing is that I'm madly in love with you. And I know that you might not be in love with me, and I know that you are having a really hard time right now, in life, and I never, never want to make things harder on you. But I figure I don't want to hide my feelings toward you because you're the best thing that's ever happened to my life, and I realize that's problematic because even then I'm thinking about you in relation to me, which is not cool, because I know that you are an amazing, amazing person and going out with you has been even better than that time I went to Disney World. Way better than Disney World. Disney World actually kind of sucked because I threw up on Space Mountain and the puke got on these people behind me and they were screaming, and I thought they were going to kill me. So as soon as the ride was over, I ran away from the ride and got lost, and I ended up in the Hall of Presidents, which is basically horrible."

And so on.

Finally, in order to stop my mouth, she kissed me. "Okay," she said. "Apology accepted."

And, about twenty minutes later, my jungle boxers with cartoon tigers were flung across the room and we made love. That's right. You heard me. We did it.

So, afterward, it was probably three thirty in the morning, and we had managed not to wake her parents, her brother, or the demon dog. The lights were off in her room, and we were lying on her futon, in her room that was so much better decorated than mine.

"Huh," she said.

"Yeah. Yessir. That's right," I said.

I was feeling what we refer to as the afterglow.

"So I guess I got that right, yeah?" I said.

"What?"

"I got that right?"

"Um . . . yeah, yeah, it was good."

"Great." I could accept that. A solid B. "But pretty good for my first time, right?"

I could hear her furrowing her brow a bit.

"Sure . . ." She sucked in a breath like she wanted to say something else but stopped herself. "Hurm."

"What?"

"I guess I . . . You were a virgin, right?"

Were *a virgin. As in past tense. Subjunctive.*

No it's not, dumbass, it's a mood, not a tense, and the subjunctive mood is about a conditional—

Shut the hell up, brain.

My brain stopped to do little celebratory high fives with my other body parts.

"I figured you probably knew," I said.

"Yeah."

"I mean I told you that you were my first girlfriend."

"Right."

"So who else would I have had sex with?"

"Hookers, maybe. I don't know."

"Do I look like the kind of guy who would go to hook-ers?" Had she met other guys who had gone to hookers? Were other people losing their virginity to them? *Were* there hookers in Janesville, Wisconsin; and if so, was there a particular street corner they hung on, or did you have to find them in the Yellow Pages or something? Also, who the hell did she think I was?

"I'm kidding. No, I mean it's stupid. I'm sorry," she said. "I guess I didn't want to do this right now, you know? I didn't want to . . . um . . . you know, your first time should be special."

"It was plenty special."

"You know what I mean? Like, I feel like this was kind of . . . um . . . I don't want you to be let down. I mean I was . . . I had a whole plan."

I turned to look at her lying next to me. Her blond hair was tangled and spread out over the pillow. Her ceiling was covered with those little glow-in-the-dark stars, and the futon was like a sea of cream-covered pillows and blankets.

"You had a plan?"

"Well, yeah—I mean it wasn't gonna be tonight. We were gonna go out to dinner, and then I was gonna make this whole Dungeons & Dragons theme—that's why I came to the game tonight, I wanted to learn about it. It was gonna be like an adven-ture. We were gonna roll dice."

At that moment, I felt like Amy was probably the greatest girl who had ever lived.

NINETEEN

The Aftermath
Or
Crap, I Fell Asleep

When the light came in through her windows in the morning, I was pretty sure my life was over. Amy's arm was over my neck; my back was hurting; and something terrible had died in my mouth during the night. I heard a dog barking and dimly recalled that there wasn't a dog alive at my house because all the pets at my house were dead.

Because I wasn't at my house.

Oh, shit. Shit.

"Shit," I said. "Shit."

Amy woke up, her eyes cloudy with sleep and then bright with terror. "Shit!" Then she put her hand over my mouth and said, "Shh!" I stopped struggling for a second and tried to send my ears out like Superman's super hearing.

There was a knocking sound. Someone was knocking on her door.

"Sweetheart?" It was her mom. I recognized the musical blend of Swedish and the thickest Wisconsin accent imaginable.

Amy grabbed my head, shoved me under the blankets, and leaped out of the bed.

"Hold on one second!" she cried, dashing to her closet.

Her mom kept knocking. "Oh, someone's a sleepyhead this morning. Can I come in?"

Amy made a little noise that was somewhere between a shriek and the sound a cat makes when you step on its tail. She had snatched a bathrobe from her closet (which was very impressive in that she had a bathrobe; she was so mature). All this I'm telling you I learned later because at that moment I was buried in the cream-colored universe of Amy's comforter. Something heavy and soft landed on me; I later learned that it was the four-foot-tall teddy bear that Amy had hurled across the room with superhuman strength just as her mother plowed into the room.

From where I lay beneath the stuffed animal, I could barely make out what was happening.

"I wanted to let you know that there are muffins if you are interested."

"Oh."

"Oh, and you're giving me a ride to the clinic this afternoon. Your father is busy; he's looking for a new snowblower. I don't know why he needs to go today, but you know how he is."

"Sure. Um . . ."

"Why is your room always a disaster area?" I saw Amy's mom bend down, pick up my jeans, and absently fold them.

"I gotta clean the room. Mom, can I get dressed?"

"Oh, sure, don't mind me, I'm just harassing you, I guess," she said, dropping my jeans on the foot of the bed just as something large and breathing like a tornado padded into the room. A giant black nose obscured my vision.

"Bear, get out!"

Bear did not get out. Amy's mom did not get out.

"Hon," said her dad, now also at the door, "there's a sale on snowblowers this afternoon and I need your advice."

"Guys, can I get dressed?"

Bear's nose started sucking air like a vacuum cleaner. He began thrusting his muzzle under the edge of the blankets.

"Bear!" shouted Amy, trying to pull the German shepherd back.

"Oh, isn't he cute?" said her mom. "Bear loves you."

I would like to comment here that a close-up look at the teeth of a German shepherd is not a pleasant experience. Especially when you are naked and you can easily imagine those teeth tearing off sensitive body parts. If you compared human teeth to dog teeth, you would come to the conclusion that the reason we walked behind them and picked up their poop is that we were terrified. Which I was.

"Okay, then," said her dad. "So the snowblower I'm thinking of is one of those Japanese ones."

"Oh for goodness' sake," said her mom.

"They're good. I'd buy American, but the Japanese are making great snowblowers these days."

"Oh, jeez, they are not," said her mom.

"I think I know my snowblowers, sweetheart."

"I keep telling him to wait till the fall—"

"The sales are now. This is the time. If we don't act now we're lost."

Amy had got hold of Bear by the neck and was struggling to force him away from the bed while keeping her robe closed, which was not exactly easy to do.

"Guys," Amy said. "Please, let me get dressed!"

"You're off your rocker, Dan. Off your rocker."

And then her parents were gone, and Amy slammed the door shut. Forgetting that I was butt-naked, I leaped out of the bed.

"Get dressed!" she hissed.

I found my boxers majestically splayed out on her desk, where a certain picture in a heart-shaped frame used to be. I took a moment.

"Come on!" she said.

I snatched them, grabbed my crisply folded pants (really nice work by her mom), and tried to put on all my clothes simultaneously, which resulted in me getting my neck in the arm hole of my sweater and two legs in the same pant leg.

Amy got dressed in her closet, which was not a walk-in, but at least she managed it.

"Okay," she said, holding me by the shoulders and flipping into ultracompetent mode. "We're getting you out of here, and we're getting you out of here now. Listen to me carefully."

The plan was for Amy to beg for doughnuts, thus sending her father on a run to Dunkin' Donuts, and for her to distract her mom with advice about all her life problems while I crept down the hallway, snuck out through the garage, and ran like hell. It worked about as well as you might expect.

Amy managed to distract her parents for just a minute—no one was going to get doughnuts because oh jeez it was an extravagance but they were happy to talk about life problems—and I was halfway down the hallway before her mom broke past Amy's defenses. I had no time to make it back to her room, so I opened the nearest door, which I figured was to the bathroom.

It was Glenn's room.

Glenn was sitting there, at his computer, deeply involved in a game of *Tetris*. The sound track to *Cabaret* was playing on his boom box.

He was thirteen years old, had an impressive Afro, and was so skinny that I seemed husky in comparison. He was also about six foot two and almost entirely legs. The basketball coach of the high school was already salivating at the prospect of having him on the team, which was a shame, since Glenn was the clumsiest person I'd ever met and was really only interested in musical theater and computer programming.

"He-ey," I stammered, closing the door behind me.

He gave me a look like I was an alien who had just crash-landed in his bedroom and was mostly on fire.

"What's up, Glenn? How's it hanging?"

"What?" he said nervously.

"I feel like we never get to hang out anymore."

"What?"

"Right. Man. Life is too short. That's all I'm saying. *Tetris*, am I right? It's pretty sweet. All those shapes. Are you kidding me? Shapes are awesome."

"What are you doing here?"

There was only one way out of this, and it wasn't the window, since I had already thought of that, and then realized that yes, I was on the second floor.

"I need your help. We're gonna walk out into the living room and you're gonna follow my lead, okay?"

He cocked an eyebrow. "Man, you're crazy."

"You owe me," I said, meeting his gaze. "Remember Christmas dinner?"

Amy looked like she had swallowed a frog when I walked into the living room, holding Glenn by the arm like a hostage. Amy's dad had already taken up his customary position on the La-Z-Boy, and was somewhat surprised to see us.

"Well, young man, I hope you've learned a lot about the project we've been working on," I said very loudly, staring Glenn in the eyes.

"Yes . . ." he said, utterly confused.

"Oh jeez," Amy's dad said. "I didn't see you come in."

"Glenn suggested we get an early start of it."

"Yup," he said. "Craig needed some help with his homework." He stared at me. "Craig needs lots of help."

"Yes. Yes I do," I said slowly.

Glenn kept going. "It's kind of amazing that a high school senior would need help with his homework from an eighth grader—"

"But that's because Glenn's so brilliant," I said, patting him on the shoulder. "You know, I've heard musicals actually help you . . . with math."

Amy's mom wobbled in from the kitchen, leaning on the doorway. "Oh, Craig, you're here! I didn't hear you come in either!"

"I've got a lot of ninja skills," I said. "I keep to the shadows."

She turned to Amy. "I thought we weren't having anyone over."

"I know," said Amy. "This is just a thing that Glenn and Craig set up . . . apparently."

"Oh." Her mom's smile withered.

I noticed then that the house was in a bit of disarray. The other times I had been there it had always seemed immaculate, like it was some kind of Swedish-Wisconsin museum of adorable kitsch and fresh-smelling flower arrangements. Now it seemed darker—dirty dishes were piled in the sink, the floor hadn't been vacuumed. Then again, I had never been there in the morning, and it was still way cleaner than my room.

Amy's mom saw me looking. "If I would've known I would've cleaned up! This place is a pigsty."

"You should see my house," I said. "We have actual pigs."

"You are too much! You are just too much! It is good to see you!" And then she opened her arms and gave me a hug. Amy's mom was skinnier than before; she felt almost weightless. She had never been a large woman, but now she was positively bird-like. She'd been losing weight in a hurry.

Your daughter deflowered me last night.

And then I let go because shit got weird.

Amy sensed the strangeness. "It's too bad you have to go," she said.

"Yep. Well," I said, suddenly aware that my hair was conspicuously jutting out from the sides of my head in a very clear case of bedhead. "Now that Glenn has . . . helped me—"

"You were really just making some simple mistakes," Glenn interrupted with a sly grin. "If you just check your work you'll get it."

"Thanks again," I said.

"Anytime. If you need help, I'm here for you, bro." He held his hand out.

I looked at it. He looked at it.

"Are we gonna high-five?" I said.

"My fee. For tutoring?"

"Ohhh . . ."

"My goodness, Glenn," said Amy's dad. "That's real industrious of you."

"Yeah, Craig's paying me ten bucks an hour," he said as I looked in my wallet and was about to pull out a five-dollar bill.

"Do you have change?" I said, taking out a twenty.

"I'll get you next time," said Glenn.

"Son."

It was a week later. I was in the kitchen, and so was my dad, elegantly draped in his most unappealing pajamas, which, considering his collection of pajamas that still existed from the 1970s, was saying something. It's not that they had holes (they did) or that they were so threadbare as to be largely see-through; it was the odd and disturbing combination of cherries and bears that seemed to dance in a satanic circle of awfulness that made them the worst. I did not appreciate it when he wore them, and yet here he was wearing the pajamas in the kitchen just after midnight.

The job search had not been going particularly well, and my dad had responded by growing a goatee. I wasn't sure if this was a midlife crisis or something, but it made him a look like Bizarro evil dad. Like, normal dad had a job and went to work and never said anything, and evil Bizarro dad expressed his feelings.

Amy had gone home a little bit ago, and he had emerged from his slumber like an ornery black bear ready to lay waste to a campsite.

"Hey, Dad," I said, pretending to yawn. "So I'm gonna . . . go to sleep."

"Hold on."

He sauntered behind me, and I could tell he had something important on his mind.

Crap. Two big hands descended on my shoulders, and he gave a halfhearted attempt between a "shake the life out of you" and "neck massage," either of which would have been very, very odd.

"So how long have you and Amy been dating?"

"Um . . . like continuously or if you put them all together?"

Dad frowned. He had no idea what I was talking about. He tried a new line of questioning.

"Are you getting serious?"

This is part of the problem when middle-aged people talk to young people about relationships. We live in completely different worlds. What the heck was he talking about? What did serious mean? Did I give her a promise ring or something? Were we going steady? We weren't engaged or anything. Was that what he was suggesting?

"Define 'serious,'" I said.

"You know what it means."

"I'm pretty sure I don't."

"I'm pretty sure you do."

"Well, uh . . . I guess we're serious, then."

"Uh-huh." He nodded, as if he had known it already. "I kind of knew that. I've seen her around here a lot."

"Yeah."

Dad took a deep breath and settled onto one of the very uncomfortable barstools. He put both hands, which he had balled up into fists, on the counter and steeled himself. This was probably worse than going to war.

"So . . . um . . . there comes a time when you and Amy are going to want to . . . explore different possibilities."

What?

"Like what?"

"Um . . . like when you, uh . . . want to express yourselves physically."

"Like charades?"

Dad frowned. This was not going well for him.

It finally dawned on me that he was trying to find a way to avoid saying "sex."

"Oh. You mean sex!"

"Yes."

"Yes. Sex. Good stuff."

Dad looked at me again and puffed out his cheeks like he was caught in a field of razor wire. "If you and Amy decide to take that step, I want you to make sure to use . . . protection."

"Sure."

"I mean it."

"Okay."

And then Dad took out a small box from the pocket of his ratty pajamas and put it on the table. I tried to avert my eyes, but I had already seen what it was. Trojans.

"These are your best friends," he said, clapping me on the shoulder again.

I kept my eyes down. My dad had just given me a box of condoms. A box of condoms, I might add, that was ALREADY OPEN. This is what happens when you anger God. He sends doom upon you.

"I'm too young to be a grandfather."

"You're not gonna be one for a while. Don't worry."

"All right."

"Are we done?"

Dad exhaled again. "Nope."

Oh, crap.

He looked down at the island again and gathered himself for another round of "embarrass the hell out of Craig."

"Are you in love with her?"

"Yeah."

"You're gonna do some dumb shit in your life, Craig. Really dumb."

"Yeah, I know. I've discovered that recently."

"When you were a baby, you used to have really dry skin. And you would claw up your face scratching it. You remember that?"

"No. Because I was a baby."

"Right. Sure. But my job was to put mittens on you. So you wouldn't hurt yourself, you know? So, basically, that's been my job ever since. Putting some damn mittens on you so you won't hurt yourself too bad."

"I think I'm doing okay," I lied, vaguely aware that my heart had been broken four times by the same girl in the past five months.

"No, you're stupid. It's okay. You're supposed to be stupid right now. The key, though, is not to be so stupid that you mess up the rest of your life. 'Cause you're at the point now where what you do is going to affect the whole rest of your life, you understand?"

"Yeah."

"So if you don't screw up, you'll be fine. And the way to screw up is to do the following: get a girl pregnant, get arrested, drop out of school, or get married. Okay? Don't do any of that shit."

"All right," I said. Apparently there were only four ways to screw up my life. According to Amy's book, women had ten. So that was a bonus.

"Good. I'm gonna go back to sleep, then."

"Good talk, Dad."

"Good talk, son."

And then he got up from the really uncomfortable barstool and shuffled upstairs, with the holes clearly visible in his pajamas.

A second later, Kaitlyn was there. She had been listening the whole time.

"Hey, give me that," she whispered, taking the box of condoms.

"No, I need those," I said, swiping them back and trying to, once again, ignore the fact that the box HAD ALREADY BEEN OPENED and at least one of them WAS MISSING.

When I took them back, Kaitlyn froze, her mouth open.

"Oh my God," she said, realization flashing over her. She pointed at me. "Oh my God! Did it work?"

"I'm not telling."

"It did!"

"I'm not saying whether it did or not. I can neither confirm nor deny the—"

"Holy shit!" said Kaitlyn, stunned. "When you were going over to her house I was like, 'This is not going to end well.' Amy Carlson." She looked at me. "You and Amy Carlson. This is, like . . . everything I believed I knew about reality has been upended. I don't even know what the hell's going on anymore. Who am I?"

"Shut up. I just had the Talk with Dad, shut up."

"Oh whatever. I had the Talk with Mom, like, four years ago."

"Four years ago?"

She hit me in the shoulder. "I didn't need the talk then, idiot."

"She probably just sensed where you were heading."

"You suck, Craig."

An uncomfortable silence settled between us. I still had the box in my hands.

"So . . . um . . . when did you, uh . . . ?" I asked.

"Oh, shut up. I'm not telling you." Then she smiled. "Like two years ago."

"Two years ago?!" I stopped myself. "Cool. I guess, right? Cool?"

"Pretty cool."

"God, we're a bunch of sluts in this family, aren't we?" And then I high-fived Kaitlyn. "Here, you can have half of these."

TWENTY

How We Got Back Together— The First Time

It was December when we had the First Infamous Family Dinner. A week after Amy had broken up with me the first time I was still in a miserable funk. I had improved somewhat, but as far as I knew, no wolves had descended on Chad and devoured him, so I was a bit bummed by that.

My mom started it. "We have some news," she said, and looked kind of sadly at my dad while she distributed the fish we were not going to eat. "We won't be going to Florida to visit Grandma this year."

"Yes!" hissed Kaitlyn.

I kicked her under the table.

"Ow." She kicked me back.

"Goddamn it," I said, trying to kick her again.

"You don't get to kick me, Craig! I don't want to go to Florida. It's horrible there. All we do is tour through old houses. It sucks."

"Okay, but still, this is a very serious moment and you're acting like a brat!"

"You don't like Grandma either!"

We had come a long way since our ninth birthday party, obviously.

My mom and dad exchanged the we-have-failed-as-parents-and-here-is-the-evidence glances.

"Guys," said my mom a little too quietly. "Please stop."

Kaitlyn put her hands in the air like she was being arrested and leaned back in her chair.

"The reason we're not going to Florida," she continued, "is that your father"—she paused, trying to figure out the best way to put a smile on this—"is going to be transitioning into a new role at the company by not being there anymore."

"I'm getting laid off," said Dad.

"But it's going to be okay! We're going to be okay. This is temporary."

"Maybe," he added, and sighed. Dad had been morose ever since the hunting trip, and it was tough to watch. Normally he prowled around the house like a panther, talking about how stupid people were, but he had been subdued lately. He barely had the strength to talk back to the weatherman on the nightly news. (Usually he'd say things like, "You weren't right yesterday, genius—why should I trust you today?" To which the weatherman wouldn't respond because he was inside the television.)

He put his hands on the table. "The job market's in the shitter right now, so . . . so we have to prepare for me being out of work for a little while."

"We're not saying 'shitter,'" countered my mom.

"I'm saying 'shitter,'" said my dad.

"It's going to be okay," added my mom, short-circuiting the discussion of whether or not we were going to become a family that cussed in front of each other. "It's not all doom and gloom."

"I'll get to spend a lot more time with you," he said. A little noise of pain escaped Kaitlyn. "But it does mean that we're going to have to tighten our belts. Not as many dinners out. We might need to sell your car."

"What?!" gasped Kaitlyn. I kicked her under the table again. She kicked me right back harder. (I was getting the worst of it— she could definitely kick harder than me.)

"If I can't find something right away, we're gonna have to get rid of it," he said. "And, um . . . there might be the possibility we have to move."

"Move where?" asked Kaitlyn.

"Wherever he gets a job, dumbass," I said, channeling my dad. *I got your back, big guy.*

"Craig," sighed Mom, trying to keep her smile going. "Not helpful!"

"But we'll see. I'll look around here first. They gave me a decent severance package, so it's not an emergency yet."

"So how about we sell the car when it becomes an emergency—"

"Stop worrying about the car," I said.

Kaitlyn turned on me. "First of all, I'm not the one who spends all the money in this house."

"What the hell?" I said.

"How much Dungeons & Dragons crap is in the basement? We should sell that!"

"No one's gonna buy that," said Dad. "That money's lost."

"Hey!" I protested.

"Oh, honey," said Mom. "You've got a lot of toys."

"They're not toys! They're miniatures!"

"What about Craig's billion comic books?"

"Kids," said my dad holding up his hands like he was the pope. "Hopefully we'll be fine."

"We'll be fine," added my mom.

"Hopefully."

"Well, what about college?" asked Kaitlyn.

That question hung in the air for a moment, just long enough for a shadow of doubt to run through me.

I had been dreading going back to Youth in Government. It was one thing to see Amy in the halls, it was another to be in a room with her, actually listening to her speak and staring at her the entire time. I had vowed not to stare at her, of course, and focus on the words carved into the desks, but I knew myself. I'd be staring at her.

"Dude, whatever," said Groash on the way there. "You should

just be like, 'Screw this, I'm not your slave anymore!' And then you just walk out."

"That doesn't really sound like a good idea."

"Are you kidding me? That's an awesome idea. That's what I would do if I were you. 'Bitch! Look at me!' Maybe I'd rip my shirt off. You know, if I was like, built, you know? Like if I had muscles or whatever, off comes the shirt—'This is what you're giving up!' And then I just storm out of there, feeling myself the whole time."

I would like to point out here that at this moment in our lives, Groash had had two girlfriends and I had had one. (And my relationship had lasted like three weeks.) Repeat: He had been more successful at love than I had.

"That's shitty advice, man."

"Well, at least you don't have to go to Madison for that thing."

"I can't get my money back. That's like three hundred bucks. It's kind of huge for my family right now."

"Just don't go. You can hide out at my house instead."

The prospect of hiding out at Groash's house for three days sealed the deal. "I'm definitely going to Madison," I said.

"You should totally get ripped first," he said.

And then there was the meeting.

She was standing near the pool table going over a list with Chelsea when we walked in.

"Hey," she said.

"Hey," I said.

Her blue eyes glittered in the light. A tumbleweed blew through. Probably a plane crashed. Time slowed down to nothing. I figured this would be the moment she admitted she was wrong, swept the billiard balls to the ground, and threw me on the pool table.

That didn't happen.

"So I'm gonna sit down," I said.

"Okay."

Then she patted me on the shoulder.

I patted her on the shoulder.

She smiled and my stomach dropped out again.

I want you back, I thought, not saying anything. *I want to be able to love you.*

"So make sure you've got your toiletries. Every year there's people who forget their toothbrush and it's not pleasant," said Chelsea, handing out the little lists of things we shouldn't forget but probably would because we were morons. "And I'm not talking about the people who don't normally brush their teeth. If you normally don't brush your teeth, start."

"Toothbrush," muttered Groash under his breath as he looked over the sheet.

"And, guys, you need to be wearing suits and ties. Please don't get the little clip-on ones. They're ridiculous. If you need help tying a tie, find one of the older guys to help you." I looked around. Groash and I were the older guys. I knew he had no idea how to tie a tie. I had about a 20 percent success rate. "Black socks with black shoes. I do not want to see white socks; I don't want us looking like a bunch of donkeys out there."

Amy cut in. "Thanks, Chelsea."

"I'm serious. Not cool."

"And remember, if you need to get your bills done, the deadline is next week, so that's your last chance to submit something. Right now we've got, um . . . four finished bills, which is kind of weak, so . . . so maybe we can do better? So . . . any questions?"

Groash put his hand up.

"Why'd you dump Craig?"

Oh shit.

Amy stared at him for a second like a deer caught in the headlights, and Groash barreled forward, throwing an arm over my shoulder in solidarity. "I mean, look at this man. This coulda been the best thing in your life. Probably not. You probably have some cool shit going on, but still. Look at him. He's a wreck. He is a shell of a human being."

I tried to sink through the floor, but it didn't work because my mutant powers had never developed.

"Just picture his heart exploding into a million pieces. You did that. He can't eat. He can't sleep. He can barely talk. He's probably not even masturbating anymore."

No one said anything for three or four years.

It was going to be a fun field trip to Madison.

"Pheromones," said Groash, rolling a twenty-sided die. "That's the secret if you want to get her back. It'll drive her wild. You just bathe in that shit. She won't even know what's going on. You'll walk by her, and then the like pheromone center in her brain will activate or whatever, and then she'll just be, like, on you. This is the perfect opportunity. You're gonna be trapped in a tight space with her and she'll be like, 'What is that powerful smell? It's Craig.' Boom."

"That's moronic," said Elizabeth.

"If pheromones work, why aren't you using them?" asked Brian from behind his screen as he readjusted his papers.

"I got natural funk, I don't need pheromones. Face it," he said, leaning over and snatching a Little Debbie brownie from the coffee table, "you need to use whatever advantage you can get. She is like so high above you on the social ladder, you basically need to cheat. Or go after easier prey. A guy like you? Sophomores. That's your sweet spot. They don't know any better."

"You're like a scholar of the human condition," said Elizabeth.

"I just understand women. On like a primal level."

"Oh, sure. I'm sure that's true."

"Is that sarcasm? Are you being sarcastic now?"

"Why would I be sarcastic when I'm clearly in the presence of an expert?"

"Dude, if you used pheromones you wouldn't have any trouble getting a guy."

Elizabeth rocked back on her chair. "Why would I want a guy?"

"You want a guy. I know you want a guy."

"You don't need pheromones for guys. Guys are sluts. All you have to do is say hi. I could have any guy I want, anytime I want. I *choose* not to, because there are no guys around that are interesting enough for me."

Groash sputtered and I looked down at the floor. Brian tripped over something.

"No offense, Craig," she said, patting me on the shoulder. "I'm just not into you that way."

"That's cool," I managed. "No worries."

"You should pick somebody else anyway," she said. "There are more women in the world than Amy Carlson."

"Not that like me—"

"She didn't like you that much, she dumped you," interjected Groash.

"Guys? Can we focus, please, on the task at hand?" said Brian. "I'm sure that Craig's love life is fascinating and all, but we are in the middle of a battle here."

That was true. And we were getting our asses handed to us. The Association of Darkness was apparently quite peeved by its non-threatening name and had used that resentment to fuel its ass-kicking abilities, which were formidable. Brian had really gone all out on this particular adventure. He put in far more time devising these games for us than he did on his schoolwork, or articles for the newspaper, or breathing.

"Rothgar. A giant mouth appears in front of you," said Brian, placing a counter on the map table.

"I leap backward," I said.

"Right into the other mouth that appeared invisibly behind you, which bites you savagely," he said, putting a second counter behind my character. He rolled a fistful of dice. "Forty-eight points of damage. You're unconscious."

"Oh, come on! How the heck—"

"You literally fell directly into the path of the spell—it's in the description." He opened his notebook to an intricately crafted spell description. "'If a character jumps backward, he jumps into a second mouth, which hits for double damage. Improved Magic Mouth.'"

"You can't just make up spells," I whined.

"The hell I can't. And I didn't make it up, I wrote it down. Evidence. I actually put work into this, Craig."

I actually put work into this.

The answer was staring me in the face the whole time. How to get her back. How to destroy Chad in a non-wolf-exploiting way.

Work.

Which immediately recalled RuPaul singing "You better *work*," which took me in a rather strange and unproductive direction in the whole winning-Amy-back plan.

Elizabeth was snapping her fingers in front of my face.

"You all right?"

"Yeah," I said. "I think I just figured out how to get her back."

Brian and Elizabeth groaned, but Groash nodded in support.

"Pheromones," he said.

TWENTY-ONE

The First Time We Got Back Together, Part Two It Was Hot (Actually, It Was Very Cold)

The Plan, such as it was, was fairly simple: Write the perfect bill. Something she would love, something that would call out to her. (Okay, yes, this was a nerdy plan.) Amy was in the House and I was in the Senate, so the only way she was going to be truly witness to my greatness is if I could get my bill passed. Damn you, bicameral government. If it passed the Senate, then it would go to the House, where it would come to her desk. Naturally, she would be amazed and thrilled that such an effective, brilliant piece of legislation had appeared before her. It would pass the House, then go to the governor's office (which was run by a junior from Appleton), she would sign it, and then it would become law, if *Schoolhouse Rock!* was to be believed. Imaginary law, but still law. And if that happened, then Amy would toss her boyfriend to the side, seize me, and kiss me passionately in the middle of the capitol building. It was perfect.

I spent four consecutive days at the library. I looked up the current state budget. I looked at funding options; I found comparable statistics from neighboring states. I made projections. I made a damn pie chart. It was glorious. If I had put this much work into my classes I would've been valedictorian—well, okay, salutatorian, 'cause Amy still would've beaten me.

Finally, beautifully, my bill was done, just in time. I slipped it into the folder for completed bills, making sure Amy didn't see it. Then it was off to Madison.

The best part of being in the Senate chamber was the chairs. They were the comfiest chairs imaginable: the plush leather was black and soft like a velvet Elvis and the wheels were made of some kind of hyper-slick material from NASA. They rolled smooth and true and held you like a lover. The chairs were probably the best reason to become a senator. A lot of people spent a lot of time spinning around in them. I was on a mission, though, so I only did that a little bit. Also, they had a whole bunch of free pencils at each desk.

The president of the Senate was a guy from Stevens Point named Jacob Hammer. I'm not even kidding. He was genetically engineered to be a politician—tall, with majestically wavy movie-star hair and a tie that was actually tied properly. When he spoke, he paused every so often and then used actual hand gestures to accentuate his points. He was mesmerizing.

Not only was he in charge, but there was a large contingent of guys from Stevens Point that had swung in like a group of Hell's Angels, if the Hell's Angels wore suits and carried monogrammed briefcases. They all spoke in complex sentences and peppered their speeches with in-jokes that made only the other Stevens Point people laugh. President Hammer recognized them all the time, and the rest of us were consigned to the back of the Senate to watch in awe and vote according to their wishes.

I looked at Groash, who was rotating slowly in his chair. "We're screwed," I whispered.

"These chairs are awesome," he whispered back.

For two entire days, the Stevens Point contingent dominated the proceedings. They introduced forty-one bills into the chamber. It was like a slow-moving revolution—they basically rewrote Wisconsin's constitution as they saw fit, slashed funding for state parks, reformed the tax code, lowered the drinking age to eighteen, and legalized pot. We voted for all of it in a delirious legislative orgy. If they would've introduced a bill to outlaw clouds, we would've gotten behind it.

Worse, though, was that they tended to shoot down bills from other cities. The bills from Appleton and Milwaukee and Eau Claire ended up destroyed, their advocates gently crying to themselves.

My stomach twisted itself into knots. The Plan required my bill to pass. If I couldn't get it passed, Amy would never see it.

"All right," said Hammer. "Next up on the docket: Bill 121, from . . . Janesville."

"I got your back, man," said Groash, giving me a thumbs-up.

A murmur of condescending laughter went through the chamber as I made my way to the podium. My heart thrummed in my ears. My vision got blurry. My stomach had come alive and was fighting to escape. My butt started to sweat. (Okay, I know, too much information. I am telling you that was what I focused on as I stood in the Senate.)

I looked out at the Senate. In their suits, everybody looked like adults. (Except for the people who were leaning way back in their chairs or otherwise rolling around.) They flipped to page 121 in the huge photocopied pamphlet on everyone's desk.

I took a deep breath and felt my stomach roiling. Then I spoke.

"So today I want to talk about something that's really important," I started. Initially, I had hoped to speak in a coherent, organized way, but the words tumbled out of my mouth in a gigantic run-on sentence. I wandered. I made awkward hand gestures. I might've pounded on the podium once or twice by accident. I forgot to reference my pie chart. But afterward, somehow, I looked out at the people deciding my fate and they were smiling.

They're basically just like me. They don't know what they're doing either.

Nobody knows what they're doing.

Hammer opened the bill to debate and Groash stood up first.

"I just want to say . . . fuck yeah." He raised his fist in triumph.

No one joined him. Then he started a slow clap. No one joined that either. Then he sat back down.

The silence afterward settled through the room like a poisonous cloud. Finally, one of the Stevens Point crew got up to speak.

"I mean," he said. "I guess we could do that, but, you know, where does this end? I think you're really overstating the problem."

From there it was downhill fast. The vote was called and Hammer pounded his gavel when it was done, officially killing the bill.

"I look around here," said Amy, "and I see failure." It was the last day of the conference in Madison, and it was the Speaker's job to give the final speech that would close the joint session. Then we'd have ice cream. If only every session of the real Congress ended with ice cream, this country might be better off. Anyway, Chelsea, Groash, and I were sitting in the wayback watching Amy talk.

I felt sick.

"A lot of us have failed. A lot of us didn't get our bills passed. A lot of us argued for the losing side. But failure is not something we should be afraid of. Failure is something we should embrace. Failure is something that should fuel us. Failure teaches us things. It teaches us to try harder, to think better, to compromise more effectively. We will not always succeed in life—there are trials and difficulties in store for all of us, and it's not our successes that are going to define us but our response to failure. Thank you."

There was a little smattering of applause. To be fair, the

audience members were not exactly in a clapping mood after they had been told they were failures. Amy gave a smile and a little wave and then took a seat up in front next to Jacob Hammer.

I had gotten used to seeing Amy every day again. The pain had dulled a bit. Instead of feeling like knives were slicing up my lungs, now it just felt like someone was taking a razor blade and tracing circles on my soul.

Since she was in the House and I was in the Senate, we didn't see each other too much during the day. But at night, our group would get together for dinner. I hadn't told her about the bill, and I didn't tell her when it went down in flames. Still, every time she entered my field of vision or I heard her laugh, my heart would twinge hopefully.

Maybe that was stupid; maybe the universe and Stevens Point were telling me to give up. Maybe I should stop. But then I thought, in Amy's speech she said "try harder," which was clearly directed at me.

Oh, God, you stupid bastard, said the Kaitlyn voice in my head.

Shut up, I said.

She cheated on you, moron, said the Kaitlyn voice in my head. *Actually, she cheated on her boyfriend with you. How about never talking to her again?*

But I didn't do that. I couldn't.

The ice cream social was largely a disaster. Amy was a minor celebrity, since she was the Speaker, so it was impossible to get close to her. Groash also found himself with a somewhat celebrated status among the Stevens Point crew as his bill outlawing visible back hair had also passed with near-unanimous support. Nobody spoke in support of back hair, oddly enough.

I stayed on the fringes, absently carving at my rock-solid ice cream with the useless little wooden spoon they give you on such occasions. Amy was laughing and chatting with a whole crowd of people, like she had a kind of gravity to her. At one point they gathered the officers together for a photo, and she was right next to Hammer. My heart deflated as she smiled. Not at me. It was like I didn't exist anymore.

I dumped the rest of my ice cream in the trash and headed back to the hotel.

Groash made it back an hour or so later. I had spent much of the intervening time facedown on the bed like any ordinary healthy sane person. It was probably completely normal for someone to moan into the comforter like a wounded animal. Groash saw me and shook his head.

"Dude," he said. "It's gonna be all right."

I said nothing.

"There is so much tail out there," he said sweetly, like a moronic guardian angel. "Suits, man. They are sexy as hell. Yes, I will vote for your bill. I will vote for your bill so hard. I'm probably not the right guy for this, but you can get out there. . . . Go into the hall, it's insane."

"I'm not going anywhere. I'm never leaving this room."

He sighed and sat on the end of the bed. "They left the pay-per-view movies on. You wanna spend the rest of the night doing that?"

I nodded, which was hard to do when you were facedown on the bed.

"They got *Godfather*. You wanna watch *Godfather*? Tons of people get killed in it. Might make you feel better."

I moved slightly. Maybe this was the right course of action.

"After that there's *Godfather II*. I think even more people get killed in that. It's brutal. Come on."

I rolled over. "You know, I kept thinking that if I did everything right, then . . ."

"That's not how it works, man."

There was a knock on our door and my heart fell out of my chest. I sat up.

She has come for me. She has changed her mind. That other boyfriend guy has been devoured by wolves.

Amanda swung open the door, grabbing hold of the frame with one hand, and not letting go of the knob, looking like a marionette being tugged in two directions. She was doing a bang-up job on her whole chaperoning gig, as you can imagine.

"He-eeeyyy," she said, wobbling slightly. "You guys in for the night?"

"Yeah," I said as my heart sheepishly crawled back into my chest, embarrassed at its own stupidity.

"Sweet," she said, hanging in the doorframe. She took a deep breath and exhaled, waiting there for some kind of mental signal that would allow her to leave. "You guys," she said, waving a finger in our general direction. I'm pretty sure she was more than a little high.

See? I did know where to get drugs! Screw you, Kaitlyn voice in my head.

"You guys are like this." She made a gesture with her fingers like we were all entwined with each other. "You know? You know what I'm saying?" No, we did not. "Like, when we came here I was like 'whatever,' and now I'm like . . . yeah."

"That's cool," I said, not having any clue what she was talking about.

"I'm the chaperone; you're the chaperone; we're all the chaperones." And then she stumbled out of the room, leaving the door open. "Ima get a turkey."

"I think she likes you," said Groash.

"What?"

"No, you're right. She's into me. That was just a test."

I heard Amanda's voice echoing in the hall. "You're the real chaperone, you're like the queen. Speaker lady. Yeah . . . like this . . . we are like this . . ."

Amy was in the doorway half a second later and my heart smashed a hole through my rib cage and fell out my back.

"Hi," she said.

She hadn't changed; she was still in her CIA spy suit, but she had let her hair down, which gloriously fell around her shoulders. In her hands she held the ceremonial Speaker's gavel. "What are you guys up to?"

Anything. Whatever you want. Origami? We'll do that.

" . . . Watching . . . movies," I managed.

"Can I join you?"

The Godfather lasted forty-three hours and I didn't pay attention to any of it. I was basically only concentrating on Amy's proximity to me. I sat on the end of the bed and she was sitting on the floor. Was there a way to move closer to her? Was she leaning in my direction? What did that mean? It meant she loved me, right? If a girl leans in your general direction it's a pretty sure indication that she is madly in love with you. Or maybe not. Every so often she would catch me looking at her and we'd make eye contact. What did that mean? Was *The Godfather* as romantic as I thought it was? Maybe when people got shot it meant that we were destined to be together? Maybe it didn't mean that at all. Maybe I was a stupid, stupid person.

Groash stretched out and got up from his spot on the other side of the bed.

"Now it is time . . . for *Godfather II*," he said.

Amy stretched. "I'm getting really tired," she said. It was after midnight.

"That's cool," said Groash. "I won't bother you. I'll just stay here watching this movie. It's awesome. There's like fifty murders."

"Oh," she said.

"Huh," I said.

"I'm gonna go for a walk," she said.

"It's really cold outside," I said.

"Nevertheless, Craig, I am going for a walk." She looked at me and raised one eyebrow a bit. "You want to join me?"

Time froze.

We were in a hotel filled with teenagers with limited chaperoning, so the whole place was a hurricane of chaos. People were running down the hallways. There were loud banging noises. In some rooms, people were singing songs. If there were any normal adults anywhere in this place, they were most likely filled with murderous rage.

We got our coats and went outside, where we could be with the drunk college students, who were, at least, respectful. It was snowing—big, wet beautiful flakes. They fell over the pavement like a fleet of feathers and caught in our hair.

We walked slowly, under the buildings that were already lit with Christmas lights. I concentrated on keeping one foot in front of the other. We walked close together, our shoulders occasionally brushing each other, which sent a shiver of electricity running through me.

"I liked your speech," I said.

"Thanks. I had to stay up last night working on it—I was sure I was going to read something wrong. I have to . . . I have to practice a lot."

"I thought it was great."

"People didn't really clap."

"Well, you basically called everybody failures," I teased.

"I didn't want it to be another rah-rah-we're-so-awesome kind of thing."

"Because clearly, some people are not awesome."

She poked me in the ribs, *which was incredible*. "That's not what I meant!"

"You should've thrown in a joke. 'Hey, what's wearing a suit and failed today? You guys.'"

"Shut up." She smiled, stabbing me with her mittened fingers.

"'It's my job to prepare you for a life of crushing disappointment. That horrible feeling you're experiencing right now—expect it to continue. In conclusion, this is the best moment in your lives; some of you will die in car crashes soon.'"

Amy shouldered into me, knocking me slightly off-balance and nearly into a squad of drunk college girls. I smiled at her.

"I did like it," I said, brushing the wet snow out of my hair.

Amy cocked an eyebrow and headed down the street. "Good." She reached out her hand and something gave way inside of me. *Why not tell her how I feel?*

"I miss talking with you," I said.

"I miss talking with you too."

"I hate this—I hate pretending I don't know you and . . ."

"I know."

We made our way down State Street, which was the heart of Madison. No cars were allowed on the street except the occasional bus, so the snow fell uninterrupted all around us.

"You know," I said, "I kind of thought the speech was directed at me. 'Cause I . . ." I stopped and looked down at the pavement. "I failed."

She brushed up against me.

"You didn't fail."

"No, I mean—I had a bill and everything and, um . . . I thought it would be cool if I got it to you, so . . . it's stupid . . . I mean, it was a stupid plan."

"I didn't know you had a bill."

"I know. . . . I . . . It was a surprise. I didn't even tell Chelsea about it. It's obviously not a surprise now, so the effect is kind of lost." I looked away from her. "Like, I almost did this awesome thing. Partial credit."

Amy stroked my arm through my coat. "What was your bill about?"

I looked down again. "Um . . . so I wrote a bill about, um . . . funding diagnostic testing for learning disabilities in elementary school. So . . . just funding for people to test for dyslexia and other things in elementary school . . . I thought it would be a good idea."

Amy's hand went to her heart. "Oh."

My eyes focused on the pavement. It all sounded so dumb. Not like the bill was real. Not like I was a real senator either.

Then I felt her forehead against mine. The fresh smell of her shampoo invaded my senses. In the background I could hear the people moving past us, laughing and joking and talking, but we didn't move. I wanted to keep my forehead touching hers forever. The snow drifted down on top of us.

"I have to tell you something," she said quietly, holding on to me. "I broke up with Chad." A chorus of angels began to sing. Rainbows sprouted from the gutters.

"Oh. Why?"

The Kaitlyn voice exploded in my head. *Did you just ask why? Are you an idiot?*

"I decided that I didn't want to be with him."

"Huh."

"Because I want to be with you."

She lifted my face and kissed me. I closed my eyes and felt the warmth of her breath on mine and the soft tug of her mittens on my back. We stood there, kissing, and the world passed by, and the snow fell, and I felt whole.

Later we found out the capitol was left open, so we laughed and danced our way around the giant Christmas tree until a security guard named Karl chased us out.

TWENTY-TWO

How I Screwed This Up

I was high as a kite when I got back from Madison, although still probably not as high as Amanda. I had been granted a stay of execution, or rather a reversal of execution. My head had been reattached to my body after the guillotine had severed it. Let's call it a resurrection, then. My entire future had once again snapped back into glowing view. Everything came back, the spring break plans, the magical night at prom, a hot, lazy summer spent skinny-dipping in lakes.

Things went downhill almost immediately. It started with our car.

The vehicle in question was a 1986 Plymouth Voyager, baby blue, with faux-wood paneling on the bottom half. It was a first-generation minivan, the primordial evolutionary leap that crawled onto the beach and emasculated every man who saw it. The Voyager had a four-cylinder engine, which whined and sputtered when the car reached the speed limit—it handled like a garbage can and had a hole in the muffler, so it sounded like one too. We loved it.

Unbeknownst to us, Dad had placed an ad in the newspaper on the day he got laid off. I'm sure it said something like *Awful vehicle available. Do you want your son to be humiliated and never get laid? Take this car.* So much for the "someday we might have to sell the car" plan. Generally, when Dad decided to take action, it was swift and terrible and involved horrible repercussions for us.

"Sure you can come take a look at it," he said on the phone as Kaitlyn writhed on the couch like she had been bayonetted in the stomach. "Tuesday at noon? No problem."

"No . . ." she said weakly.

Within five days, he had three calls. Clearly the *Janesville Gazette* was a hotbed of people salivating over the latest minivan offerings.

"But it's Christmas," moaned Kaitlyn. "You can't sell the car over Christmas. That's not how we honor baby Jesus."

I rolled my eyes. "Baby Jesus does not care if we have a minivan or not."

"The hell he doesn't!"

"Jesus, get over it," I said. Inwardly, of course, I was dying too. Losing the car was going to reverberate in my life as well, but it was more fun to needle Kaitlyn about it.

"Am I gonna have to take the bus to school? Is that what you're saying? This is a nightmare."

Taking the bus to school in the winter was no fun. And by no fun I mean, life-threateningly awful. We took the bus every day in middle school, which was a kind of living hell—the buses were old, 1960s vintage, with art deco stylings and a tendency to break down. One February the buses' windows froze open, and we rode to school every day in temperatures below zero, shivering and huddling together for warmth, while the exhaust stink of the dirty engine flooded our mouths with the taste of corruption. When you waited for the bus, you stood on the side of the street, ensconced in snowdrifts, before the sun rose. It was cold and dark and horrible; that's not even counting the fact that you were likely to be bullied by the tribes of mean kids that rode the bus like some kind of apocalyptic biker gang from hell. When we had gotten the car, I had said good-bye to that life forever. I had thrown a little party for myself. Now I was sliding back down the ladder.

"Guys," sighed Dad. "There's just no way we can keep it—"

"How much are you even gonna get for it? It's not like it's worth anything."

"It's the insurance," he said. "Someone in this family has a pretty poor driving record. Think of it this way—I have to pay a lot of money because the insurance company is convinced you're going to wreck the car someday."

Kaitlyn frowned and twisted her hair. "Can I borrow your car, then?" she said.

I realized the side benefit to the absence of the car almost imme-diately: I could ask Amy for rides home from school. Her car was not exactly a paragon of functionality, but it worked, and it had heat, and it also happened to have Amy in it. The rides home usually ended in make-out sessions in the car as we contorted ourselves around the stick shift.

Of course, her duties as student body president and President of All the Clubs kept her after school most days until five thirty. But it was a small price to pay. I would wait in the hall, or in the back of whatever room she was in, reading some monstrously large Russian novel and sighing dreamily. When I wasn't doing that I was surreptitiously trying to draw sketches of her, but I kind of sucked at that, so her nostrils usually ended up kind of piglike.

Maybe I overdid it. (Okay, yes, definitely, I overdid it.) But I had lost her once, I had felt the pain of having her ripped out of my life, so I was going to make sure that she never made it out of my sight again.

I called her every night. I waited for her between classes. I thought about her continuously.

I'm not going to lie: I was annoying as hell.

Maybe things would've naturally settled down. Maybe I could've found a way to navigate the new feelings without becom-ing overwhelmed by them. I probably could've managed that, had it not been for the fact that it was Christmas. And Christmas required getting her a Christmas Present. And the Christmas Present must be so amazing that it must perfectly encapsulate all of my feelings for her, if the continuous commercials for diamond companies were to be believed.

Elizabeth had suggested a couple of funky-looking charm things that her mother got from the hippie crystal store, and I got one of them, and then I got something else, and then I returned that present and got something different. Then I went back for a third thing.

Then it was time to visit the Janesville Mall, where I wandered about like a phantom, stumbling from store to store, hoping for inspiration. The mall was home to roving bands of middle school kids, who clustered together, sometimes linking arms and legs (don't even ask, it was a thing) as they flirted and annoyed everyone. Even the mall Santa hated them. (Probably because when they got bored they would get in line to sit on his lap and ironically ask for presents.)

I spent a miserable Saturday there until Kaitlyn spotted me and verbally harassed me to cut it out.

Then I had to get a card.

Anyway, that was my mind-state: total insanity. And that's probably why when Amy invited me to have dinner with her family on December 27th I stupidly agreed.

The letter from Gustavus Adolphus arrived the morning of the fateful dinner.

I stared at it. With all the drama with Amy and my dad, college had drifted into the back of my mind. It was there, and I knew it was happening, but I wasn't focused on it.

Had they liked my Dostoevsky essay? Had they been impressed by my list of two or three extracurricular activities? It wasn't a super-fat letter. Two sheets of paper at most. *Is that good or bad?*

What happens if I don't get in?

You could always move to Los Angeles and live in Amy's closet next year.

That is a terrible idea and you are stupid.

If I don't get in I'll go to Madison. See my sister every day. Want to die.

I opened it.

WE ARE DELIGHTED TO OFFER YOU A POSITION IN CLASS OF 1998

"Fuck yes!" I yelled.

"Why are you swearing?" called my mom from the other room.

The second piece of paper was instructions for completing the financial aid application, which I pressed into my mom's hands immediately. GAC cost $25,000 a year, which was more than half of my mom's salary. If you put that together with the cost of Kaitlyn attending UW-Madison, my parents could afford to send us both to college if they moved into a cardboard box and ate saltines for every meal. So, yeah, financial aid. Fingers crossed.

But I was in a terrific mood when I arrived at Amy's house in preparation for . . .

TWENTY-THREE

Breakup Number Two

December 27, 1993.
Time: 6:00 p.m.
Her house. Again.

Dad managed to unload the minivan for a handful of magic beans (and $500), so I was forced to drive my mom's Buick LeSabre over to Amy's. I got there about an hour early and slowly circled the neighborhood like a stalker in order to not seem overeager.

Amy's mom had set up the dining table and put out the good china. There was a red tablecloth with fancy embroidering. Actual silver silverware. Fancy goblets for our water.

I shit you not, they had *dressed up.*

They had dressed up for dinner in their own house.

I was doomed.

I was wearing a tie-dyed T-shirt under a flannel shirt, and my jeans had holes in them. I had embraced the whole "grunge" thing, which basically meant that I was trying to look homeless. It was not a good look on anyone. It was an especially poor look for a fancy post-Christmas dinner at your girlfriend's house.

Glenn wore a fucking tie.

I wondered what would cause a thirteen-year-old to put on a tie for dinner in his own house. They must've been torturing him behind the scenes or something.

I set my little sack stuffed with an ill-advised number of presents near the Christmas tree and embraced my doom.

"What's Chad doing this break?" asked her dad about halfway through.

"Um . . . I don't know," said Amy. "I haven't talked to him."

"Oh. Why not?"

"Dan," said her mom. "They broke up."

Amy's dad rocked in his chair a little bit. "Nobody told me that!"

"It was like a week ago," said her mom.

"It wasn't a week ago," protested Amy. "It was like three weeks ago."

"I can't keep up," said her dad. "First it's one guy, then it's another guy. There's like a revolving door."

"There's not a revolving door. I was going out with Chad and now I'm going out with Craig."

"Oh," said her dad. "What was wrong with Chad?"

Amy put her face in her hands.

"Hon," said her mom. "You're embarrassing her. She obviously doesn't want to talk about it with us."

"All right, I won't talk. I won't say anything. I'll just sit here confused."

"Craig," said her mom. "Did you have a nice Christmas?"

"I did," I said. "Actually I got my college acceptance letter today."

She made a high-pitched happy sound. "Oh my goodness, that is wonderful! Did you hear that, Dan?"

"Chad's already in college."

"Oh jeez, get off of Chad! He's gone! It's over!"

"Fine."

"Of course, Gustavus is close by. Not too hard for his parents to come and visit. Maybe you should've applied, sweetie." Amy bit her tongue. "Of course, it's a tough school to get into. You might not've made it."

"Mom, I'm the valedictorian—"

"Oh sure, but they look at all sorts of things. There's your SAT scores, which, come on—"

I envied Glenn. Glenn had his head down and was focusing on his food. He had heaped a thick swath of gravy on his turkey and was trying to plow through dinner without being noticed.

"I did fine on the SAT."

"Fine isn't great. I told you you could take it again."

"I didn't need to take it again."

"I'm pretty sure Amy would've gotten in anywhere she applied," I said. "I mean she's freaking brilliant."

Amy's mom lifted her eyebrows. "I'm sure she is."

"Glenn," said Amy, noticing that he had escaped unscathed so far. "What's new with you?"

"Nothing," he mumbled, then kept eating.

"Sometimes I wonder what's going on in his noggin," said Amy's mom. "Whatever it is, it's profound. He's a thinker."

Glenn tried to focus on his food.

"Whatcha thinking about over there, Glenn?" she asked.

"Nothing."

"I find that hard to believe."

"Mom," said Amy, trying to call off the torrent.

"You know it was so funny," said Amy's mom. "The other day Glenn came home with a CD—what was it? He was hiding it in his backpack, it was the funniest thing."

Glenn froze.

"What was it, sweetheart?"

"I don't—I don't remember."

"Oh, it was so weird. It was from *Cabaret*. The musical."

Everyone was dumbfounded. Glenn tried to hide. "Um . . . I heard it was really outrageous," he said.

"Oh, sure," said Amy's mom. "There's a man dressed like a woman on front. I mean, whatever floats your boat, right?"

"Why is he dressed like a woman?" asked her dad.

"That's what the Nazis did, hon."

"The Nazis didn't dress like women."

Amy tried to leap in. "I think that's kind of a subversive take on club life."

Let me pause for a second: I had no idea what *Cabaret* was. I guessed, according to these people, it was about cross-dressing Nazis, which did indeed sound dangerous. It also sounded like something a thirteen-year-old black boy in Wisconsin would have trouble explaining to his parents.

"You know who loves musicals?" said her dad. "The gays."

I pictured the dining table in flames. Glenn put his head down. Amy started twitching. Her dad shoveled food into his mouth, oblivious.

"I love musicals," I said.

"You do?"

"Oh sure," I repeated. "*Cabaret* is awesome, in fact. It's um . . . really super good. Yeah—I listen to it while I play football and, um . . . lift weights. Pumps me up. In a manly way."

There was a brief pause. Glenn exhaled.

"But what I really want to talk about," I said, "is the Green Bay Packers."

I survived the rest of the dinner. The conversation remained on the Packers' playoff chances and storied history for at least an hour. Once her dad got on that subject, there was no stopping him. Glenn finished dinner like a Hoover vacuum and escaped to the kitchen.

In the Carlson household, it was the kids' responsibility to clean the table and wash the dishes. Glenn came back, snatched as many dishes as would fit in his hands, and darted back into the kitchen. Amy got up to follow him and I leaped up to help.

"Oh no, Craig is a guest," said her mom. "He can stay out here with us while you guys clean up."

"No, I'll help," I said.

"Oh, nonsense!" she chortled. "Sit."

"I—I'm actually . . ." I stammered, "training—for restaurant work, so it's really important for me to get this experience." I scooped up the gravy boat and escaped to the kitchen.

Glenn was already hard at work filling the sink with suds and staring out the window with a haunted expression.

Amy was still fuming, but managed to pat him on the back. "It's okay," she said. "It's cool, don't worry about it. It's cool." Glenn kept filling the water and squeezing dish soap into a sponge. "Hey," she said. "It's gonna be all right." She smiled at him.

I stood there for a second, holding the gravy boat, not sure what the protocol was. "Um . . . here's a gravy boat," I said, handing it over.

"Thanks," he said, running it under the faucet as Amy went back for the silverware. I stood there for a second and he added, "Thanks for, um . . . intercepting my dad back there."

"No problem. I don't know shit about *Cabaret*."

"It's cool."

"I'm sure." I picked up one of the dish towels and started

drying things off. I will add that, remarkably, I was not good at this. I had never been good at drying dishes. It was one of my many failings as a human being.

"Are there like a lot of kids into *Cabaret* in middle school? Is it a whole thing now?"

Glenn smiled and shook his head.

"Really?" I said. "Man, I woulda thought that it was huge. Like whole gangs of kids beating you up if you don't know the lyrics to the songs."

He laughed.

"Nope. Just me."

"Oh. Well . . . it's better in high school. There are people into musicals. Not like a ton of them. But there are some. People don't judge you quite as much. I remember middle school; people thought I was a dork. And now look at me." I spread my arms, keenly aware that I had paired a tie-dyed shirt with a flannel. "It probably can't get better than this."

Which was true, in a way, because it was about to get a whole lot worse. By nine o'clock Amy's parents were watching television in their bedroom and it was time for the Christmas present debacle. Glenn had retreated to his room after the dishes were done, presumably to listen to show tunes and play *Tetris*.

I retrieved my unwieldy sack of presents that included the weird charm thing, a VHS tape of *Fantasia*, and a pair of earrings. She had a tiny little present for me.

She looked at what I'd got.

I looked at what she'd got.

Both of us thought, *Shit.*

I made sure to hide in my pocket the twelve coupons I'd made for neck massages. Maybe I'd give them to her at our two-month anniversary. (At this point, I was counting total time going out, rather than the amount of time since she had taken me back in Madison.)

"Wow," she said.

"Yeah, I was . . . um . . ." I couldn't really even speak. There were no words to defend this.

"So I got you this." She handed me her present.

It wasn't even wrapped. Because it was a hat. Was it a romantic hat? Not really. I'm not sure there is such a thing as a romantic hat.

"It's a hat," she said.

"Yeah."

"You might need it if you go to college in Minnesota."

Maybe I should've gotten her a bikini for UCLA.

That would be even weirder than what you did get her, Craig. You are stupid.

My stomach was beginning to drop into the floor when something stopped me. Her card. She had written, *Merry Christmas, Craig!* And then, next to that, she had drawn a heart and written the word *Amy.*

She had drawn a heart!

Sure, it wasn't the best present in the world, but it was the thought that counted, and the thought behind it was clearly summed up by the drawing of the heart. She wouldn't have put the heart there if she didn't truly feel the heart, right? Right?

CRAIG IS ABOUT TO DO SOMETHING RIDICULOUSLY STUPID

Of all the dumbest things I've ever done in my life, this probably stands as number two or three, just edging out the time when I was sixteen and said, "Wow, these pickles really look like cucumbers." And then everyone stared at me like I had three heads, and I slowly realized that pickles were, in fact, cucumbers.

I looked at the card and the admittedly nonromantic hat.

"You heart me, huh?"

"What?"

"You heart me?"

"What are you talking about?"

"You drew a heart here."

"Oh. Yes. Yes, I did."

"So does that mean . . . you love me?"

Amy's eyes went wide like she was watching a meteor about to hit the earth. Her mouth quivered just a bit.

"What?" she said.

There should've been something in my brain screaming *Abort mission! Abort mission!* at this point, but I had shut down all rational thought.

"Does that mean you love me?" I said, repeating the stupidity.

"It's just a heart," she managed.

"Which is a symbol of love."

"It's a heart."

"But it means love. It's like a symbol."

"Ninety percent of girls put little hearts over their *i*'s!"

"Yeah but there's no *i* in Amy! All right, never mind."

"We've been going back out for three weeks!"

"Well, you're throwing out mixed messages here!"

"IT'S A CARTOON HEART!"

"IT'S A SYMBOL OF LOVE! And—and—if you add the three weeks this time with the four weeks last time, that makes seven weeks. And that's enough time."

"Time for what?"

"To fall in love."

Amy freaked out a little bit. She put her hands through her hair. One eyelid didn't blink in unison with the other one. She was still really pretty, though.

"Are you in love with me?" she asked.

Yes, obviously. Yes, madly, 100 percent.

I said, "Uh . . ."

Amy reached down and snatched the card I had got her, which had a pug in a Christmas wreath on it because I hadn't been able to find anything better. She flipped it open. There was a heart next to my name.

"There's a heart here!" she shrieked.

"Yes!"

"You love me! You freaking love me!"

This was not going how I had planned. Not that anything ever went like I planned, but having your girlfriend shake an accusing finger at you and guess that you loved her wasn't how I imagined this going.

"Seven weeks!" I shouted like a madman.

"You can't love me yet!"

"Too late!"

"Argh!"

Jump in, Craig. What's the worst that could happen?

"All right. Fine, I love you! Okay? I love you like crazy."

And then I just started making dumb-ass metaphors because I couldn't think of anything else to do. These were the honest-to-God things that came out of my mouth:

1. I love you like chocolate cake.
2. I love you like those mother bears love their bear cubs.
3. I love you like a bald guy loves Rogaine.
4. I love you like a heroin addict loves like a million pounds of heroin.

Hey, Craig. Those are similes, by the way. Not metaphors.
Shut up, dorky part of my brain.

"Craig," she said, putting both of her hands on my shoulders like she was trying to restrain a madman. "This is not normal."

"I know."

"And . . . I know you're new at this, but you're really kind of freaking me out right now."

"I'm a little freaked out too," I admitted. "But I've never been in love before."

"Okay. Okay," she said, trying to come up with an argument. "I just . . . It's just too much, okay? The after-school stuff?"

"We get to spend more time together—"

"Right, but, like, I see you out in the hall when I'm in a meeting or something and, like, you're pacing."

"I like to walk."

"Right, but you're walking back and forth in front of the door. Like . . . that's weird. And the calls and the . . . it's kind of suffocating. And tonight at dinner and now . . ." She looked down at the pile of presents in her hands. "I don't think this is working."

What's not working? Us? We're not working? But I'm awesome at this!

I stared forward in dumbfounded silence. The room began to tilt.

"How about we take some time off?"

"Time off from what?"

But I knew the answer to that.

Later, I made some poor choices, which included standing on her snow-covered lawn and shouting up at her window like a deranged lunatic.

"I'm not giving up!" This is exactly what stalkers say. "I love you, Amy! And I know that you're scared of our love right now, but I'm going to keep on burning like the shooting star that I am!" I was still on the simile kick apparently.

Amy's mom opened the door. "You're going to catch cold, sweetie."

"That's a price I'm willing to pay."

She wrapped a scarf around herself and walked out into the cold, moving gingerly and wincing against the cold. It was funny, because at that moment she kind of resembled Amy—the way she walked, the way she talked, everything about her reminded me of Amy.

"Oh," she said with her big Wisconsin O. She took a deep breath; there was something calmer about her now, like the tension at dinner had dissipated.

"She's making a terrible mistake," I said. "I mean, she's obviously really smart and again I want to reiterate that she could get into any college she wanted to, but it's clear that she's making really stupid choices here," I stammered, freezing, vaguely recalling the fact that Amy's mom had given her a book about stupid choices.

Amy's mom put her hand on my shoulder. "Oh, honey."

I stared down at the ground. I could feel the tears welling up behind my eyes. "I thought both of our feelings were the same."

And then I was crying, again, on Amy's lawn.

Her mom pulled me closer. "That's why you talk to each other. You talk about it." She punched me on the shoulder a little bit, which was weird.

"I'm not gonna say it's meant to be. I don't know that anything's meant to be. But you never know. And she likes you, I know that much. She really likes you. Okay?" She grabbed hold of both of my arms and looked up at me. "She's gotta figure things out. So give her some space."

" . . . Okay." I sniffled.

She held me another second.

"You want some brownies to take home?"

" . . . Yes, please."

When we were inside, the house was cool and dim. Bear had rolled onto his back and was showing his belly to the world, only slightly opening his mouth to reveal his massive set of terrifying, genital-destroying teeth.

Amy's mom had gotten out some Tupperware and was cutting brownies.

"Oh, well—you know, we had wanted kids for a long time. We had our hearts set on it. Dan—I mean, he pretends to be a goof, but it just crushed him when we found out. That it wasn't gonna work out. But that's life, right? Sometimes it doesn't work out. Sometimes the big things don't work out.

"So you start thinking, *Okay, well, I'll do what I can, then, and we'll get to take all those trips we wanted to take. And we'll get a dog and we'll make a full life anyway.* So we went all over the place—we went to Europe, we went to Thailand, we were both working, but every time I'd see, you know, little kids, I kept thinking . . . *That's not for me. . . . We don't get to have that. . . .*

"So then—it was my forty-fourth birthday and Dan came in and he said, 'How would you like to adopt?' And I said, 'Our whole life is gonna change,' and he said, 'Sometimes that's a good thing.' So we got Amy. She was six days old. And it was like somebody flipped a switch and suddenly the world was in color. And I know I'm tough on her, and I'm tough on Glenn, but I just . . . I want everything for them. I couldn't even imagine how happy she would make us, and how happy Glenn would make us. So you never know."

She finished putting the brownies in the Tupperware.

"You can keep this, okay?"

"Thanks," I said.

"You gotta bend, you know? With whatever life throws at you. Okay?"

"Okay."

I looked at the floor and she drew me into a hug.

"It's gonna be okay," she said. "You'll get over it."

But I didn't.

TWENTY-FOUR

How We Got Back Together Again—And Then Again Again

Brian held up a picture of the *Sports Illustrated* swimsuit issue. "This is a picture of a human female," he said. "There are about three billion of these on the planet. Pick another one."

But I didn't want one of the three billion. I wanted the one.

Oh God, said the Kaitlyn voice in my head, rolling its eyes.

The aftermath of the second breakup was similar to the first. I face-planted in the snow again ("Are you gonna do this every time?" asked Elizabeth), I moaned, I lay about, I rolled around on my bed and drove my friends nuts. No amount of coral would help.

Youth in Government was over, and I bummed rides from Elizabeth now instead of Amy, so our contact was limited to awkward interactions in the hall. I would see her coming, and I'd break out into a sweat and panic about whether or not I should make eye contact. And then I'd decide, *Yes, eye contact, she will see my eyes and she will come to regret this decision and also, I want to show with my eyes that I'm no longer clingy and am actually a functioning human being and shit I missed her, where did she go?*

And it continued that way for about two weeks until the night my friends kidnapped me, shoved me into the back of Elizabeth's car, and dragged me to Perkins.

Perkins was a twenty-four-hour diner by the interstate which functioned as a community center for all the freaks, weirdos, nerds, and lunatics who couldn't find anywhere else to go. It had a smoking section, which was typically packed to the gills with teenagers, and serviced by one waitress who wanted everyone to spontaneously combust. The fluorescent lights buzzed brightly, but the vaporized cloud of nicotine in the air served to make the place as hazy as a fog-shrouded Scottish moor.

"I hate this place," said Brian, as soon as we got there.

Elizabeth wrapped her arm around his shoulder and pulled him toward his doom. "We are here to cheer up Craig. Solidarity." Elizabeth promptly left us to drop in on a table of skate punks in the corner.

"Perkins is awesome," said Groash, fishing in the "wishing well," which was a (you guessed it) well-shaped bucket containing cheap plastic toys for small children and, apparently, Groash. He snatched a blue jumping frog and pocketed it like it was gold.

Perkins had the benefit of having a bottomless cup of coffee, which came in a metallic canister reminiscent of a missile silo. The coffee tasted less like coffee and more like liquefied asphalt.

Sheryl, our waitress, dropped it on the table with a *thud* and went to the back to resume hating us. Probably because we stayed for hours.

"I bet I can stay here longer than you," Groash said, pointing his plastic frog at Brian.

"I have a curfew," said Brian.

"I don't care. I can still stay here longer than you."

"I don't want to stay here. This place is a boil on the ass of Janesville."

"And I can stay on this boil longer than you can."

Sheryl returned to collect our menus. "Are you going to get anything to eat or are you just going to sit here for hours drinking coffee?"

"This guy is gonna have pie," said Groash, invading my personal space.

Sheryl was not impressed. "What kind of pie."

"All the pie."

"You can't have all the pie."

"This man was dumped. His heart was broken."

"I'll have the cherry pie," I said, before Groash could comment on my masturbation habits again.

"Great," said Sheryl, continuing to hate us.

"You know what?" said Brian. "I will stay here longer than you. I don't care. I will beat you."

"It's on, man."

An hour after I finished the pie we were on our third silo of coffee. Brian, who was unused to caffeine in large doses, was a twitching, frothy mess. He giggled at nothing at all, and was constantly pushing his fingers through his hair. Groash had steadied into a rhythm, but the coffee was hitting him hard too. My stomach was a boiling, radioactive waste dump. The immense pain in my gut was taking away from the pain in my heart, so the Perkins jaunt was a success.

Elizabeth returned with a skate punk named Reggie and dropped in next to Brian, unsettling him further. Reggie had six earrings and an infectious sense of joy.

"You want to hear my poetry?" he said, slapping a leathery journal on the table and flipping it open to reveal page after page of poetry written in a thick Sharpie.

Oh shit.

"This one is called 'Pain.'"

"Sweet," said Groash, twitching.

Reggie sucked on his teeth and flattened out his book. "'The pain is everything I feel.'" He grinned. "'It is the only thing that's real.'"

This must be what I seem like to my friends. I am a horrible human being.

Reggie beamed and plowed onward, savoring every word.

I tried to look for an escape route, and that's when I saw Amy and Chelsea sitting down in the non-smoking section.

The world shrank instantly to a circle surrounding their table. *What are they doing? They're laughing a bit. They seem to be enjoying themselves. Amy's picking up the menu. Maybe she's hungry. Yes, that's why people normally order food, dumbass. I wonder what she'll get.*

"'My tears fall like rain,'" continued Reggie enthusiastically. "'And remind me . . .'"—he paused—"'of the pain.'"

Amy was tying her hair back into the clam thing and was totally unconscious of the fact that she was moving in slow motion.

"This one is called 'Exit wounds,'" said Reggie, grinning, and turning to a page that had cheerful drawings of skulls.

"Dude," said Groash, following my eyes. Brian and Elizabeth turned to look. Reggie, oblivious, kept going.

"Don't even look, Craig," said Brian. "Just pretend she's not there."

But it was too late. Amy had turned in my direction. She waved. *She waved.*

"I'm going over there," I said, before Groash could reach out to restrain me.

"Hi," I said.

"Hi," she said.

"Hey," said Chelsea.

My stomach, which churned with the unholy acid of four cups of Perkins coffee, started performing a gymnastics floor routine.

"So what's up?" I said, trying to stay cool.

"Just hanging out," she said.

"Yup," said Chelsea.

"Um . . . there's a really painful poetry reading going on at my table. Mind if I join you?"

So I did. And we talked, and it was kind of normal. It was better than normal. It was easy and it was fun, like we had never broken up. Most of the talk was about Chelsea's secret hookup with Jacob Hammer back in December that absolutely no one knew about.

"You were gone from the room for like four hours," she said to Amy. "What else was I going to do?"

"I woulda done him," I said. "He was like a living god. Then again, I guess I have a thing for authority figures."

Amy laughed. "Oh, so that's what it's about. I still have the gavel, you know."

"Say the word," I said in that I'm-not-serious-but-yes-I-am-totally-serious-please-take-me-back sort of way. Amy smiled. I smiled. The roiling coffee-like substance in my stomach lurched in anticipation.

Chelsea looked at both of us. "I'm gonna go see what that poetry's about," she said.

I looked into Amy's eyes.

She looked into my eyes.

The smell of cigarette smoke wafted over from the smoking section. The clink of coffee cups sounded like an orchestra of manic toddlers. In the background I could hear Sheryl's musical voice say, "Fuck this."

I thought about the previous times we had gotten back together: the bridge, the capitol. I needed something romantic. I needed something amazing to look at.

"You want to go for a walk?" I said.

"It's cold," she said.

"Nevertheless, I am going for a walk."

She smiled.

About a block from Perkins was a Janesville institution known as the Big Cow. The Big Cow was, as you might have guessed, a very large cow. It looked like it was concrete but was made out of fiberglass and loomed majestically over a parking lot near a gas station. On some nights, after sports victories, enthusiastic teenagers would throw toilet paper on it to celebrate greatness.

We stared up at it, hunched in our coats to protect against the cold. Nearby, we could smell the exhaust from diesel engines and hear the high-pitched beeping of a tanker truck backing up.

It was slightly less than romantic.

Damn it.

"What do you think went through the person's head that ordered that?" I said. "Do you think he was like, 'Get me the best fiberglass cow artist in America, damn it! I want it big!' And the artist was like, 'How big?' And he was like, 'Use your imagination, son.' 'Like a hundred feet tall?' 'Not that big.' 'How about slightly larger than life-size?' 'Done.'"

Amy laughed. "Probably they were thinking of a way to distinguish this gas station from the other gas stations and a giant fiberglass cow seemed like the way to go."

"You're taking the mystery out of it."

"Are you hoping for mystery? Is that why you brought me here?"

"Maybe just inspiration," I said, and then she was right next to me and I could feel our coats connect with each other.

"For what?"

"For this."

I kissed her.

Two weeks later she dumped me in the park, mafia-style. (See chapter one.)

And one week after that, she stopped coming to school.

Unlike our two previous breakups, this one seemed to affect Amy the most. You could tell when you saw her—there was a hollowed-out look to her; sometimes she hadn't even showered. The first two breakups had wrecked me, the third one seemed to have wrecked her.

After her second straight absence, I sought out Chelsea after school. When she wasn't doing YIG, she was on the gymnastics team, which was banished to the auxiliary gym, because the basketball team ruled the regular gym with an iron fist. It took me about ten minutes to find her, but then I spotted her practicing the vault. Her brown fluffy hair was tied into a huge bun and bounced on top of her head like an attached balloon when she ran. She hit the vault, flipped over once, and stuck a landing on a blue crash mat. It was impressive as hell. I thought about my friends. None of them could do flips. They mostly didn't even try.

"Do you know what's going on with Amy?" I asked, when she was taking a break.

Chelsea looked to the side and sighed. "When was the last time you talked to her?"

"Last Saturday. She was breaking up with me again."

"Huh."

"Is that what she's upset about? She's normally not that upset after she dumps me."

"She feels bad when she dumps you. Trust me."

"Oh. Well, that's good to know, I guess."

She took a swig from her water bottle. "Maybe you should go talk to her. She might . . . appreciate that."

"Do you think I should? I mean, like, when we broke up last time, it seemed like she didn't really want to talk about things. So maybe I was thinking I could write her a letter." Chelsea groaned. "Should I not write her a letter? Should I just drop by, then? Would that be okay?"

"How the hell should I know? Am I inside your relationship?"

"Do you think we still have a relationship?"

"Ugh. Dude. Whatever you want to do, okay? I think that a visit from you might be a good idea. But if you're going to be bizarre about it, then probably not. So if you can contain yourself, you should go. If you are incurably strange, then don't go."

Shit. That's a tough choice.

After her third absence, I drove to her house after school. Her teachers had let me collect the homework she had missed, so I had a small folder with her assignments. I had thought about slipping a heartfelt letter into the stack, but decided against it, because that seemed to be in violation of Chelsea's requirements. My mom had let me borrow her car after I promised that I would stop by the grocery store on the way home to retrieve more fish product.

The lights were on when I got there. Her car was in the driveway. My heart did that thing where it stopped working, and I started sweating unreasonably. My typical reaction.

Glenn let me in after Bear leaped on me and drove me backward with his massive paws. I tried to pet him, which was hard, since he was a brown-and-black blur of motion and teeth.

"She's in her room."

Amy was in her butterfly chair, listening to Miles Davis and reading.

"I brought you your homework," I said, setting the folder on her desk.

"Thanks," she said weakly, looking pale in the light of the floor lamp. Her nose was red and there were deep shadows under her eyes. She hadn't been sleeping.

"Whatcha reading?"

"*Invisible Man*. For AP English."

I nodded. "You know, I bought the wrong version of that. I was so stoked—yes, finally some science fiction in school. So I read the whole H. G. Wells Time Machine collection."

She smiled.

"Then people started talking in class about race relations and I was, like . . . *Shit, I did not get this book at all.*"

"But now when you read the real version you'll have a lot more to say. About the connections."

"You've got a theory about those?"

"I've always got a theory."

I put my hands in my pockets.

"So, um . . . are you doing okay?"

". . . Yeah."

"Good. 'Cause I was a little worried about you. I figured you might have the plague or something."

"So you decided to come over to my house? Even if I had the plague? You could catch it, you know."

"That's a price I'm willing to pay."

My smile died. I was too far away. I had managed to take two steps into her room, but couldn't go any farther—I was still wearing my heavy coat. The hat she had given me was on my head. It felt like we had migrated to two entirely separate worlds. She was ensconced in a place I couldn't reach.

"I can go if you want me to go," I said.

Amy looked down.

"No." She started chewing on the end of her finger. Her eyes flicked back and forth.

"You can tell me," I said.

She took a deep breath. "My mom's cancer came back," she said, finally, wiping her nose. "It's, um . . . it's not good—it's in her pancreas this time." Her eyes fell to the side like she couldn't look at me.

My feet felt like they were locked in concrete, but I took a step toward her. "I'm so sorry," I said, realizing that the words felt hopelessly small and stupid. I was sorry? What did that actually mean?

She got up from her chair and grabbed hold of me.

"That's why . . ."

"It's okay," I said.

"I found out two weeks ago and I . . . That's why I had to break up with you. I didn't want to . . . It's not fair to you to make you go through this with me—"

"No, it's okay," I said, tightening my grip on her.

"I didn't want to do it. But I really thought—I thought I needed to do this myself, but I can't. . . ." She was crying now, pressing into me. "It's so fucking awful, Craig. Every time I pause for a second I feel like the whole world is going to fall apart. . . . I wanted to just wall you off from it."

"You don't need to do that," I said, holding her.

"So if you need to bail, this is the time. . . ."

I grabbed her and held her tightly against me. "I said I was going to take care of you last time I was in here. And I meant that."

Amy's nose was running now, and she was burrowing into me. I could barely move, but I managed to pluck the box of Kleenex from her futon.

"You want a Kleenex?" I said.

". . . Yes."

So that's how we got back together the third time, clinging to each other like we were in a storm-tossed lifeboat.

TWENTY-FIVE

The Downfall of Amy, Queen of Everything

Up and down we went, circling each other.

Two months later we were together again, after the fifth breakup, delivered by the letter of doom, didn't stick.

Amy's mom took the diagnosis with aplomb. "I beat it before, I'll beat it again," she said, but there were good days and there were bad days. I tried to support Amy the best I could. She continued to deteriorate.

It started with her classes. Class rankings were frozen after the first semester, but Amy had received a pretty serious scholarship to UCLA and it depended on keeping her grades sky high. UCLA cost something like fourteen billion dollars a year, her parents didn't have a ton of money, and with her mom's sickness, there was no way they could pay for her to go without the scholarship.

So she had to keep working. With her dyslexia, everything took twice as long. Spell-check caught a lot of her mistakes, but she'd often substitute the wrong word for things, so the only way to make sure it was right was to double- and triple-check everything.

That's not even mentioning the fact that she was student body president, in charge of Youth in Government, and organized two or three other lower-profile clubs. As president she was also in charge of prom, which was a logistical nightmare of Lovecraftian proportions—just imagine an evil octopus-headed giant sleeping in the ocean and ready to wake up and devour humanity. Amy had to rent the space, get the money, approve the theme, and come up with a decorating plan. It was too much. It was too much for any two or three human beings, and it was definitely too much for a girl whose mother had cancer.

"Quit," I said on the phone late one night after a particularly brutal conversation.

"I can't do that."

"Amy. Quit. Other people can do the work. You don't have to do everything."

She was quiet for a moment. ". . . I know."

"You can do it. You can quit. Please."

We had an all-school assembly a few days later. Amy sat up front, just like in the state capitol. The teachers announced a few things, and then she stood up. I had tried to be next to her, playing the role of the crying spouse during the public resignation, but they wouldn't let me. She was alone in the gym.

"I just wanted to let you know," she said, trying to keep it together. "That I've really enjoyed being student body president, and I have tried to do the best I could." The crowd murmured. Amy was holding on to the podium, and I could see her hands trembling just a bit. "I've really enjoyed this . . . but, um . . . I need to . . . resign." She stopped. "My vice president, Tricia Minor, is going to take over as president."

And then she just *deflated* a little bit, and some assholes in the back started clapping, not for Amy, but for Tricia taking over. And you could hear other people mocking her, saying "Aw, poor baby" or conjecturing about the sex scandal that was bringing her down.

I couldn't do anything. I tried to make eye contact with her, but she sat back down on one of the stupid folding chairs and the curtain of blond hair fell again, and I couldn't help thinking about when she had broken my heart for the first time.

Now her heart was breaking, and there was nothing I could do.

I hoped that going to prom would cheer her up, or at least provide her a break from the tragedy at home. I'd been dreaming about it since the first time she kissed me—I could see us, under the balloons and the lights, forgetting about our lives and celebrating being in love. There was a whole musical number in my head to "In Your Eyes" by Peter Gabriel. We'd hold each other on the dance floor, swaying slightly, since even in my imagination I couldn't dance for shit.

I know it's shocking, but I had never been to prom. I had never been to any dance, ever. It had always seemed like that was something for other, cooler, more attractive people who had decent hair-care products and rhythm. But this time—this time I was going to go. This was my only chance.

There was only one problem.

I had no money.

Renting a tux cost at least a hundred bucks, and that wasn't even counting dinner at a semi-fancy restaurant, which was going to be at least fifty. My dad was entering his fifth month of unemployment; the five hundred bucks and magic beans we'd gotten for the minivan were long gone. There was no way I could ask Mom and Dad for the money. They had already told Kaitlyn she wasn't going to be able to get a new dress this year, at which point she said everyone was ruining her life, and then apologized, and then decided that she could go ahead and use the dress from last year.

But I needed cash, and there was only one way to get it, since I couldn't sell my blood plasma until I was eighteen. Stupid laws.

Rick's Collectibles was located downtown near the Y, next to a movie theater that had closed when I was ten. It had opened to great fanfare my sophomore year, which had sent my friends into an extended paroxysm of joy until Groash was banned six weeks later. (He would skateboard there after school, take a Dungeons & Dragons book off the shelf, and read it for two or three hours before leaving. He'd repeat the process the next day, slowly working his way through the entire collection and buying exactly nothing. We all understood why he was banned. "I would totally ban you from my store," Brian had said at the time. "I wouldn't even let you on the same block as my store.")

Besides the D&D stuff, Rick also sold comic books, which formed the crux of my plan. I packed the best ones from my collection (the ones whose covers weren't crucified on my walls) and biked downtown.

Rick was a young black guy with a beard, maybe twenty-five, who spent all the time when he wasn't selling things to nerds working out. Apparently he was in training for the moment in time when secret agents would burst into his geek store and try to rob him with ninja skills, at which point he would rip off his shirt, flex his impressive pectorals, and open up a can of whoop-ass.

"I would so open up a can of whoop-ass," he said, staring longingly at the door. He kept a pair of nunchucks behind the counter because he was *that* guy.

"They're called nunchakus," he would say.

Great.

I set my collection on the counter. The valuable comics that I hadn't dismembered and stapled to my wall were placed in Mylar sleeves, with cardboard backing, and I hadn't so much as breathed on them in years. I had some good ones: *Silver Surfer* #1, *X-Factor* #1, *Wolverine* #1, *The Amazing Spider-Man* #298 (it was the first Todd McFarlane issue—trust me). I figured that all told my collection was worth just under three hundred bucks.

"Fifty," he said, looking them over.

"Are you kidding me?"

Rick tensed, wondering if this was finally the moment he could open up his can of whoop-ass. I could read his thoughts: *Just try it, kid, I have nunchakus right here.*

I calmed down a bit and flipped open my copy of the official *Comics Buyer's Guide.* "Okay, if you actually look at the values listed here—"

"That's sales price, not purchase price."

"Fine, but accounting for that, you're giving me less than twenty percent of their value."

Rick scratched his beard. "I'll give you twenty-five percent. Seventy-five bucks for all of it."

Kaitlyn's words came back to me: *We should sell that Dungeons & Dragons crap.*

"I do have one more thing," I said.

This is going to take some setup for non-geeks; please bear with me. The first Christmas my dad accidentally bought me Dungeons & Dragons crap, I received the single greatest rule book in the game: *Deities & Demigods*, published by a company known as TSR. It was an illustrated book with a series of gods from world religions that you could fight if you wanted your character to be brutally destroyed. (They hadn't included Jesus, but maybe the game designers thought they were skating a little close to eternal damnation as it was.) The book itself wasn't so unusual, but this was a first-edition copy of it, which contained both the Cthulhu mythos and the Melnibonéan myths (I'm not sure I can think of a geekier sentence than the one above, but with a little effort I might be able to manage). Both of those were the intellectual property of someone else, so TSR took them out of the next printing because they had been threatened to be sued into the fires of a non-copyrighted hell. So the version I had was a collector's item. A valuable collector's item.

History lesson over.

I set it down on the counter like I was twirling my own nunchakus.

Rick gave a low whistle and turned it over in his hands. "Well, well, well . . . now we're talking."

I had planned on asking Amy to prom after school, but I had forgotten about Kaitlyn's track meet.

"You never come to my track meets," Kaitlyn had said earlier in the week. We were in our usual arguing spot: the kitchen.

"You never come to my Dungeons & Dragons games. I think that's for the best."

"Why would I come to one of your stupid games?"

"Thank you," I said, putting my hands in the air like I had just won the Heavyweight Crown of Stupid Arguing.

"Do you get cheered on in D&D? Is that what you need? You need someone saying, 'Yay, Craig, out-nerd those other nerds!'?"

"Craig, it would be nice for you to go to the meet," called our mom from the living room.

"No it wouldn't!" I called back. "Track meets are an oppressive wasteland!"

"This could be my last high school meet," said Kaitlyn. "You haven't come to one in two years."

"Yeah, I learned my lesson."

My dad groaned from the living room. "Jesus, Craig."

"The only reason she wants me to go is to suffer," I complained.

Dad sauntered into the room, smoothing out his goatee. "Son," he said, "sometimes we have to do things because women want us to suffer. That's part of growing up."

So I had agreed to go to the track meet. Despite an awful day at school, Amy didn't want to go home after school, and that's how we came to be sitting in Monterey Stadium in a miserable drifting mist for thirty-one hours while I planned my big romantic moment.

Maybe it wasn't thirty-one hours. But it was probably close. You think, at some point, the track meet might end, but you've been caught inside the event horizon of a quantum singularity, and time has warped into a circle. People run around the track. Then there's a pause. Then people run around the track again. Forever.

Monterey Stadium had long metallic benches that had been installed in an earlier era when people had tiny butts and endured pain because it was good for you. They dug into the backs of your legs like razor-sharp teeth and transmitted the cold like a block of ice. It was not fun.

My parents had acquired little puffy cushions from a car dealership and sat in relative comfort near the front of the stands. They both had umbrellas and blankets and were prepared. Amy and I huddled together twenty rows back, trying to preserve our body heat, so that part was nice at least.

I kept my arm around her and held her tight against my side, noticing, as usual, that she smelled great.

"Are you okay?"

She nodded.

"If you need anything, just let me know."

"Maybe like twenty more degrees and sunlight."

"That might be beyond my capabilities. I keep hoping those mutant powers are going to develop, but . . ."

"Just keep holding me, then."

"Done."

The benches squeaked as I saw Elizabeth striding up to us in her combat boots.

"Hey, guys," she said.

"What the hell are you doing here?"

She pointed down to the track. "I came with Brian. He's being forced to cover the meet for the paper." I spotted him on the sidelines, holding a notebook and looking as miserable as the rest of us. She wiped off the spot next to Amy with the arm of her jacket and settled in. "I liked your speech the other day," she said.

"Oh," said Amy.

"No, it was cool. I mean, you know, honest."

"Thanks."

Kaitlyn was slated to run the 200, the 400, and the 110 hurdles. That meant she would be in action for approximately a minute and forty-five seconds out of the thirty-one hours.

She won the first heat of the hurdles easily. She ran angry, her ponytail flying in the wind behind her. She hit almost every hurdle, but she smacked them so hard they didn't slow her down.

"Wow," said Elizabeth. "I'm amazed you guys share the same genetic material."

"We don't share the exact same genetic material," I said. "Otherwise, we'd be identical twins."

"She got the better shit, then. Maybe she stole it from you in the womb. Like she reached over with her umbilical cord and sucked the good stuff out of you." Amy giggled. Elizabeth was on a roll. "You realize she could, like, beat the shit out of you. If you got down there and raced her—"

"I'm not gonna race her."

"But if you did, she would destroy you. Like, it wouldn't be close. She could probably turn around halfway through and run backward, laughing at you the whole time."

"I don't enjoy running. And be honest: Is there any real reason to run these days? It's not like there are wolves chasing us."

"If there were wolves chasing you, they'd get you first. She'd get away."

A little while later, Brian joined us. "Your sister's doing well," he said.

I groaned. Amy patted me on the back.

"He's sensitive about it," she said.

"I'm not sensitive about it."

"Really sensitive."

"He's got like an inferiority complex," added Elizabeth.

"Understandable," said Brian.

"Shouldn't you be like, reporting on this?" I said.

Brian took out his little notebook. "Here's what I've got so far. 'On and on runs the wheel of time. People run. They jump. They fall. This will undoubtedly be the high point of some of these people's lives. The drizzle continues indefinitely, like the incessant buzzing of a barely repressed nightmare. Is there a God? Not on this day.'"

"I feel like sports reporting might not be your thing," said Amy.

"I do straight news," he said. "This whole sports thing is bullshit."

We laughed and I held Amy's hand. Despite the mist and the misery, it felt like sunshine.

After Kaitlyn's last run (she took second in the finals and there was much cheering), I turned to Amy.

"So, um . . . I wanted to talk to you about prom."

"Oh my God, don't even get me started on prom."

"Right."

"It's such a disaster right now. There was a huge fight because one of the people on the committee has a cousin who's a DJ or something—I don't know—and they started going back and forth about it, and I was like, 'I hate all of this. It is so pointless. Why am I doing this? Why am I in this room right now when I should be at home? And maybe I'm in this room because I don't want to go home,' and then . . ."

She clutched the edge of the cold bench. "Sorry. If I could make prom explode in a giant fireball right now I would do it. I should have resigned from that, too."

"Yeah."

"I don't even want to go."

I bit my lip and looked down. A black hole opened up inside my chest.

"You don't want to go?"

She sniffed. "No. It's not fun. It's stressful. I can't even— I don't have a dress, and that's one more thing I gotta do, and then when I'm there everyone's gonna be asking me to do stuff— I don't want to be responsible for it, you know? I've got enough to fucking worry about."

"Right."

I took a deep breath.

"Um . . . well, maybe we shouldn't go, then," I said.

She looked at me. "Is that okay?"

"Of course that's okay. It's just a dance. I don't have the money to go anyway."

"I thought you probably wanted to go," she said weakly.

"It's fine." I smiled. "It's fine. We'll do something else."

She took hold of my hand in hers and leaned her head on my shoulder.

"I love you," she said, and for a brief moment a ray of sunlight split the clouds and warmed my back. Maybe it was going to be okay, after all.

TWENTY-SIX

The Night from Hell

By May things had gotten bad in our house. Of course, my off-again, on-again relationship with Amy wasn't helping things, but my dad still hadn't found a job. The severance pay was gone, the unemployment was gone, and now we were just on my mom's salary.

My dad took it pretty well, considering. He undertook a project to build a deck behind our house, which was deliriously nonsensical. Since I was the other male in the house, I was drafted into the unhelpful task of holding pieces of wood and bringing him tools. I was the least handy person ever and my dad wasn't all that much better. So most days he could be found swearing his head off behind the house, cursing the gods, wood, nails, hammers, and anything else that was infuriating him.

Things fell apart on May 3, two weeks after Amy resigned the presidency.

It started with my comic books.

"So I was wondering if I could get my stuff back," I said to Rick, slowly gathering up my comics like old friends.

"You can buy 'em back."

I looked at the prices. He was selling them for four times what he'd paid me. My *Deities & Demigods* was now encased in some kind of Kryptonian-crystal shield and illuminated by tiny spotlights. It was ninja-proof.

"Here's the thing, Rick. I have a lot of nerdy friends. So many of them. And if they hear what an awesome guy you are, they're gonna shop here. They're gonna buy stuff at your store." Okay that was probably a lie, since most of my friends were dirt poor. "So think of this like a business decision: You don't lose any money from this transaction, and you get a whole bunch of good karma. I can tell karma is important to you."

Rick leaned over the counter, his triceps bulging. "I like you," he said. "And I like karma. But I got a guy interested in that book already if his girlfriend will lend him some money. So I can't give them back to you. But if you ever need a job, you let me know."

That was the best part of the day. Then came the letter from Gustavus Adolphus.

The financial aid letter.

I wasn't an idiot. I knew what it meant. The college fund

wasn't huge, and in danger of being tapped to pay for things like food. So this was it. I could find a job over the summer, but without significant help there was no way I was going there.

I literally trembled when I held it. My hand shook. A shiver ran over my cheeks.

I took two deep breaths and tore it open.

CONGRATULATIONS—we have determined . . . blah blah blah—I skipped forward to the numbers.

Your expected contribution: $10,450 per year.

Grants: $6,600 per year.

Loans: $9,800 per year.

I set it down. I knew what it meant.

Shitshitshitshit.

It went downhill from there.

I showed the letter to my parents and they were just as crushed as I was.

"I don't think we can make that work," said my dad, giving me one of those vise grips on the shoulders that meant serious trouble.

The whole family was sitting around the couch under an ugly thundercloud that had gathered in our living room. Meteors were streaking toward us.

"So . . ." sighed my dad.

"So I guess it's Madison, then," I said. I had been accepted there too. It was my safety school, but it was still a fine university and not the end of the world and—

I realized no one was saying anything.

"Honey," said my mom very slowly. The smile that was almost always on her face was gone. "Um . . ." She exhaled and looked over at my dad.

"That might be really hard," he said finally.

"What are you talking about?" I said.

"Well . . . um . . . I'm really sorry. We talked this over and I thought I was going to be able to find something . . ." I started to feel sweat sliding down the back of my neck again. What the hell was going on?

"What are you saying?" asked Kaitlyn.

"Well, I mean, Kaitlyn didn't get much financial aid, and it's pretty late in the game to—"

"Don't bring me into this," she said.

"Wait a minute!" I protested.

"I don't think we can afford to send you both there at the same time. Your mom and I have been talking about this—a lot. Once I get a new job we should be able to make it work, but . . . there's just no way right now we can make it happen."

I felt the future disappearing in front of me, like the bridge out of Janesville was collapsing into a bottomless pit. I had trouble breathing.

"Are you serious?" asked Kaitlyn.

"What does that mean?" I asked, trying to breathe.

Kaitlyn jumped in before my dad could answer. "What about our college savings?"

My dad's voice was like gravel. "There's less in there than we hoped—"

"How much?"

"About four thousand dollars."

Kaitlyn stood up. "Are you kidding me?!"

My mom's eyes went red. "We tried to save and—with two at the same time we can't—"

"It's not like this is a surprise!" yelled Kaitlyn. "You've had seventeen years to get ready for this! What the hell have you been doing? You saved four thousand dollars in seventeen years? How did you think you were gonna pay for this? We could've skipped one vacation and we would've saved that much!"

My mom wilted under the barrage. The cheerful smile was gone, the person who always tried to soldier through the pain, who had endured her husband being out of work for six months and the relentless conflict between her children—it all came crashing down right then. Her face fell into her hands.

"Jesus, Kaitlyn," I said. "Lay off! So you take a year off school—"

"I take a year off school?! *I* take a year off?!"

"Like you give a shit about college," I said, feeling my face burn from adrenaline. "You can still go to the parties and get hammered. You don't have to live there to do that."

"Are you fucking kidding me?" She spun on me.

My dad tried to intervene but she barreled forward. "I'm not going to college to party, you asshole. I want to get a degree and a good job—"

"Oh, come on, we all know you're not gonna study any harder in college than you did in high school—"

"Shut up."

"It's true. College doesn't matter to you. It's just something your friends are doing; it doesn't matter to you if you go this year or next year or three years from now—"

"I'm running track in college, dick. I'd lose an entire year of eligibility—"

"Oh, gee, I'd hate to have you lose the ability to run," I said, mocking her. I was in it now. Part of me screamed *stop* but the rest of me didn't care anymore. "You can run down the street if you want. We can set up hurdles if it's that important to you. Society is going to be a lot worse off if you lose a year of *track* eligibility. Are you going to the Olympics? Are you getting a big track job after school?"

I'd seen my sister angry a lot of times. But I don't think she had ever come close to what I saw then. Little thermonuclear blasts exploded behind her eyes. It was a good thing she was on the other side of the ottoman, because I could sense her tensing up to beat the actual shit out of me. I imagined a little sign dropping down from the ceiling, WELCOME TO THE END OF ALL THAT IS.

"Fuck you, Craig," she said slowly. "You don't give a shit about anyone but yourself. You walk around here like you're better than me because you do well on standardized testing or whatever, but you can't even fucking go to a party—"

"Oh, I'm missing out on the—"

"'Cause you can't talk to people! So you sit with your little friends in the basement like a freak, imagining yourself so superior. And you look at me with *contempt*, don't you? Contempt. I don't do that to you. I don't look down on you—"

"The hell you don't—"

"'Cause you hate me," she said. "You hate me. Because you're jealous of me. And you gotta go and pick the most expensive school in the damn country because you don't give a shit about Mom and Dad, you don't give a shit about me. You just figure, *Somebody's gonna cough up the money for it, 'cause I'm Craig and I get whatever I want. I never* get what I want. It's always you first. Well, fuck you!"

My mom was weeping at this point, yelling "Stop it!" through her hands.

Kaitlyn stormed off to her room, slamming her door like a shotgun blast.

I looked over at my dad. He had his eyes on the ground too. I didn't say anything else and retreated to my room.

When a family represses its feelings like good Midwestern folk, and the shit hits the fan, the shit really hits the fan.

Four hours later, the cataclysm seemed to have subsided. We decided on exactly nothing other than it might be a good idea for all of us to eat ice cream and bury our feelings again. It was like we had all taken a family field trip to the Void, snapped a few pictures, and then decided to go home.

Believe it or not, Kaitlyn recovered first.

"Hey, I'm going to Debbie's tonight," she announced around eight.

Dad just looked at her in exhausted, dumbstruck horror.

"Are you sure that's a good idea?" asked Mom.

"Yes."

"Are you sure, though?"

"Yes."

Mom was at a loss. I could see the gears turning in her head—she was trying to come up with just the right amount of guilt and sadness to keep Kaitlyn home for the night. It wasn't going to work.

"I'm gonna need a ride," said Kaitlyn.

It's important to mention here that Kaitlyn had lost her license because she was the worst driver in the history of humanity. Literally, she had been pulled over three times in two weeks because every time a happy song came on the radio, she floored it. I think the police had a bet about how many times they could pull her over.

"I'm not taking you," said my dad, shaking his head. "Not doing it."

"This is totally unfair!"

"Sorry. Not doing it."

I tried to make myself as inconspicuous as possible, which was hard because I was stuffing my face with Cheetos. (It was Saturday night, after all, which meant that my friends were coming over for Dungeons & Dragons, and if I didn't eat all the Cheetos now my friends would steal them all before I could have any. Yes, I had priorities. And sure, the world had kinda ended, but that was not going to stop me from playing D&D.)

"Craig," she whined, turning to me.

"What?"

"Give me a ride over to Debbie's. She's having a party."

The word *party* caused my mom's danger sense to activate. "Are Debbie's parents going to be there?"

"Yes," lied Kaitlyn.

"If I call over there, are her parents going to answer the phone?"

"Yes," lied Kaitlyn again.

I had to hand it to my sister. It was total bullshit; my parents knew it was total bullshit, and yet here she was, lying straight to their faces, daring them to call her bluff.

"Okay, I'm going to do that, then," said Mom.

"Great. Her parents will love to hear from you. Their names are Chip and Jen." It was astonishing how quickly the lies piled on top of each other.

I narrowed my eyes. *There's no Chip and Jen. Chip and Jen are lies.*

There was a time when I had been amazed by Kaitlyn's ability to get away with this kind of thing, but she had explained it to me like this: "If Mom calls over there and Debbie's parents aren't there, that's going to cause a lot of effort on her part. Mom and

Dad're going to need to get mad and come over to pick me up, and then they're going to have to go through the whole ordeal of grounding me and making speeches or whatever. They don't want to do that."

She had a point.

"Craig, give me a ride to Debbie's."

I laughed. "No. You were fucking horrible to me today."

"What?! You were fucking horrible to *me* today! You owe me a ride for that."

Mom had had enough. "If the f-bomb gets dropped one more time tonight, I'm canceling everyone's birthday."

"All right, fine," I said. "Kaitlyn. No. I will not give you a ride to Debbie's. You were horrible to me tonight."

"Because you were a selfish asshole."

"Whoa," said my dad.

Mom began the process of making unhelpful suggestions. "Can you take the bus?"

Kaitlyn's eyes rolled out of her head. "No, I'm not taking the bus." She turned to me again. "Craig."

"No! We just had a huge fight!"

"And I'm slowly getting over it."

"I'm not over it."

"You should be. That's your fault you're not over it."

"I'm not taking you there. My friends are coming over tonight."

"Nerdfest can survive without you for an hour."

"I don't even like Debbie."

"So what? She doesn't like you, either. It's not like you're invited to the party; you're just giving me a ride."

"Maybe you could say please," suggested Mom, as if that would solve things. *Oh. Oh, you said please? I'll just abandon my principles, then!*

"Craig, please, don't be a loser."

"I'm not taking you," I said.

"Yes, you are," said Kaitlyn. "Yes. You. Are." She started staring at me, doing a Jedi mind trick.

"It's. Not. Working," I said, staring right back at her.

Dad put his head on the island. "For God's sake, Craig, just give her a damn ride."

"Language!" protested my mom. "This is where they get it from."

"Fine!" I said. "Let's go, then."

"I'm not ready yet," said Kaitlyn.

It took Kaitlyn an hour or so to get dressed and do her makeup and make sure that she wasn't early to the party. I will add that after an hour of preparation, Kaitlyn's auburn hair looked exactly the same as it did before, which was still perfect. I sat around in the kitchen, twitching, hoping that Debbie's house was burning down or zombies would attack.

Since her first experience with Dungeons & Dragons, Amy had had the good sense to stay away on Saturday nights. On the night from hell, she was staying home to take care of her mom.

Anyway, around nine or so—just when Groash had showed up—Kaitlyn announced that she was ready for me to give her a ride to the party that I hated.

"Dude," said Groash. "Aren't we playing?"

"Yeah," I said. "I have to give my sister a ride first."

"You want me to give her a ride?"

"No. No, I do not."

"Are you sure? 'Cause I would give her a ride all over town."

"Shut up," I said.

"What do you think she's looking for in a boyfriend?"

"Obedience."

"Cool." Groash thought about it. "I could do that."

"Just wait here for Brian and Elizabeth. I'll be back as soon as I can."

"So what am I supposed to do?"

AN IMAGINARY CONVERSATION
BETWEEN GROASH AND MY PARENTS

DAD: So . . .

MOM: You want something to eat?

GROASH: Dude. Yes. My family doesn't feed me.

MOM: Oh, I'm sure they feed you.

DAD: Why the hell do you have a safety pin in your ear?

GROASH: Helps with my aerodynamics.

Debbie lived in the rich section of town, which was located in the woods on streets named after planets. Each house was like a medieval castle and had superfluous lighting showing just how much bigger it was than your house. The streets were all dark and curved around each other a hundred times, which I'm sure was designed to keep poor people out. We were basically lost for most of the night.

We drove in silence.

Kaitlyn's words were still pinging around my skull, cutting me up. *You don't give a shit about anyone but yourself.* Was it true? Of course it was true. I tried to think of a way out, some evidence that she was wrong, something that proved I wasn't the selfish jerk she thought I was. Was my whole college search all about selfishness?

Nothing had been resolved. I felt like my future had been ripped out of my gut. Was I going to college or not? Was Kaitlyn going or not? Were my parents going to make us fight it out, *Highlander*-style?

I'd had my heart set on GAC since the weird visit in the fall. I hadn't thought about the money. I guess I had just always figured it would work out. Maybe that was blindness on my part, maybe that was evidence that I didn't really think about other people, but the place seemed so amazing. I imagined myself there in the fall, maybe hanging out with those women, having discussions into the middle of the night, drinking tea and eating popcorn. Or braving the elements in the winter and running to classes about literature and philosophy and Winnie-the-Pooh-inspired Taoism. I'd write deep, thrilling letters to Amy and we'd call each other as often as we could, and we'd fall deeper in love and then get together on breaks and then we'd get married and have kids and Amy would probably take a job in a think tank in Washington, DC, and I'd write the Great American Novel.

Not that I'd thought about it.

And now? Nothing. A black hole. I had no idea what was going to happen.

"You suck at this," said Kaitlyn helpfully after the first hour.

"*You* suck at this," I said.

"I'm not the one who got us lost."

"You suck at giving directions."

"I'm not the one driving."

"Because you suck."

"You suck."

"You suck more."

"You suck infinity," she said.

"That doesn't even make grammatical sense."

"Your grammatical sense sucks."

It was nice to have a friendly discussion with her again, instead of the apocalypse that happened earlier.

Finally, after about an hour and a half of this, we arrived at Debbie's stately manor. There were a few cars parked outside, but I knew that at high school parties, kids parked randomly in a two-block radius. That way it wouldn't be so obvious that a party was going on if police happened to drive by. Of course, it's not like police were driving by the rich houses anyway, and if the cars didn't clue them in, perhaps the shitty pop music blaring from the well-lit manor might have alerted them.

I had been to exactly one high school party in my life, and that was by accident. I was there for an hour, standing around awkwardly and terrified that the police were going to smash through the windows and haul me away to prison. It had been a relief when someone finally shouted, "The cops are coming!" and I broke into a blind run and hid in the kiddie pool at the nearby park. Later I learned that the cops were not, in fact, coming; that was just something you said when you wanted the dorks to leave. And given my experience in Minnesota, I wasn't exactly champing at the bit to go to another party.

"All right, come on," said Kaitlyn after I had parked in front of the house like an idiot.

I looked at her like she had just suggested making out with an alien mushroom.

"What?" she said.

"I'm not going in there."

"It's been a shitty day. Come in and blow off some steam and then leave. Jeez."

"I thought I couldn't talk to people," I said, pouting.

"Well, here's a chance to find out."

I think this was her idea of a peace offering.

I'm sure that the inside of Debbie's house was normally really nice. They probably had a cleaning lady or a maid or a team of servants to polish the floors or whatever. At the moment, however, the whole place stank like cheap beer and sweat and a rather terrible sweet smell, which I recognized as marijuana.

Oh yay. Just what I was hoping for.

I affected my usual party demeanor—stand awkwardly for a few minutes without talking to anyone—before I started to make my escape.

"Craig!" shouted someone I didn't know. He was a meaty, red-faced blond guy lightly coated in sweat. "Dude!"

"Hey," I said.

He wrapped me in a bear hug and put one shiny massive arm around my shoulder. "Oh my fucking God, this guy! This guy is awesome!"

I'm not sure anyone was listening to him, but he kept going anyway. "This guy is like the smartest guy in the world! You know that, right? You know that?" He leaned in really close so that I could see the red lines surrounding his pupils. "You're gonna be running shit someday, right? Like, companies and shit? Like, all the companies?" Then he turned to the imaginary crowd again. "This guy is like Bill Gates and the other guys! He's like a genius!"

Don't bet on it.

Again, I wasn't exactly sure who this was. He seemed nice, though.

"You know what you need?" he said, pulling me into his armpit. "Beer. You need a beer!"

"I'm actually the designated driver," I said.

"Awesome! That is so awesome. THIS GUY IS AWESOME! You wanna do a keg stand then?"

"No, I'm pretty sure I'm still the designated driver."

"Oh yeah. Yeah. Good point. Can I ask you something? Honestly, man-to-man?"

"Sure."

"You hate me, don't you? You fucking hate me."

"No. Not at all."

A wave of sweat and relief passed over his face. "Oh, man, that is so great. I was worried, dude! I was like, 'Craig hates me.' And I just couldn't stand that, you know. Like, these other people, I could give a shit, you know? But you . . . that means a lot to me. I want to hug you. Okay? I'm gonna hug you now."

"You're kind of already hugging me."

"I know. But I'm gonna hug you more. Like a real hug. You know what I'm saying? Come on." He spread his massive bear arms wide. "Gimme some."

So I hugged him more, and then he lifted me into the air and shouted, "Yes!"

At this point, I had lost track of Kaitlyn, but he wasn't about to let me go.

"You should come to more parties," he said. "The beer is in the basement. Come on."

Then he headed for the stairs, missed one of them, and caught himself on the railing just before he tumbled down twenty steps to the concrete below. "Holy shit I almost died!" he shouted, and then people started clapping for him.

At this point, the party was not exactly what I had expected. Because the gigantic sweaty person was not the only one to hug me or declare that they were honored to be partying with me. I was not, in fact, partying with them. I was looking around, and then I was getting the hell out. We were slated to fight a green dragon tonight, and there was no way I was going to miss that. If I wasn't there, Groash would have to play my character, which basically meant that he'd charge stupidly into battle and end up dead. Every time.

But these were people I had gone to school with for years.

You don't give a shit about anybody but yourself.

Some of them I had gone to elementary school with. The faces were familiar, but the names escaped me. I didn't really know any of them. I didn't know Amy before this year either, and yet here I was, her sometimes boyfriend. I was graduating in a month, and I didn't really know anyone. There was a whole ecosystem of other humans who were living their own separate lives, and I didn't know anything about them.

Maybe Kaitlyn was right.

The basement had been finished into a bar-type area. They

had a pool table, which was surrounded by boys with little cups. There was a dartboard, a huge TV, and half a dozen couches. Someone had strung up Christmas lights everywhere, so it was even a little bit magical. Okay, it wasn't magical. But it was otherworldly.

I was just starting to relax and contemplate perhaps getting one of those red cups and seeing what the beer tasted like.

So I made my way toward the keg, which was sitting in the bathtub.

And that's when I saw a girl with blond hair who walked slightly like a duck. She had her back turned to me, but it was Amy.

There was a guy standing next to her, with his arm over her shoulder. He was taller than me, a little heavier, with a wide neck and a scraggly beard. When he turned to the side, I could see his face in profile.

He seemed familiar. But I couldn't place it.

And then he smiled for a second and whispered something in Amy's ear, and I knew where I'd seen him before.

In a heart-shaped frame on her dresser.

TWENTY-SEVEN

The Night from Hell (Part Two)

The room turned freezing cold as I stood there, watching them.

Amy was leaning into him. He was holding her shoulder.

Then she put her arm around his waist.

The arm that had held me. The arm that I loved. There was a tingling in the back of my neck as I lost my balance a little bit.

Amy laughed and tossed her long blond hair and then accidentally looked in my direction.

"Shit," said Kaitlyn, who was apparently standing right next to me.

Amy's eyes went wide when she spotted me.

The next thing I knew I was getting the hell out of there. I was up the stairs and past somebody saying, "Dude, it's Craig!" and then I got turned around and pushed past someone until I was on the back patio. I heard Amy behind me; she was saying something, but I couldn't make it out from the noise of the party.

Then I was out into the darkness, on the edge of a long sloping yard that led down into a forest. It was a warm night, and there were wisps of clouds snaking through the sky, covering up the hordes of bright stars above. I stumbled down the cool grass, past the smokers, and headed for the trees.

I don't know why I was heading for the forest. Obviously, there was a whole fight-or-flight response going on at this point, and since I was genetically disposed to run away from danger, this was the flight instinct. Clearly, I was channeling the deer that had run away from me in the woods.

"Craig!" called Amy, racing after me.

I didn't say anything. I kept going.

"Craig, come on!"

I had reached the edge of the forest, and, stepping over the roots and passing by the trunks of huge trees, I plowed into it. Amy caught my elbow.

"Stop!" she said. "It wasn't what it looked like!"

I spun on her. "Did you know he was going to be here?" She didn't answer. "Did you know he was here? Did you plan this?"

"There was nothing going on!"

"You had your arm around him! I'm not an idiot!"

"He's a friend. He's just a friend."

"He's your ex-boyfriend!"

"He was just being nice!"

I believe I made some kind of coughing noise. "What the

hell, Amy? You said you were taking care of your mom tonight! And instead, you're out here with that guy!"

"Listen to yourself! You sound like a jealous boyfriend right now!"

"WHAT? I am the least jealous person in the universe! I'm also the fucking dumbest! You're lying to me! You lie to me all the time!"

"No, I didn't!"

"How long have you been back with him?"

"I'm not back with him!"

"Is this just like us? Do you break up with him all the time too? Do you just alternate between us? Who the hell are you?"

Amy was clutching me now, and though her face was obscured by her hair again, I could tell she had started crying.

Not gonna work this time, I thought.

"My mom fell asleep, and he called me up and . . ."

"And you didn't think to call me?"

"I don't need your permission to go to a party, Craig!"

"Especially when you're going to be making out with your ex-boyfriend!"

"I didn't kiss him! He was being nice!"

"Yet. You didn't kiss him yet."

She threw up her hands. "All right. Whatever. Think what you want to think."

"Well, what am I supposed to think? You tell me a lie about

what you're doing. I come to a party, and I find you with your arm around your goddamned ex-boyfriend!"

"I can't do this," she said, burying her face again. "I can't! I'm sorry." She put her hand against a tree. "I wasn't going to do anything with him. I was just feeling really sad, so I wanted someone to talk to."

"You looked really sad," I said, being mean.

Amy screwed up her eyes at me. "Fuck you," she said. "You don't know."

"You didn't tell me! Call me if you're sad! Talk to me! That's what I'm here for! You can lean on me!"

"I don't want to lean on you all the time!"

"That's what I'm here for! About your mom, about school, about prom, about everything! I have been nothing but kind and thoughtful and great with you and you're out here cuddling with your ex-boyfriend!"

She turned away. "I can't do this," she said again. "I'm sorry—I just . . . I can't do this right now." She waved her hand like she was swatting some kind of imaginary bug. "I just wanted a minute where I wasn't dealing with all the shit in my life; and he called up, and I thought it would be fun. You hate these things; you didn't want to come out, so I went with him. And, fine, I was having a good time, but I can't . . . You can't force these expectations on me like I'm supposed to be perfect! I wasn't doing anything. I love you, but I just . . . I can't be with you right now."

Fine, I thought. *Fine. You want to do this now, let's do this now.*

It was all piling up, the fight with Kaitlyn, the collapse of my future, Amy . . .

Let's just burn it all down, then. That's how this is gonna go.

"You can't be with me?! You weren't with me! You were with him!"

"Stop it! I'm not having this stupid fight—"

"Maybe you should've thought of that before—"

"My mom's got chemo on Monday, okay? She's going in on Monday. All right?"

I stopped.

"It's bad, Craig. It's bad this time."

"I didn't know that," I said.

"My mom's probably going to die, okay? And I'm the one who's taking care of her! My dad has checked out; my brother isn't helping; it's all on me! Okay?! I'm the one who has to give her her medicine! I have to make sure she eats! I'm the person who gets up in the middle of the night and has to help her get back to sleep! I'm fucking doing everything and it's too goddamn much! I deal with that every night. My mom is dying. Every. Night. And I'm supposed to be going to school and running things and being your girlfriend—I can't do it!"

A void opened up inside me. All the words I wanted to say tumbled out of my head.

"And I just keep hurting you. I keep hurting you all the time, and I can't help it!"

Then she put her head down and stumbled away from me,

deeper into the trees. "You want so much from me that I can't give you right now! And I'm sorry that I keep blowing things up and—"

And that's when she ran face-first into a low-hanging tree branch.

Amy's head snapped back, and she dropped to her knees like a rock.

"Oh . . . FUCK!" she shouted, holding her forehead.

Even in the dark, I could see the blood coming from her face. The branch had torn a long horizontal gash above her right eye, and blood was pouring out of it like a geyser. Maybe not a giant geyser. A small geyser of blood. Still, a worrisome geyser.

"Holy shit!" I said, running to her and barely missing bashing my face against the same tree.

Amy was going fetal, and I put my arms around her shoulders and pulled her to her feet.

"Oh, man," she said, looking at the blood in her hands.

"It's fine . . . it's fine . . . it's just . . . oh, man, it's not fine . . . oh, Jesus," I said, displaying the calm resolve that would disqualify me for military service. Or being a firefighter, policeman, nurse, doctor, or trash collector.

We stumbled out of the woods.

We were quiet on the entire drive to the hospital. Afterward, I sat in the waiting room of the emergency center. It was probably about midnight, and their magazine selection was horrible.

Mostly *Ladies' Home Journal*, which appeared to be only articles about doilies and baking stuff.

So I sat there, in a blue plastic chair, staring at the wall.

You don't give a shit about anyone except you.

Her mom was dying. She wanted to be out of the house to be away from it for a while.

There were people at the party who liked me.

There was a whole world I didn't understand. A whole world that didn't center on me. I might not be going to college next year, and I thought it was the end of the world. But it wasn't. And I'd been fighting over that like it was life itself. And meanwhile, Amy's mom was fighting for her life. And Amy was taking care of her. What was that like every day? What was going on in her head every day? I had no idea. Of course she needed to get out. I had thought I knew her, but maybe I just knew my idea of her. Maybe she was a different person than the one I had imagined. Maybe her life didn't revolve around torturing me.

There was a youngish mom there with me. She had checked in with a sick little boy and was now fidgeting in the corner, trying to read a *Ladies' Home Journal* and probably hating it.

What was going on in her mind? What was her life like? I wondered what problem the little boy had. Maybe he was dying too.

And then it occurred to me that even though things had been pretty tough the past six months, my whole life had been basically untouched by tragedy. Apart from the litany of dead pets, nothing bad had really happened to me. My grandfathers had died before I was born; I had never broken a bone; my parents were still together. Groash had it worse. Elizabeth had it worse. Brian had it worse. Amy had it worse. I was the luckiest person I knew.

That thought didn't make me feel good, though. It made me feel like kind of a dick.

Amy came out at about one in the morning. They had bandaged up her face. She had eleven stitches.

"They said I might have a scar," she said, trying to give a weak little smile.

"It'll make you look badass," I said.

"Maybe."

"Like, *I will fuck you up. Do not mess with me. You know the tree that gave me this scar? It's dead now.*"

She laughed a little bit and sat next to me.

"Maybe we should go back there," I joked. "With, like, a chain saw. *You tried to take me out, tree? Say hello to my little friend!*"

"Have you ever used a chain saw?"

"No, I'm totally scared of them."

"Yeah, me too."

Amy sat there for a second. "Thanks for taking care of me," she said.

"To be fair, I think I caused this."

"No." She shook her head. "You didn't do any of this."

"Did you call your parents?"

"No. I guess that's the benefit of being eighteen. I don't need to bother them with it."

"Do you need a ride home?"

"I think so."

When we stopped at her house, it was nearly one thirty in the morning. I pulled into the driveway and shut off the car.

"Sorry," I said.

"It's okay."

Amy bit her lip and looked down. I had turned the car off, and it felt like a coffin in the dark. I tried to think of the words I needed to say—anything that would stop this, or let her know that I understood. But there weren't any.

"I should go," she said, after a few minutes.

"I love you," I said.

"I love you too." She said it like a death sentence.

Then she gave me a hug, and I started crying. That was breakup number six.

TWENTY-EIGHT

The End of the Beginning

Kaitlyn was pretty annoyed with me when I showed back up at the party. Apparently, someone had said that the cops were going to show up. That had cleared out most of the house, but there were still a few diehards there when I found it again. (I only got lost twice!)

"So what happened?" she asked on the ride home.

"With what?"

"With Amy."

I sighed. It was only a twenty-minute ride home. There wasn't enough time to tell the whole story. "We broke up. Again."

"That sucks."

I turned to look at her. She was staring out the window. Clearly, she had been lobotomized during the party or replaced with an alien replica. Then she turned to me.

"Are you doing okay?"

"Am I doing okay?"

"Yeah. It's a question."

"No, I'm not doing okay. I'm doing fucking horrible. I found out I can't go to college and I got dumped and her mom is having chemo on Monday. It's been a banner fucking day."

Kaitlyn nodded. "Yeah." She turned back to the window. "That all sucks."

"Yeah."

"I'm sorry about what I said today."

"Me too."

There had been no resolution in the college thing. What were we going to do? My friends were already making their plans for next year. Brian had gotten into Michigan. Groash was going to U-Rock, the community college in Janesville, which, come on, sounds fairly stupid. It's like everyone who showed up there needed a little validation.

I suck, I'm going to U-Rock.

No, you rock!

Thanks. I feel better.

You rock!

I do rock, thank you.

You rock!

Now you're overdoing it.

Elizabeth had gotten accepted to Madison and was going to try to make it work. (Her mom had less money than we did, but

Elizabeth had the benefit of being an only child, so it was a little easier to swing it.)

But for Kaitlyn and me it boiled down to this: On my mom's salary we couldn't afford for both of us to go to college at the same time. Even though tuition was fairly low at Madison, it wasn't cheap, and the cost of living in the dorms, or even commuting every day on the bus from Janesville, would be enough to break us.

One of us could go.

One of us would need to stay and get a job.

I felt like a plant withering in the dark.

This is how it happens. This is how they shrink you. You take time off, and the next thing you know it's five years later, and you're at the GM plant, or the Parker Pen plant, or you're working in some fast-food place and trying to be assistant manager. And then you get married and you settle and you have kids and your life washes away from you before you ever had the chance to start.

I looked at my stack of college mail. All the shiny pictures; the sunshine; the smiling students wearing sweaters and laughing about Descartes. (He was the French guy behind the whole revolutionary "I think, therefore I am" idea that swept through Europe at the end of the Renaissance. Like, before that, were people confused or something? *Hey, am I real? Get back to digging that poop trench, Bob.*)

My room started to look like a prison.

No more Amy, no more northern lights, no more eating pop-corn with cute girls on a co-ed floor . . .

Jesus, quit your whining. It's not all about you.

Oh, sorry, where was I?

So the Wednesday after breakup number six I decided to go to the hospital after school. There was only one hospital in Janesville: Mercy Hospital, which was enormous, so it was fairly easy to call them up and find out where Amy's mom was staying. With two visits in four days, I was pretty sure they were going to recognize me soon.

Amy's mom was propped up in one of those adjustable beds watching *Jeopardy!* when I showed up. There were about ninety-five vases of flowers around the room. I recognized Amy's handwriting and terrible spelling on one of the cards. Glenn had made a mixtape, apparently.

She looked worn-out. Her eyes were sunk in a bit. She hadn't lost her hair yet, but you could tell that it was going to go. It didn't have that whitish sheen anymore. It seemed brittle. Everything about her seemed brittle.

"Hey there," I said, immediately recognizing the fact that I had forgotten to get flowers or a card because I was a dumbass once again. A little more planning would have gone a long way here.

"Craig! How are ya?"

"Oh, you know." *Girlfriend dumped me. Might not be going to college. But I didn't have chemo on Monday, so that's a bonus.* "Hangin' in."

"Yup," she said.

"How about you?"

"Well, they took the tubes out, so that's nice."

"Oh." I did not want to hear about tubes. "You got a lot of flowers."

"Oh yeah. Amazing."

"It's kind of weird when you think about it," I mused. "Like, is it supposed to make you feel better? I mean, think about it. You take something beautiful, and then you cut it up, and then you watch it slowly die next to you."

She frowned. "You're kind of a downer, Craig."

"Sorry."

"You gotta cheer up. It could be worse." She laughed a little bit.

"Tubes?"

"Let me tell ya. Not fun." She shuddered. "So what brings you over here?"

"Figured you could probably use some company. But I see you have the flowers."

"Don't talk about the flowers again."

"I won't," I said. "I thought maybe I would do something funny that would cheer you up."

"Okay. Do it."

"But I didn't really think of anything."

She laughed. "Oh, that's good."

"That wasn't even really a thing."

"Good timing, though."

"I guess. At least I've got good timing in something." I smiled bitterly.

"Amy broke up with you again?"

"Yeah. Did she tell you?"

"Oh, sure. We talk all the time."

"Cool." It was weird to even think it. I never talked to my parents if I could help it. The thought of Amy explaining yet another breakup to her riveted mother kind of gave me pause.

"How are you at *Jeopardy!*?" she asked.

"Mediocre."

"Good. Pull up a chair."

So that's how we spent the next fifteen minutes or so. She got tired pretty easily, so I was able to shout over her and answer the questions first—I even remembered to answer in the form of questions.

"Who is Muhammad Ali?" (He was my go-to answer.)

"Who was Billie Jean King?"

"Who was Socks the Cat?"

"Who the hell knows?" She laughed.

"Who is probably Muhammad Ali again?"

"Why would I know that?"

"What is the Marianas Trench?"

She was asleep. Her breathing was shallow, but steady.

I sat there for a bit, not sure what to do. Maybe she would get better. Maybe the chemo would work. I hoped so. But it all seemed so incredibly huge to me, so utterly beyond my ability to understand. I didn't know what Amy was going through. I couldn't know what she was going through.

"Hey."

Glenn was standing in the doorway. He had his backpack slung over one shoulder and was a little out of breath.

"Hi," I said.

He gave me a little nod then went over to his mother.

"I think I put her to sleep," I said. "Not like . . . not like an animal at the vet or anything, but, you know, she fell asleep while I was here. . . ."

He smiled. "I walked over here from school. I was hoping that I could talk to her."

"She probably needs to rest. She's gonna be okay, though."

"You think so?"

"Well, I mean—I'm not exactly a medical professional, but . . ."

Glenn looked back down at her. "The doctors don't think so."

"What the hell do they know? If they knew what they were talking about, would they have to take so much time in medical school?"

That got a little chuckle out of him. Then it seemed like a curtain fell in the room, cutting out the light. The place grew dimmer.

"I guess I should go," I said. "You got a ride home?"

"Amy's coming to get me."

"Okay. All right. Well, um . . . take it easy."

I was halfway out the door when he said, "Can I ask you a question?"

"Sure."

"You think I should tell her?" His eyes were huge and dark under the industrial lighting.

I had half a mind to pretend I didn't know what he meant, but I didn't.

Glenn kept going. "I was thinking on the way over here . . . if she's gonna die, would it be better if she knew, or would it be better if she didn't know?"

"What do you think she would say?"

He looked back at her and opened his mouth to say something, but nothing came out.

"So . . . I don't know your mom all that well, but . . . she did tell me that adopting you was one of the happiest moments of her life. And I think, if you have enough space to open your heart to a baby that isn't yours, if you're a person who can do that, then you can probably open up your heart to accept whoever that child becomes. And maybe sometimes it's best to assume the best about someone. That's what I think."

He nodded, hands on his knees. "Thanks."

I heard Amy's shuffling steps before I saw her. She was halfway down the hall, coming toward us. She probably hadn't heard me, but that was all right.

Just in case you were wondering, we didn't get back together.

But she got there and we talked a little more, and Glenn stayed by his mother's side. Amy put a few fresh flowers in a vase. All three of us walked out together, and Amy and I didn't hold hands.

And it was okay.

TWENTY-NINE

One Last Adventure

The weather turned warmer. The rain stopped and people started wearing shorts again because they were idiots and it was only fifty degrees, but that's what you do in Wisconsin. Amy and I said hi to each other in the halls. We didn't have to pretend we didn't know each other. It was kinda cool, actually. Being friends.

Nothing had been resolved between me and Kaitlyn regarding the college situation. I was worried she was going to begin a relentless singing campaign against me, but mostly she just glowered when she saw me. My dad redoubled his efforts to find a job, but the job market was still deeply ensconced in the shitter.

Anyway, with two weeks left in the school year, Amy called me up.

"Okay," she said. "This is going to sound nuts, but I kind of need your help."

Yes. The day has come. Of course I will give you a back rub. We'll see where it goes. No worries.

"What is it?"

"Well, um . . . My mom got out of the hospital the other day and we were talking . . . about my birth mom and, um . . . since I'm eighteen I can go to the adoption agency and I can find out who she is. And I think I want to do that."

That hung in the telephone for a moment. It was kind of like saying *I have decided to fly to the moon.*

"Oh," I said.

"I was born in Milwaukee, so that's where the adoption agency is."

"Wow."

"So . . . do you want to go with me?"

Milwaukee was about ninety minutes away if you had a car, which I did not anymore. Neither did she, actually. Her car had died an unheralded death when the engine broke. There was a complicated explanation involving belts or cartridges or other things, but it basically meant that the car was dead.

I can imagine my dad right now reading the above paragraph and concluding that he has failed as a father.

Borrowing our parents' cars for a day trip to Milwaukee was out of the question, so that left us with no way to get there except the bus.

And Brian, whose early graduation gift was the keys to the

family's 1984 Dodge Omni, a car designed for elves with a death wish.

"Are you kidding me?" he said, when I asked if he wouldn't mind ferrying us halfway across the state out of the goodness of his heart.

"It's like five hours, maybe six or eight, max," I said.

"EIGHT hours?!"

"Well, if she wants to try to find her birth mom afterward, and if we figure that it's gonna take some time at the adoption agency."

"Dude, I am not giving your girlfriend a ride to Milwaukee. That's crazy."

"She's not my girlfriend. Right now. At this moment."

Brian blinked his eyes in dumbstruck horror. "You have problems. There are probably counselors that can help you."

"Please?"

"No! What am I gonna do in Milwaukee while you're hanging out with your not-girlfriend?"

Then it occurred to me. "Gen Con," I said.

A low noise almost like a grunt emerged from Brian's mouth. I had found his weakness.

Okay, if you don't know what Gen Con is, congratulations, you are most likely a socially competent human being. I'm sure that you will enjoy your life in the upcoming years with your well-adjusted family. If, however, you know what Gen Con is, then you may skip the next three paragraphs and continue on in the story as if I had said something like *It's the biggest gathering of nerds ever witnessed on earth.*

I'm being ungenerous. Gen Con was short for Geneva Convention, which had nothing to do with human rights and everything to do with Dungeons & Dragons.

Brian began to quiver. So imagine him quivering in a non-sexual yet still disturbing way while I explain this thing.

Gen Con is a yearly event in which enthusiasts of gaming gather together for a week of more gaming, competitive nerds-manship, and trying to find girls in chain-mail bikinis. There are seminars. I repeat: There are seminars. There are sections devoted to gaming with little monster miniatures or inventing new games or designing new elven races or playing Dungeons & Dragons with a group of really weird strangers. It was like a moving town of ten thousand of the oddest, nerdiest adult men and ten or twelve women. (Okay, there were more women than that—I'm exaggerating for comic effect.) There were shimmering clouds of body odor and vaporized Mountain Dew in the air. It was, in short, awesome.

None of us had ever gone. We had dreamed of it, sure. We had read the brochures. But none of us had ever set foot in the hallowed paradise that was the Milwaukee Convention Center. (Side note: TSR, the company that created Dungeons & Dragons, began the convention in Lake Geneva, which, again, is in Wisconsin, not Switzerland, because people just got tired of coming up with new names by the time they made it to Wisconsin, so they just started repeating shit. Gen Con grew too big for Lake Geneva, so it packed up and moved to Milwaukee, but instead of being called Mil Con, it was still Gen Con.)

Brian put his hand on his forehead and stopped quivering. "I don't know, dude."

"What?!"

"It's a long drive, and we wouldn't be there for very long—"

"We'll get a hotel room. We'll stay one night and then we'll spend a whole day at the convention," I said, fabricating this plan faster than speed of thought.

His eyes went wider. "What am I gonna tell my parents?"

"Lie to them. Look, I've watched my sister do it for her whole life, and it's mostly worked out for her. Come on—you've wanted to go to Gen Con forever. We all have. Groash can come. Elizabeth can come. We'll make a thing out of it."

He wavered. "I don't know . . ."

"Brian," I said, looking him in the eyes. "This is your chance to do something stupid. After you get out of high school, you're gonna say, 'Why didn't I do anything dumb? Why didn't I try anything?'"

"You've been doing dumb stuff all year long," he said. "And look what's happened to you."

I put my hands on his shoulders. "You know what? That's probably a fair point. But I gotta tell you—and I mean this—this has been the best year of my life. Period. Because I went after something. So you can sit at home safe and not get arrested—"

"We're gonna get arrested?!"

"Probably not. Unless Groash does something. But you can be safe, or you can take a chance. And it's better to take a chance."

He took a deep breath. "Okay," he said, gathering steam. "Okay. Yes."

"Yes!"

"Fuck yes! Take the chance! I'll just tell my parents I'm in jail."

"Not sure about that part of it."

"But how are we gonna afford it?"

"Don't worry about it."

"Dude," said Groash, later that night. "I'm in. Gen Con." He made some kind of invented gang-hand-signal gesture.

"But you can't get arrested or anything," I said.

"Brian's so sensitive about that shit," said Groash.

We were on our own for the night. Brian was a having a solo adventure with Elizabeth—we were facing the prospect of ending our campaign at the end of the summer, which was bumming everyone out. Playing together had been one long story; we had started sometime during our freshman year and now it was coming to a close in three months. It's like our show had been canceled. So, anyway, Brian was trying to get everyone caught up in the narrative before the final boss battle.

And then . . . who knows?

"By the way," Groash said. "I'm gonna need money for an entry ticket."

"Okay."

"And the hotel room."

"All right."

"And probably some food."

THE PLAN

STEP 1: Convince parents to let us spend Saturday night in Milwaukee. How to do this? Lie our asses off. Brian said that he was going to an incoming Michigan student social. Groash didn't say anything to his mom because she didn't give a shit and wouldn't notice. Amy told her dad she was going to a sleepover. Elizabeth, because she had a very strange relationship with her mom, was able to tell the truth. That left me.

"So . . ." I said. "I'm going to a sleepover at Groash's house tonight."

Mom was incredulous. "Is his mom going to be there?"

"Sure. Absolutely. You can call her. Her name is . . . Esmerelda." I smiled.

"Okay," she said.

Thanks, Kaitlyn.

STEP 2: Rent a hotel room in Milwaukee.

This proved more complicated than it sounds. My money from selling the comic books was already slated to buy entry passes and food for everyone. None of us had credit cards, and the rest of my friends managed to scrape together forty dollars between them (well, actually them minus Groash, since he could contribute nothing except unhelpful suggestions like "We should get an awesome room"). For that price, we could get one room at the Motel 6, as long as we didn't tell them there were going to be five people staying in it. I called up and reserved a room, which shocked them, since the Motel 6 was pretty used to people showing up with a wad of cash and the cops hot on their tail.

STEP 3: Drive there without killing each other.

Also harder than it sounded.

The nightmare was already well under way by the time I folded myself into the Omni the next morning.

If I had been a cat or Spider-Man, my danger sense would have immediately activated. Something was terribly wrong. The air in the car, which you might expect to be breathable, was thick with terror. Groash looked at me from the shotgun seat and mouthed the words *Get out now* as I ducked in. Elizabeth sat in the middle of the backseat, and Amy was scrunched up against the driver's side rear window. There was room for an additional five or six molecules of oxygen if we squeezed.

"All right, then," said Brian, trying to keep it together. "And we are on our way."

I tried to make eye contact with Amy, but she was looking out the window. What was going on?

No one said anything. When we got to the highway, Brian floored it. The Omni's engine, composed largely of Tinkertoys, whined and surged to life.

"Don't you think you're going a little fast?" asked Elizabeth.

"Nope."

The car started to vibrate. Even Groash looked uncomfortable.

"Brian," Elizabeth said.

"Just a red-blooded American male driving fast in my fucking car," he said.

"Okay, then," mumbled Groash, holding on to his seat belt.

"You don't have to prove anything, you know," said Elizabeth.

"I guess not," Brian said, gritting his teeth.

"If you want to say something, say it," she said. Brian shook his head and kept flooring it. "This is always your problem, dude. You try this whole circuitous route to get what you want, but you can't ever actually say what you want."

Groash let out a low whistle.

"I tried to say what I wanted last night," said Brian. "I've been trying to say that for months and you don't want to hear it."

Oh shit.

"I didn't say I didn't want to hear it!" cried Elizabeth.

"You laughed!"

"Because it was *weird*! I reacted to the weirdness!"

"It was *original* and *romantic*!" He fished in his jacket pocket and produced a piece of coral. "Did you even see the coral? Did you even realize the coral was in the room?"

I looked for an eject button somewhere in the Omni. There weren't any.

"Just be clear," said Elizabeth. "That's all I'm asking from you."

"I tried to put a little mystery in it. I tried to actually think about your experience."

Elizabeth groaned and looked at the ceiling. "You can't be the Dungeon Master of our relationship. You gave me a box to check! What the hell? Are we in middle school?"

"There was a box?" asked Groash incredulously.

"It was a RIDDLE from a SPHINX!" growled Brian, as the Omni zoomed around a curve in the road. "The answer to the riddle was whether or not you wanted to embrace someone who liked you."

"Which is DUMB!"

"I put a lot of time into that! Okay? I put effort into that!"

"You planned a whole solo adventure just so you could manipulate me into going out with you at the end!"

"Oh, come on!"

"You said I'd get a vorpal sword if I chose correctly!"

Groash erupted in indignation. "You can't give her a vorpal sword for going out with you! That's ridiculous! I don't get a vorpal sword! I would totally make out with you for one!"

"It wasn't in exchange for making out!" protested Brian. "It was in exchange for—"

"You said," interrupted Elizabeth, "that if I chose the right answer to the riddle then I'd get a vorpal sword, and there would be more riches than I could possibly imagine—"

"It was a fucking METAPHOR!"

"That's not a metaphor, dude," I said.

"Why not just ask me out? If you want to go out with me, ask me out! Don't put it in a stupid game!"

"Fine! I'm asking you out, then!"

"Why?"

"Because I like you!"

"Why?!"

"You can't ask why!"

"I can ask whatever the hell I want, I'm the one being asked out."

"Because I think you're awesome. You're hot as hell and you're smart and you're funny, and you're the only one of these dumbasses that role-plays worth a damn."

"What?!" said Groash.

"You're mostly just into it for the dice-rolling," said Brian. "Elizabeth actually plays her character. I respect that."

Elizabeth smirked. "Go on."

Brian gripped the steering wheel. "And I mean I feel better when you're in the room. I think about you all the time. I think about what you're doing. I think about us, together. My whole day gets better every time I see you—I want to spend as much goddamn time with you as I possibly can because my life is better when you're around."

"All right," she said.

"What does that mean?"

"That means all right." Elizabeth unhooked her seat belt and leaned forward in the Omni to kiss him. She found that rather difficult, as the car was still speeding, so she ended up putting one hand on Groash's head and managed to kiss the side of Brian's face.

It was still pretty awesome.

There was silence for a moment.

"So do I still get a vorpal sword?" said Groash.

"Everybody gets vorpal swords."

"Is it a two-handed sword or a long sword, 'cause I'm not proficient in—"

"It's whatever you want, okay?"

After a brief and awkward pause at a rest stop ten miles down the road, we made it to Milwaukee that evening. When we arrived at the Motel 6 we came to the realization, just like everyone who has stayed at a Motel 6, that we had made a terrible mistake. There were two twin beds that looked like they had been the site of several bloody crimes going back decades. It was perfectly romantic if you enjoyed horror films.

Brian and Elizabeth attached to each other at the shoulder and went on a "walk" as soon as we got checked into the motel. They giggled incessantly and made little chirping noises at each other, which I gather was some kind of reference to the previous night's solo adventure, but I really had no idea what they were doing. "This is bullshit," complained Groash after they left. "She's getting all the magic items now. We're fucked, Craig. I think it was better when they were fighting with each other."

Amy stayed in the state she had been in all day: silent contemplation. She had spent most of the ride looking out the window, lost in thought (or simply trying to avoid the flailing nerdstorm raging around her), and when we got to the motel she continued to keep to herself. She had brought along her journal and sat on the ratty couch, tucking her knees up to her chest. What was the protocol here? Should we be talking about this? Did she need space? Did she need me next to her? I decided maybe the best thing was for me to leave her alone.

When Brian and Elizabeth came back, there was some serious negotiation for bed space. They spent a few minutes trying to discover whether or not their fresh relationship could survive sleeping in the same bed. After much discussion and some unhelpful noises from Groash, it was decided that Brian would sleep on his own and Elizabeth and Groash would sleep in the other bed together. But, for propriety's sake, Groash would sleep upside down, with his feet on the pillows and his head at the foot of the bed. Somehow, this seemed to make sense to them. ("This is how I sleep normally," said Groash.)

If you've been paying attention, you probably have a good idea what Groash's feet smelled like. He hadn't been back to his house for at least two weeks, and the showers he took at my house might not have been the most thorough. So Elizabeth was in her own special kind of hell.

That left the couch for me and Amy.

We had spent the night together exactly once when we were going out, so this was definitely something new. A test of our newfound friendship. Also, I should mention that this wasn't even a pull-out couch; it was a regular-size couch. And when I say "regular-size," I really mean very small.

So there was that.

Amy took the inner edge of the couch and wrapped herself up, burrito-style, in the spare sheet from the closet. That left about six inches of cushion for me on a couch about four feet long. I also had no sheets or cushions. This was gonna be awesome.

As you can imagine, falling asleep was impossible. Amy kept to her spot, but I could feel her breath on the back of my neck. Should I turn around and face her? Should I stay totally still, petrified, like a statue? What did this mean? Were we getting back together? Surely there was nothing more romantic than a Motel 6 in Milwaukee with three of your best friends? Clearly it was working for two of the people in this place.

It surprised no one that Groash fell asleep first, probably because his odorous feet were gently nestled on a pillow. Somehow Elizabeth crashed too, and then it was just me and Brian who were awake.

I stayed as still as possible, but it didn't help. After about five hours of this, I saw Brian get up. He yanked on a shirt and walked into the hallway, letting the door click shut.

I followed him.

I found him on the "porch" of the Motel 6, which was a slab of concrete with a couple of chairs and the overwhelming sensation of despair. A couple of trucker guys were smoking cigarettes and downing Miller High Lifes in a circle. They regarded Brian a little wolfishly.

I tried to ignore them.

"How's it going?" I said, settling in next to him.

He smiled and shook his head. "Crazy, man. I think my whole world just turned inside out."

"Yeah."

"I've liked her for two years. I didn't say anything. Because, like—why would I think she would go for me?"

"Wow."

"Then I watched you and I was like, 'Well, if that girl likes Craig, then I've probably got a good shot.'"

"Glad I could help."

"But I'm serious, right?" He stopped and bit his lip. "You internalize things. You start seeing yourself the way you think people see you. But maybe they don't see you that way at all. She told me, tonight, that she'd had a crush on me for a while. And I was like, 'You couldn't have made that clear earlier?'"

"And if you hadn't done that stupid solo adventure you wouldn't have known."

"Yeah."

"You know, Groash wants a solo adventure now too. He says it's not fair she gets one and he doesn't."

Brian put his hands through his spiky hair. "That's gonna be a little weird."

I looked up at the sky. The lights of the Motel 6 made it impossible to see the stars. The clouds overhead were a sickly orange color.

I had basically missed this entire thing. Brian was my friend; Elizabeth was my friend, and I had no idea what was going on. I had been so wrapped up in Amy and my own problems that I was completely blind to everything going on around me. Once again.

"I'm happy for you," I said, and I meant it. Oddly enough, it felt like diving into a deep pool of water.

"Thanks."

"Are your parents gonna be cool with it? I mean, I know Elizabeth's mom is cool with it—she already saw your sexual power and everything."

He laughed. "Um . . . I think it's gonna be okay. My mom's gonna be like, 'You think that's love? Your father was in a prison camp for sixteen months while I raised your sister, that's love. I brought him food every week or he would've starved to death. That's what love is. You wrote a Dungeons & Dragons adventure.'

"But I think—you know, my parents want me to be happy.

And if the white girl in combat boots and a nose ring makes me happy, then . . . go for it."

"Cool." I thought about my parents. "I think my parents want me to be happy too."

A semi was backing up in the parking lot, sending an obnoxious beeping sound reverberating over the patio.

"Hey, man," he said. "I'm sorry about what happened to your college plan."

"Yeah."

"What are you gonna do next year?"

"I have no idea. I thought maybe I'd go to Madison, but . . . I don't know what I'm gonna do."

Brian looked over at me. "I think it'll work out."

"I don't know."

"Think of it this way: Maybe it's better to wait and see what happens. You push and you push and you push and maybe the answer is just to relax."

Pooh just is.

"Huh."

"And create a solo adventure with a sphinx and then fight about it in a car the next day."

When I got back to the room, Amy had stretched out over the entire couch.

I settled in on the floor.

THIRTY

You Can't Always Get What You Want

"Whatever you do, don't hurt the car," said Brian.

"I'm not gonna hurt the car," I said. "But let's face it: It's an Omni, something is going to go wrong. A squirrel could jump on it and the bumper would fall off."

"Craig—" He took off his glasses and rubbed his face. "I don't really feel good about you taking the car."

"It's okay," interrupted Elizabeth, squeezing Brian by the shoulder. "Craig's really boring. He's not gonna do anything."

"Thanks," I said.

We were already at the convention center, which was thronged by ecstatic nerds from all over the country. Ironically enough, I did in fact spot someone in a chain-mail bikini. As a result, we had already lost Groash. Of course, once he realized I gave Brian all the money for the tickets he'd be back.

"Promise?" said Brian.

"Yes."

"All right," he said, finally.

"Thank you," said Amy.

The adoption agency was on the south side of Milwaukee, theoretically only three or four miles from downtown. It took us about three hours to get there because Milwaukee is basically designed like a deathtrap. Once you're inside, there's no getting out; every road is both one-way and under construction, and the signs are nonexistent and contradictory. To make matters worse, the Omni accelerated like it was being powered by a hamster wheel and handled like a cardboard box.

Amy was still quiet. When I wasn't actively praying that the car would live through the day, I wondered what was going on in her head. Was she going to find out her birth mom's name today? Was it possible she lived nearby? What would happen then? Suddenly the immediate future was an unknowable gulf. "You okay?" I said, realizing I had just turned the wrong way down a one-way street.

"I'm sorry," she said, shoulders hunched. "I'm just thinking."

"You want to talk about it?"

"Not really."

"Okay."

The agency was in a nondescript white brick building, hanging low to the ground like it was embarrassed. There was an insurance office, and an accountant, and a bunch of other tiny businesses housed in these buildings—people live out their whole lives working in places like this, and everyone else drives past.

"You want me to come with?" I said.

She nodded.

We entered the first waiting room, which had been decorated in the 1970s and hadn't recovered. The tile was a gold-and-gray geometric pattern that was probably designed to subliminally make you buy popcorn. The chairs were created in the same vein—stiff-backed, and too deep to sit in comfortably. We signed in and fidgeted.

A teenage couple. That's what we looked like. *Were we a teenage couple?*

A middle-aged woman behind the counter called Amy up and handed her a raft of papers on a clipboard. After she finished them, they called her into the back and she disappeared down a wood-paneled hallway. I stayed in the waiting room and poked at the magazines on a side table. *Ladies' Home Journal.*

Why is it always Ladies' Home Journal? *Who are these ladies that need instructions on doily construction so much?*

There was another couple there, dutifully filling out paperwork. They were older, probably in their mid-thirties—the man had a tie like he had just come from an office of some kind. The woman was tall, dark-haired, and nervous as hell. Every once in a while she would look over at me and give me a faint smile like I was a dying animal.

Ten minutes later, Amy came back. She held a white envelope

in her hands and stopped in the middle of the waiting room. Tears were already brimming in her eyes. I stood up and wrapped her in a hug. In my mind, while I was waiting, I tried to picture what I was going to say to her, but I hadn't come up with anything. I just held on to her.

"I just want you to know," said the woman, getting halfway up from her chair, "that I think you guys are doing the right thing."

It took me a second to realize what she was talking about.

"Oh, we're not a couple. I mean, we were a couple. Six times actually."

"I see," she said, slightly horrified. "It's a good thing you're giving it up, then."

We burst out laughing when we got in the car.

"Do I look pregnant?" said Amy. "Shit."

"I shoulda been like, 'We're not really sure who it belongs to. I'm one of a number of possibilities.'"

She smacked me on the arm. "You're horrible."

I kept laughing. "They probably saw you and were like, *Dibs*."

Amy put her face in her hands, losing it.

"Then they saw me and were like *Eh, maybe not*."

She shook her head. "Those people were doing a good thing."

"I shoulda said, *I'm just here for the* Ladies' Home Journal. *I can't find it anywhere*."

Amy snickered, then looked down at the envelope in her hands. It had the name of the adoption agency on the outside, typed in a wide, official-looking font. It was a cloudy day, the light was soft, and when she looked down, her hair fell just over her shoulders, reminding me of that first time in Youth in Government. She looked so beautiful it hurt.

I tried not to look at her. The feelings that I'd been pushing down the whole trip were swelling inside of me, like my whole skin was just a thin covering of my heart, which was about to burst.

The envelope crinkled in her hands. She took a deep breath.

"So . . ." she said, exhaling. "It's not quite how I thought. They're not gonna just give me the name; I have to write my birth mom a letter and then they have to let her know that a letter exists, and she has to decide if she wants to read it. And then, if she reads it, then she can send a letter back. And then . . . then we can meet."

"Oh."

She let go of the envelope and threaded her fingers together under her chin. "I don't know that I'm ready to do this. Can we maybe go somewhere?"

We settled on McDonald's, which seemed like a perfect place to have a public breakdown. We got some lunch and tucked into a hard plastic booth in the back, as far away from the malignant play area as possible.

Amy kept looking at the envelope. "I really thought I wanted to do this, but every time I think about what I would write to her . . . it gets scary."

"Of course it's scary."

"If I start going down this path, then I can't go back."

"You can stop at any time."

"I know, but . . . once I write the letter, then it's out there. Then those words are out there. I mean, this is the person that made the most important decision in my life, and I've never met her. And I don't know if I want to meet her." She took a deep breath. "But then why come here if I'm not gonna follow through with it? I dragged you all the way here—"

"It's okay," I said. "It doesn't matter. Do what you need to do."

"I can't tell you how many times I've thought about her—what she'd be like, if she had a family. All I know is that she was really young and from the wrong side of the tracks, but . . . I don't know."

She still had the envelope, which had been crinkled, uncrinkled, crinkled again, then finally smoothed out on the surface of the table.

"What's she gonna say? If she meets me? Maybe she has a whole different life now. Maybe she doesn't want to be reminded of what happened?"

"I don't know," I said. I'd been saying that a lot. I had no clue what to say.

"But then what if she wants to be a part of my life? What if she's doing great, and is in a place where . . . where she can have a relationship with me?" She plucked a Kleenex and blew her nose into it. "At first I thought I wanted that—I mean, I think in the fantasy, that's what I dreamed about for years, but now . . . now I think about—what does that mean for my dad and Glenn? Glenn can't even try to find his birth mom for years, even if he wanted to. And then I just kind of imagine us all . . . separating . . . after my mom . . . dies. . . ."

Amy started to collapse.

"I don't want her to go," she whispered.

I was sitting right next to her. I had my right arm around her shoulder, and my left arm was wrapped around her stomach, like I was preventing her from falling to pieces. I wasn't succeeding.

"And I know she can be difficult, but she's the thing that holds us together," she managed.

"I know."

"What's gonna happen when I go to college? If she's . . . not dead, then who's gonna take care of her? If it's just my dad and Glenn . . . what's gonna happen to my brother?"

Amy stopped to blow her nose again and then dropped the used Kleenex in the white mountain that was forming on the plastic bench next to her.

"I'm not staying," she said, steeling herself. "She's not gonna make me stay. I can't do that to myself. I mean—why do you think I'm going to UCLA? I'm going as far away as I could. . . ."

She took the envelope in her hands again. "Maybe this is just the same thing: an escape route. . . ."

She was shaking a little bit, and I still had my arm around her and was trying to think of something to say that was going to make all this better.

And there wasn't anything.

I didn't have any words that could make this less shitty.

So I stayed silent, and I held her for a long time. Finally, she got up, took the envelope, and pushed it into the trash.

THIRTY-ONE

The Basement Project from Hell

"So let me explain my vision, here," said my dad as we tromped into the basement.

It was the week before graduation and my dad had chosen this moment in time to destroy my world.

The basement consisted of exactly four rooms:

1. THE SECRET GUN ROOM—This room was off-limits. What happened in here? No one knew, but there were many guns. This was where all my friends had declared they would go in the event of the zombie apocalypse.

2. THE OUTER LIVING-ROOM-TYPE PLACE—The wood-paneled room with the nasty couch, chair, and television. Site of breakup number five.

3. THE LAIR—The unfinished part of the basement, which was where we gathered to consume Mountain

Dew, nerd out, and play Dungeons & Dragons. Also, curiously, it contained our washer and dryer.

4.   THE COLD STORAGE ROOM—Beyond the Lair was a cave-like place that housed our many, many Christmas decorations and abandoned dreams. I had been in there exactly once and it scared the hell out of me.

The Lair had a bare floor and exposed beams. There were drains in the floor in there, and the walls were plain cement that were stained with water marks. Spiders had grown powerful over the years and had created a small empire in the areas behind the chairs. You tried not to look too hard in any area of this room.

And it was here that Dad had a vision.

He opened the door to the Lair and took it in with a deep sigh. "So here's what I see. We pull everything out of here. Get rid of the junk we don't need. We clean the hell out of everything else."

I may have let out a little gasp of pain at this point.

Since the job hunt had been a continuous failure, Dad had been coming up with more and more projects to keep himself useful. So far he had reorganized the garage, built the shaky deck, and had now moved on to his white whale: the basement. His real goal was to reach the cold storage room and discover what terrors lurked within.

"I know we've got some wedding presents we never opened in there," he said.

The mere act of taking everything out of the basement and

cleaning it would take a normal, industrious human a week. For us, it was going to be longer.

"And you're gonna help me," he finished, clapping his hands together.

"Okay," I said.

I think most disasters in history begin with someone proposing a plan and then some other idiot saying the word *Okay*.

We yanked all the furniture into the outer room first. That was the first nightmare. Because there were things beneath that furniture—crumbs that had dropped months or perhaps years ago, which had developed their own ecosystems and resented being exposed to the light of day again. Large, bloated wormy things slalomed away from us. We found about nineteen dice.

The cleaning process took longer. We swept the floor, and my dad took a break while I mopped everything.

"That's not how you mop," he said.

"This is how *I* mop."

"It's not effective." He took it from my hands. "You go side to side, in an arc, okay? Side. To. Side." He went back and forth with the mop, wetting the floor. "You know my first job? I worked in a restaurant." He kept mopping. "The last thing we did—every night—mop the floor."

"They probably thought you were a mopping genius."

He chuckled. "I was, actually. Everyone else was terrible."

He kept mopping.

"So I think I got a job lined up," I said. "For the summer."

He paused and leaned on his mop. "Don't get a job in a restaurant." Then he took a breath and looked at the wall. "I might be able to talk to some people at Parker Pen. They usually hire some kids for the summer."

"Actually there's a guy who owns a comic book store who needs some help."

"Huh." You could tell the wheels were turning in his head to see if this was a "real job" or not. "Just don't let him pay you in comic books."

"Sure."

He stopped and put the mop back in the bucket, resting his hands on his hips. "Oh shit, Craig." He sighed deeply with his back to me. "I thought I'd have something by now."

"I know."

"Buddy, I'm really sorry." He still wasn't looking at me.

"It's okay—"

"No, it's not. It's not okay."

"Dad—"

"We didn't have a whole lot when I was growing up. Grandpa had that store, but it was always just barely scraping by. We had to borrow money from Grandma's family—she had to take extra work when she could get it. There was never a possibility that I was gonna go to college. . . . I got that job at Parker Pen early."

I knew the story. Usually it was followed by something along the lines of *I worked my ass off and that's why you need to do your homework, damn it.*

But his eyes were red when he looked at me. "And I thought that it wouldn't be the same for my kids. No matter what I did, I was gonna make sure that you and your sister had the chance to go to school. I mean, that's why I went to work every day."

He wiped a tear away from his eye.

"I mean, that was the point, Craig," he said, his voice cracking. "To make things better for you than they were for me."

He wiped away another tear with a shaking hand. I took a step toward him, feeling the space between us for a moment, then reached out and held him.

"The shitty thing is that I thought I had done it," he said. "I was on the path—and they just throw you in the garbage right at the end. They don't give a shit. It's all about money for them. I wanted to send you to that fruity school, damn it. If that's where you wanted to go, with all the lesbians, that's fine."

"I don't really know how many lesbians there were, Dad."

"Seemed like a lot." He took a deep breath. "I feel like I failed."

After he left, I stayed in the basement, taking in the emptied room. How many hours had I spent down here with my friends? How much money had Mom and Dad spent on all this stuff? All the Christmas presents they'd gotten me, all the birthday presents. It was all still right here. They'd given me the space to be weird, to find my own way. And here it was, the gray concrete mopped down and clean.

I'm sure I wasn't the son my father was envisioning. *Welp, I'm a red-blooded American male with a big gun collection, I sure hope I get a trench coat–wearing Dostoevsky-ish nerd with no athletic ability whatsoever. I hope he hangs out with a guy who has a safety pin for an earring. That would be peachy.*

And yet he loved me. He didn't understand me, but he loved me. And he had given up so much.

I knew what I had to do.

Kaitlyn was watching a *90210* marathon when I found her.

"This is rotting your brain," I said.

"No doubt." She had a bowl of Cheetos and was popping them into her mouth one after the other.

"So . . . uh . . . I want you to go to Madison next year."

She turned to look at me, her cheeks chipmunked with Cheetos. "Wha . . . ?"

"I've thought about it. I'll stay at home and take some classes at U-Rock. You go to Madison. You can run track and do whatever it is you need to do."

Kaitlyn tried to argue. "I thought we were gonna arm-wrestle for it."

"Just accept it, okay? I'll be fine. I'll transfer in after a year or two, once Dad gets a job. All right? It's not the end of the world."

Kaitlyn seemed moved. She looked back at me.

"Thanks."

"This show sucks, by the way."

"Screw off."

THIRTY-TWO

Graduation

THINGS TO DO ON GRADUATION DAY

1. Put on a weird dress thing.
2. Take pictures with relatives you've never met.
3. Sit in the sun for a long time.
4. Not think about Amy.

How do they find the guest speakers for graduation day? Does someone just throw a dart at a wall? We had a guy who was the president of a bank or something. I guess the administration felt that, since he had made a lot of money, he would be a good person to give the graduation speech. Like, *Hey, kids! Look at the man in the suit! He made money! You can too! I bet he worked hard in school and had high expectations!*

I'm going to call him Bob.

Bob was the worst speaker in the history of humanity. My guess is that they made Bob president of the bank because he had started talking and it had been the only way to shut him up.

When you're a twin, you quickly realize that, through the magic of alphabetical order, you will be sitting next to your twin at every event ever. As if I hadn't seen enough of this person in the womb. Someday, when Kaitlyn and I are both dead, we will be buried next to each other. Anyway, so we were both in plastic blue dresses with funny hats and listening to Bob.

I had told my parents about my plan and it had caused an uneasy atmosphere of kindness to fall over the house. We weren't quite sure what to do with it. I could sense Kaitlyn wanting to say something mean, then remembering my niceness, which kind of short-circuited her a little bit. Anyway, as she sat next to me listening to Bob, I could sense the weirdness coming from her.

Bob spoke slowly, as if all of us had both hearing and mental problems. "When. You. Look. Around. At. Your. Class. Mates. You. Will. See. People. Who. Changed. Your. Life."

"Kill me now," I said to Kaitlyn.

"You. Know. How. I. Became. Presi. Dent. Of. The. Bank?"

I started imagining that scene from *Raiders of the Lost Ark* when the Nazis open up the ark and murderous spirits melt their faces off. Blood spurts out of their faces, and they clutch their evil Nazi hats; and then they turn white (because they were made out of wax), and then they all scream and dissolve. I started hoping that would happen to Bob.

"It. Might. Be. A. Cliché. But. Hard. Work. Pays. Off."

After two or three hours of this, in which no fewer than four birds committed suicide overhead, Bob was finished. There was a smattering of weak applause from the assembled graduates, who were too numb to do anything but bump their hands together like brain-dead seals.

Our principal, whose name was Mr. Johanssen and who was inexplicably from Sweden, took the microphone and wiped the sweat off his pale forehead. "Okay! Ya. Okay! And now a few words from our valedictorian, Amy Carlson."

Amy somehow managed to make a shapeless blue dress and weird hat look great. Her hair fell over both shoulders, and there was probably a chorus of angels somewhere in the background.

"Don't even look at her," said Kaitlyn.

She started her speech.

"Don't even think about her."

"I can't help it. She's up there."

Kaitlyn elbowed me. "Stop looking at her."

"I'm fine," I said. "I'm cool."

"You are so not cool."

"I want to talk about our dreams," said Amy. "About holding on to our dreams in the face of reality. About holding on to the people who are important to you. Because we are going to face tragedy in the future. It is inevitable that there will be pain and suffering in our lives, and it's a fact that we aren't all going to make it to our reunions."

Kaitlyn elbowed me and whispered, "This speech is a downer."

"Yeah," I said, smiling. "She's doing great."

"But, according to Fyodor Dostoevsky, suffering is the sole origin of consciousness."

She paused just a bit to let that sink in, but I was the only one with a tear in my eye.

Afterward, there was a gauntlet of photos to survive. Elizabeth's mom was first in line. She made eye contact with me and gave me a little wink.

"Okay, smile!" she said, bracelets jangling as Groash, Elizabeth, Brian, and I crowded together. We smiled.

"Okay, now just Brian and Elizabeth!" Brian and Elizabeth stood next to each other, arms around each other. They were adorable.

"Can we do one where we're kissing?" asked Elizabeth. "Before his parents get here?"

"Yes!" said Brian.

"I'm in," said Groash, grabbing Brian and trying to hump him just as his parents arrived with their tripod.

Brian's father was lean and wiry, but you could tell by the crows-feet around his eyes that he was the kind of guy who smiled continuously. Even though I'd been friends with Brian for eight years, I'd only met his dad a few times. He spoke English fine, but his accent was thick and sometimes it was hard to understand him.

Brian's mom was there as well—she was petite, and her black hair was swept up into a complicated bun-thing. She had a dazzling smile and was deeply involved in telling her husband how exactly to set up the tripod.

I thought about the sixteen months she had spent bringing food to Brian's father while he was in a prison camp. That was longer than my entire six relationships with Amy. They spent two weeks together in the bottom of a cargo ship. They somehow managed to make a home in the middle of Nowhere, Wisconsin, and they were still in love.

And now their son had graduated, was going to a good school next year, and was a pretty damn good Dungeon Master.

They had made it. Maybe I could make it too.

"Hey," Amy said, coming up from behind me.

"Hey," I said.

"My mom wants to get a picture of the two of us."

"Really?"

"Don't act so surprised! Did you like the speech?"

"It was awesome. You're great at making everyone feel terrible."

She poked me with her long fingers. "I didn't want it to be clichéd, you know."

"Reminding everyone how some of us were going to die soon was a great way to do that. I'm kidding. It was great. It really was."

"Thanks."

"You probably should have made it more depressing. Talked about how most of us were going to fail."

"They made me take it out, actually." She smiled. "I was going to say, 'Remember that half of you are below average.' Or maybe I should have been like, *Prepare for your low-wage jobs at Walmart, subhumans!*"

"You should have been like, *Kneel before Zod!*"

Chelsea swept over. As vice president of the junior class, she was forced to attend because there was some sort of passing of the torch that needed to occur. She was wearing a red floral dress specifically designed to make everyone feel self-conscious in their shapeless blue wizard robes. "Oh my God," she said. "That bank guy? I felt my brain starting to slide out of my ears. I thought about passing out just to liven it up."

"Yeah, he was wonderful," said Amy.

Chelsea hugged her. "You were wonderful. You kicked ass."

"Thanks."

"We should have you back next year to give the speech again."

"Oh, there they are!" It was Amy's mom.

She had a bandana over her head and was walking using a cane, but at least she was walking. Amy's dad was helping her along, and Glenn was there, listening to his Walkman.

"Hey there," I said as she hugged me.

Amy's dad held out his hand. "You're wearing a dress."

"Yep. Yes I am. I was thinking of going nude under this—"

Amy's mom laughed. "He is so funny! Don't you think so, Dan?"

"He's a comedian."

"You know, Dan here did stand-up once. 1971. Milwaukee. He gets up—"

"Um . . . guys?" said Amy. "Can I talk to Craig alone for a minute?"

"Oh, sure, don't mind us. We'll just be over here."

Chelsea raised her eyebrows and smiled.

Amy and I walked toward the side of the school. She kept her shoulder close to me.

Her hand slipped into mine.

I REPEAT: *HER HAND SLIPPED INTO MINE.*

In my mind's eye I could see my friends screaming in slow motion, leaping to stop me. *They're too late. It's over. All my dreams are coming true.*

"So, hurm," said Amy, taking a deep breath. "So here's what I'm thinking."

"Uh-huh."

"I feel that now school is over, I'm in kind of a better place."

"Uh-huh."

"And I know that we have tried this before. . . ."

"Uh-huh."

"But I was thinking . . ."

"Yes. Absolutely."

"Can you let me say this first?"

"Sure."

Basically my negotiating stance was total surrender. Amy took my hand.

"I was thinking about the year. And about us. And my theory is that I've been thinking too much, you know? Like I'm resisting things because I'm worried about outcomes that I can't really control. I should just let things . . . occur. You know what I'm saying? Like, change."

"Change is good."

"And just . . . I felt this way when we were in Milwaukee, that if there was one person I wanted with me, it was you. It was you. So . . ."

"Yeah."

"So I think maybe . . . let's go back to that place."

"Done," I said.

Amy shook my hand a bit. "I want you to think about it first."

"Already did."

"No, I mean take some time. Ask other people. Really think about it. Is this something you want to be getting back into?" There was a little pause when she realized what she had said. "That was a poor choice of words."

"Okay, I'll think about it."

"Take twenty-four hours. After twenty-four hours, if you still want to go out, we can do that."

"I feel like I should tell you now."

"No, I want you to wait."

"But what if you don't feel the same way tomorrow?"

"Twenty-four hours. Okay? And I want you to think about what I wrote in the letter."

My eyes went blank. "What letter?"

"The letter I wrote to you when we broke up."

"Which time?"

"The fourth time, maybe."

"Oh." I hadn't read that letter. "Yes. The letter." I was about to play it off and then I stopped. "You know, I didn't read that letter. I'm sorry I was . . . I was messed up, obviously, so I . . . I couldn't really look at it."

"Oh."

"But I will. I'll read it, and then I'll find you tomorrow."

THIRTY-THREE

AMY'S FIRST LETTER TO CRAIG (As read for the first time in June). (Holy shit, this is long.)

Craig,

I've thought a lot about how to say this. That's probably my problem in a nutshell: I think too much. Always thinking, even when it would be better to just be.

I think, and this sounds weird, that I know you better than you know me. You're always open, and I think I'm always closed. I'm sorry about that. Maybe this letter will help explain me to you.

I'm just gonna come out and say this: I can't be the person you want me to be. I don't know that I'll ever be that person for you.

Mabye you'll say I'm scared and running away from you—maybe I'm doing that. Mabye I'm so fucked up on the inside that I don't think I deserve love. Or I'm going to destroy it. Or destroy you. I watch my parents and I think about them, and their relationship is far from perfect, and I think my mom is controlling and everything, but that's not it either.

I know I told you I got held back when I was little. But I was also tall and awkward and ugly as a kid. Other kids thought I was dumb. Add to that the fact that nothing I ever did was ever good enough for my mom—I could never be prety enough or skinny enough or smart enough. I was a very sad girl for a very long time.

I made a conshus decision in middle school—I was going to make myself something better. I wasn't going to be the wierd girl anymore. I spent a lot of time building Amy Carlson. I pretend to be something. I built some kind of statue of myself. Her skin is like marble, and she's beutiful and smart and gets straight A's.

She got popular. She started getting invited places. She started having boyfriends. She went out with Chad Darby because she thought it looked good. But none of that was true. None of that was the real me.

The blow-up with my friends—I told you about that—but mostly I told them all to go to hell. I broke up with them too. I broke up with Chad. I break up with everything. I have a theory it's because I'm expecting to get hurt. I am wounded on the inside and I can't be there for you. It hurts me to admit this. I feel like I'm carrying around an anchor. I need to be honest with you. You have tried so hard, you're trying to do everything right, but I can't have someone that does everything right in my life.

There's that Amy that I built in middle school, and there's the real Amy, who is a frightened, scared little girl still in there some-where. There's the girl who got picked on in school, who was ugly, who was dumb, whose real parents didn't even want her. I was that girl. So I don't trust it when people say they like me. Why would they like me? Would they like the real me? Maybe they just like the fake Amy Carlson that is the student body president and the valedictorian. Maybe they have no idea who I am.

So I run. I blow everything up. Because I don't trust anyone. Because I'm afraid that I'm a lie.

I keep hurting you. I know I'm breaking your heart all the time. It kills me that I do this.

I realize your letters are funnier than mine. Sorry. I feel like I should put jokes in here.

I wish this letter was better. I wish I was better.

But I can't keep doing this. I have to find a way to stop. And I think that has to mean being by myself for a while—until I can figure out which person is the real me, and be able to love you in the way you love me. And I know you love me. You love me in your way—openly, sweetly. And I can't love you like that.

I'm sorry.

I'm so sorry.

Amy.

THIRTY-FOUR

The Seventh Torment

I set the letter down on my bed.

The window was open; the cool breeze fluttered in, reminding me of the night we had spent together, when we had kissed for hours in my bed. When it seemed like kissing was all that was necessary to be in love, to be in the same space with someone, full of joy. Maybe that had never been enough for her.

Goose bumps ran up and down my arms and I stared at the wall, unmoving.

There had been so much I wasn't aware of. Just like Brian and Elizabeth. I had missed a huge part of what was going on around me. How could I have failed so completely to understand the person I loved? How was I blind to her pain?

I started crying and I didn't even know why.

Maybe the Amy I created in my mind wasn't the same one

that was standing in front of me. Maybe I was in love with that version I invented.

The more I thought about it, the more I realized I had never bothered to question myself. I was just doing things; I wanted out, I wanted her, I wanted something, anything, but I didn't know why I wanted it. I wanted a bigger life, but I didn't know how to get it.

Pooh just is.

Change is good.

I went over to her house the next day. She was in the backyard. Her dad had set up a hammock between two of the pine trees, and Amy was sitting there, deep in a Joseph Campbell book.

"So I thought about it," I said.

"Good."

A cold shiver ran down my spine. My ears buzzed. I had trouble finding my breath.

"What do you think?" she said.

The words caught in my throat. And then I heard myself saying them:

"I think the answer needs to be no."

All the sound drained out of the world. Amy's eyes started to water.

"I know this seems like revenge," I said, "but it's not revenge. Because I'm still gonna be here for you. And we're still gonna be friends, and we're still gonna spend time together. Because I think you're an amazing person. . . . I know that sounds stupid and cliché, but it's true, and sometimes stupid and cliché things are true . . . but . . . I can't do this again."

I took hold of her with both hands. "I want you to know that this is not about you baring your soul to me and me rejecting it—because I love your soul. I love your mind. But if we do this again, and if we break up again . . . ?" I shook my head. "I don't know what would happen then." I said more, and there were a lot more words that came out of us.

"It's funny, you know," she said, finally. "I keep picturing us in the future, and someone asking us, 'How did you two get together?' And then I'd say, 'You're never gonna believe this story. But I broke his heart six times and he kept coming back.' And they'd say, 'Wow, he must have really been in love with you.' And I'd say, 'Yeah. It's a pretty cool story.'"

We were both crying now, and I was hugging her.

"It's still a pretty cool story," I said.

EPILOGUE

Epilogue?

What the hell?

I should've warned you that that was the stopping point. At least, it was one stopping point. There are no endings until the people are dead, and our story wasn't over. So there's one last part I want to tell.

Tragedies end in death. Comedies end in weddings.

So I guess this one is a tragedy because Amy's mom died at the beginning of November.

I had continued to visit her from time to time. She told me stories about Amy's childhood, and things that they had done together. She told me when Glenn had decided to come out to her, and how happy she was that he was finding out who he was.

I even wrote rather funny letters to Amy when I got the

chance. At U-Rock I got an e-mail address, and she had one through UCLA, so we were able to communicate frequently, actually. I told her when my dad got a new job; I told her about the insanity of our continuing basement clean-out, which had stretched from a three-week project into five months; I told her about my classes at U-Rock and my plans to transfer at the end of my first year. (I didn't tell her that I applied to UCLA, 'cause that sounded pretty sad and desperate.)

Rick hired me for the summer and then extended that through the year. I loved being in the store; I even sold my *Deities & Demigods* to a guy from Lake Geneva who turned out to work for TSR. He invited me to stop by and I started an unpaid internship two days a week. It was almost like a dream come true.

The funeral was November 3—a year to the day from when Amy and I first got together.

She came home to be there.

There were a lot of people at the funeral. Some I recognized, like Chelsea, but most of them came from a world that I knew nothing about. Amy's mom had taught elementary school for years; a lot of her former students were there.

Amy sat up front. She had cut her hair, not chopped in a victory breakup haircut, but still, it was shorter. Just over shoulder length. It looked amazing.

Was I a jackass for thinking about how pretty her hair looked at her mom's funeral? Of course, but I think we've already established that point.

Her dad got up to speak. He had gotten a haircut too, and he looked small in the black suit, as if he had shrunk somehow.

He stood at the podium for a moment and looked down at his hands.

"So," he said, with that long Wisconsin O. "Uh . . . if you know me, you know I don't . . . do this a lot." He stopped again. "Barb and I . . . uh . . . we've been in love a long time." He stopped again, trying to keep himself from crying.

"I've been tryin' to think about what to say. How to talk about her. I met her in high school . . . and we were in love for a long, long time. You know, we wanted a family—and then we learned we weren't gonna have one . . . but then we decided to anyway." He looked out over the congregation—he looked at Glenn, then he looked at Amy.

"And you guys . . . we're so happy to have you . . . and Barb was thrilled . . . every day . . . she got a chance to be your mother."

His voice was cracking, and the words barely trickled out. You could hear people blowing their noses now.

"My whole life was her."

He stopped again, and managed one last word before Amy came up to help him down.

"Good-bye."

The snow was falling when they lowered her casket into the ground. It was the first snow of the year, and the flakes were huge and wet—they stuck to everything, landing on the black shoulders of my trench coat and tangling in Amy's hair. Everywhere they fell, they melted.

I stood there for a moment with my hands in my pockets like an idiot as the snow dropped around us. Then she was hugging me, and I wrapped her in my arms like I had done so many times before. I could smell the cotton of her hat.

We went for a walk. And we were quiet for a long time, but then we started talking, like we always did. She told me about a philosophy of religion class she was taking, which she liked a lot, and that she was considering being a religion major. I told her about getting to work in a building with all my nerd heroes. We talked about Brian and Elizabeth and Groash and Chelsea; everyone was doing okay. Life was good.

We didn't kiss, and we didn't hold hands.

Maybe someday, I told myself.

Later, after she had left, I got in my car and heard the rhythmic squeak of the windshield wipers. I sat there a moment, not wanting to go anywhere at all. Not wanting to let this moment escape into the past. But we all have to go sometime, I guess. I adjusted my hat, put the car in drive, and headed out.

ACKNOWLEDGMENTS

It's a cliché that every book is the result of the work of dozens of people, but like most clichés it has the benefit of being true. This book you have in your hands would be infinitely worse and probably unreadable without the contributions, sweat, and kind assistance I've received at every step of the way. I'd like to take a moment to thank everyone who pitched in.

First, Shannon Geiken Horn, without whom there would be no book. Shannon e-mailed me in the spring of 2014 asking to commission a play to take to the Edinburgh Fringe Festival the following year. At first I was going to do a play about an astrophysicist, but we lost an actress, so naturally my thoughts turned to heartbreak. That's where the idea of the seven breakups occurred to me.

The students we took to Scotland, who performed the original roles, were invaluable to me. Chris Ramirez, the original Craig, and Alex Hammersley, who played the original Amy, were absolutely perfect in their parts and gave me so much insight into their characters. I don't think I ever would've understood Groash without Bo Hiel's performance, and Amelia Kassing, Eric Jewel, Grayson Yerich, and Emily Dial were instrumental in fleshing out this little world I created.

Next, the amazing Holliana Bryan, who edited the very first, very rough manuscript I sent to her. Without her brilliant ideas and suggestions, this book would be far weaker.

I need to thank my incredible agent, John Cusick, who took me under his wing and has been there for every stop of this whirlwind process. I completely rewrote the book under his guidance, and the result was a novel that is far more nuanced, complete, and hilarious than anything I could have done on my own.

I need to thank Carol Nguyen, who gave me invaluable insight into her experiences growing up in small-town Wisconsin and provided some much-needed context.

My entire team at Hyperion, including super editor Laura Schreiber, who has been a champion for this book, has laughed along with me, and still managed to protect my fragile author feelings while delivering all-important suggestions for improvement. I also need to thank Hannah Allaman, whose input was incredibly helpful, and the careful comma and hyphenation corrections of Dan Kaufman, who solved my numerous, numerous errors. I clearly never learned how to use commas or dashes correctly, and any remaining mistakes are my own.

I also need to thank the No-Vibe Tribe, who unwittingly provided much of the material in this novel, even though they didn't realize it at the time. So to Matt, Ken, Dan, Sky, Ray, Tiff, Mike, Russ, Aaron, and Jon: Ha-ha-ha-ha-ha. It's in print now.

Though she probably isn't aware of it, Jennifer Finney Boylan is also partly responsible for this novel. I had wanted to be a novelist for years and years, but working alongside her at Ursinus College showed me a pathway to my dreams. She helped me along the way with my first book, and for that I am eternally grateful.

I would also like to thank the good people at Starbucks and various other coffee shops in the United States and Scotland who generously provided me with enough caffeine to do this.

Lastly, I need to thank Anne Godfrey. I don't have enough words left to say how much you mean to me.